DEAD CALM

a novel

MAIA ROSS

All the characters in this book are fictitious, and any resemblance to actual persons, living or dead, is coincidental. This is a work of fiction.

V1.8

www.maiarossbooks.com

Cover by MiblArt

ISBN: 9798742822899

For John

CONTENTS

One — Irma

I simply refused to die before teatime. Unfortunately, I was locked in what could only be described as a life or death struggle. My heart thumped in my chest, all my focus pinholed on my opponent. “No surrender!”

Giggles erupted from my left flank. I narrowed my eyes and returned Lucas García’s killer serve with a backhand I’d spent a lifetime honing. The ball rammed down the middle of the court and clipped him in the shoulder. Lucas wouldn’t mind; he was the club pro and was used to being occasionally pummelled by his clients. Plus, he’d aimed his last serve right at my left eyeball. I pumped a fist in victory.

The aforementioned giggler and current house guest, Violet Blackheart, broke into applause. And more laughter.

“What on earth is so funny?” I asked.

“Irma,” she said, her shoulders jiggling. “‘*No surrender*?’”

I shrugged, feeling no embarrassment, which was a wasted emotion. I was not quite five feet tall and had recently retired from a lifetime in intelligence work for the British government. It had been my experience that puffing up a bit helped keep one's opponents off balance. "Heat of the moment, dear, you understand."

"Oh, of course."

Lucas loped over, his hand held out to shake mine.

"Great work, Irma," he said with a grin. "Always nice to see that level of aggression in a retiree."

"Thank you, dear," I said, beaming. I'd once gone undercover as a tennis coach at Wimbledon and perhaps took my game a bit too seriously. "Violet? Your turn."

"Sorry, what?" she said, narrowing her eyes. Like usual, Violet was wearing all black, the waves of her lovely chestnut hair falling to the middle of her back. Her amber eyes were often trained on a screen of some sort. In fact, she was currently nose-deep in the laptop computer she dragged along with her everywhere, sort of like an adult version of a binkie.

"It's time for your lesson, dear," I said again. She was looking at the computer with one eyeball already, and the second was going to follow shortly, if past behaviour told us anything, which of course it did.

"Thank you so much, but I don't need a tennis lesson," she said. Her second eyeball was still focused on me, but I could see it drifting. "Because I am not a tennis player."

"That's why you need the lesson, my dear. And it's only ten minutes. My treat. Why don't you just try? You can stop if you don't like it."

"I'm…uh…" She hit a few random keys on her keyboard. "Busy…and…did you know that the irrigation system here is open to attack?"

Here was the Beaver Island Country Club, which island residents always referred to as *the Club*. And I didn't bother to ask how she was aware of the intimate details of its water works. Engineers always seemed to know this type of information. Just like I knew there was a tiny nerve in the hand that could be activated with a little squeeze, putting the victim's entire arm into spasm. Different strokes and all that.

"What kind of attack?" Lucas frowned as his necklace fell to the ground. It was a simple gold chain with a little charm, an *8* his mother had gotten him before she passed away a few years ago. It was his lucky number. He picked it up and secured it back around his neck.

"Cyber," Violet said. "I have an IOT device scanner on my phone and it went off. The sprinkler system is wide open to attack and—"

"What's IOT?" Lucas said, his nose wrinkled.

"The Internet of Things. You know, doorbells spying on you, Barbies recording you with their beady little eyes, that kind of thing."

"Well, as long as we're not getting cyber-attacked at this exact moment, we might as well play tennis, eh?" Lucas said with a winning smile. "It's just a mini-lesson. A micro-lesson, even." He held out a racquet.

She looked up and paused, like she was suddenly mesmerised. Which was understandable; at twenty-seven, Lucas was in the prime of his life, lean and muscled and tanned, his not-too-long brown locks streaked with blond from the sun. With a winning smile and gorgeous face topping it all off, he really was quite fetching. Today he was wearing slouchy white tennis shorts and a t-shirt that said *Lucky #8.*

"Uh..."

"It's all right," I said, walking off the court. "If you don't want to try new things or learn new skills, that's fine with me. We'll just go sit in a ditch and count the cars going by—"

Violet held up a hand. "You know, you're like a cult leader."

"Thank you, dear."

"Not a compliment, Irma."

"It felt like one," I said reasonably.

She shot me a half-smile before wrestling a hair elastic over her lovely curls, and I did a few cooldown stretches while Lucas led her through an easy warm up. It was puzzling, her refusal to exercise. Or wear a colour not favoured by morticians.

She'd been an elite athlete when she was young, which was how we'd met years ago. My chosen retirement location was my childhood summer retreat: Beaver Island. A tiny Lake Ontario getaway, it was home to a few vineyards, some five-star dining, and some of the best sailing on the lake. It also boasted an excellent pre-professional ballet academy. She'd been here on scholarship the summer she was sixteen. By the time the season ended, she had offers in hand from two ballet companies, but she'd decided to go to university instead.

Now forty-three, Violet was on the ballet school's board, and so was I. When she told me a few months back that she'd never gone on a real vacation, I'd offered to host her at my place and introduce her to an island lifestyle. Thus far, she'd been reluctant to actually leave the house and *see* the island, but luckily I was not one to give up easily.

Lucas stood beside Violet, reviewing proper form for her grip. Right now, it looked more like she was about to smash someone over the head with her racquet, which, it had to be said, was also an excellent life skill for young ladies to learn.

"Hello, Irma." Snookie Smith, an old island nemesis, had skulked over while I was stretching out my triceps. She was holding an enormous plastic cup full of a frothy pink substance. I kept some distance between us. A few weeks ago, she'd let the air out of my tires while I was brunching. More recently, she'd tried to trip me at a formal event and I'd almost succumbed. I didn't mind a few scrapes and bruises, but everyone had their limits. Some in my former line of work were afraid of knives or explosives or being strangled with piano wire while tootling down a zip line; my greatest fear was shattered hips. Life was a rich tapestry.

"I always do," I responded.

She snorted, her pince-nez reading glasses sliding down her nose. She was so thin, she bordered on scrawny, but she was taller than my almost five feet, and would never let me forget it. "You looked not bad out there."

High praise, coming from Snookie. I raised an eyebrow but said nothing. I was trying to figure out if she was going to make another attempt at tripping me, or perhaps throw her drink on me. The adrenaline that had spiked during my game with Lucas made another appearance in my veins. If I was going to head-butt her in self-defence—and in public—I'd have to make it look good.

I glanced around the court. Like any normal mid-June day at the Beaver Island Country Club, tennis whites-wearing spectators mingled around us, a smattering of pastels in the crowd. I had a mint green tennis dress on, myself. Violet was wearing a black t-shirt and similarly grim-hued yoga pants. On the bright side, she was wearing excellent tennis shoes. Honestly, when I gave them to her as a gift this morning, she should have known something was up, although, to be fair, she was half asleep at the time.

"Your friend appears to be…struggling."

Snookie might have been just a little bit evil, but she wasn't blind. Violet, bless her heart, was not a natural. Lucas seemed to be directing his efforts at teaching her to rally instead of serve. He'd always been a smart boy. Violet was still holding the racquet like it was a weapon, but it was hard for me to find fault with that.

"So, what is this I hear about Stuart being accepted into the Beaver Brooke community?" Snookie said.

The nasal undertone in her voice was unmistakable. She was having allergies again, and I made a mental note to take advantage of that fact sometime soon. Her known allergens were ragweed, shellfish, and me.

Then I tried to squelch the irritation bubbling up inside me at her words. Stu Barker was one of my oldest and dearest friends, and Beaver Brooke was a new condo development on the other side of the island that they were breaking ground on tomorrow.

Stu owned his own hardware store in town, but other than that, was utterly disinterested in capitalism. He'd never dabbled in real estate before, and he'd bought the place at Beaver Brooke without speaking to me or a financial planner or even the good folks at the island credit union. I'd been worrying on and off about this for over a month now, and I was struggling to tamp it down. Being overly emotional was always bad for business.

"Irma? Are you having age-related hearing problems again?"

"Snookie," I said, as calmly as I could possibly manage. "You are only four years younger than me."

She gasped, resting her hand on her chest in outrage. "I will have you know I am fifty-nine!"

My head tilted, all on its own. I'd always been drawn to viewing the world from an off-kilter perch. "I will have you know that you were born at St. Michael's Hospital in Toronto on June 17th at three thirty-two in the morning. Sixty-seven years ago." I wasn't positive about the time, but she probably didn't know either, so it felt like a safe bet. Plus, three a.m. was the perfect time to take care of evil business. Everybody knew that.

She sputtered, her ears sticking out even more than usual. I felt momentarily dejected that there was no ragweed whatsoever on Club grounds.

Another member, Rose Campbell, shuffled past us with a faint, "Excuse me."

My eyes followed her. She was wearing a wrinkled tennis ensemble, which was the equivalent of showing up at the Club in a housecoat and curlers. Her head was down.

"Rose, nice to see you," I said to her back. She was one of the owners of Spa Lala, Main Street's delightful aesthetics centre, although I'd always thought she seemed a little uptight for a self-care business owner. "I had a massage at your spa the other day. I was all in knots after running the island half-marathon. Fixed me right up."

"Did you?" Snookie said, like I'd just rattled off the cipher to an enigma machine. This was actually Snookie's most dangerous trait, her gossiping. She'd ruined relationships, weddings, a competitive sewing circle, and, most memorably, a potato sack race in the early nineties.

"I certainly did."

"Oh, how nice," Rose said, her voice flat. She was wearing oversized sunglasses, so I couldn't see her eyes, but I was pretty sure she'd been crying recently. One got used to noticing such things after a career like mine. A pang of sympathy ran through me. "I'm just about to have tea, dear," I said. "Would you care to partake?"

Rose pressed her lips together. "Thank you," she said. "It must be nice to have time for tea, but I do not."

"It is, indeed," I said, my eyes narrowing as she turned and left. I made my way to one of the tables at the edge of the courts, the one in the corner that allowed me to keep my back to a wall and see all the comings and goings of the club members, and ordered *the usual.* The usual was a pot of Earl Grey tea, strong as they could possibly make it, slices of lemon on the side. Strong tea helped fortify the soul, Mother had always said.

Then I cast a glance at Violet, who seemed to be able to return the ball over the net now. At least sometimes. But she was smiling—probably in spite of herself—and Lucas was grinning at her. Ha! I knew she'd have a good time.

I turned back to watch Rose shuffle off to the parking lot. I didn't know her well; she was newly married and had only been coming to Beaver Island since last summer. I hoped nothing was seriously wrong with her.

Snookie had followed me to my table, and was hovering beside me like a velociraptor, the cords on her neck at attention. She let out an evil little laugh. "I hear she's already cheating on her husband. And they haven't even been married a year."

My stomach tightened. If Snookie already had a snootful of gossip about Rose, whatever was going on with her was very bad indeed.

Two — Violet

It was a bit creepy how much I was enjoying tennis. I was not the outdoorsy type and I had the hand-eye coordination of a drunken manatee. But after lots of warm-up and instructions like: *keep your eye on the ball, Violet. Violet, the ball! No, the ball!* I was returning Lucas's easy serves occasionally, which as far as I was concerned, was pretty awesome.

"You're doing great!" he said, with too much enthusiasm for it to seem authentic, although I could never tell about that kind of thing for sure.

"Thanks, Lucas. I think I'm getting the hang of it." It felt like a small moment of glory, until I glanced over at the next court. A pair of six-year-olds were bashing the ball back and forth like pros.

"Don't look at them," Lucas said. "Keep your focus here. On the ball. No, *the ball!*"

I watched a streak of yellow whizz past me, then jogged to the back of the court to get it, where three twenty-somethings in tennis dresses were arranged in a gaggle. They were blonde-brunette-redhead, so it looked like they'd covered all the bases there.

"Excuse me," I said, trying to squish the ball between my racquet and the clay surface of the court. And failing. I finally grabbed the little sucker and walked back to the court's centreline. I was sweating in the heat, the sun beating down on me.

Lucas and I batted the ball back and forth until the short lesson came to an end. I glanced over to see that Irma had somehow wrangled herself a courtside tea service delivery, which she was enjoying with a fervour normally reserved for the Queen of England.

Her petite, elegant form was tucked into a chair, her silver, chin-length bob still perfectly coiffed even though she'd spent an hour tearing up the court with Lucas. I sometimes wondered how someone so tiny could ingest that much tea. It had to be a British thing.

"Thanks very much," I said, shaking Lucas's hand. He looked a bit awkward at that and my stomach tightened. Was I supposed to tip him? I'd have to google what to do when I got out of his sight.

"I'm going to come with you, if you don't mind. I need to talk to Irma about something." He fell in step beside me.

"What's up?" I asked, immediately feeling awkward over my nosy question.

"Just some weird letters I've been getting," he said with a shrug. "Irma's on the board of the Club and I thought I'd run it past her. I don't want to make a big thing about it."

"Lucas," the blonde from the gaggle called to him. "I need to speak to you. *Now.*" She was probably a size zero, with long frosted blonde hair, big, blue eyes, and dainty, girlish features. Her outfit contained so many different shades of pink it looked like a Barbie factory had exploded on her.

"Tiffanni!" Lucas said, his voice slightly exasperated. Across the court, Irma brought her cup to her mouth, then raised her eyebrows at me. I sent her an *It's-your-club* shrug.

Tiffanni hissed loudly, her cheeks reddening. "How could you do this to me?"

I cast a glance around the court. Everyone had stopped playing. Tennis skirts that were swishing came to a rest. Feet that were running froze. Mouths hung open. I briefly considered taking a picture to show my friends back home in Toronto but decided it would be in bad taste.

"I...I don't know what you're talking about," Lucas stammered, backing up. Red was creeping up his neck and into his ears.

"You're going to pay for what you've done to me!" Tiffanni shrieked. She brought her racquet—still nestled in its bedazzled pink covering—down on the clay with a smash. Rhinestones flew off like popcorn.

"Tiffanni," he said more firmly. "Stop that, please." He turned away to calm one of the other club members.

Another shriek, which she punctuated by throwing her racquet. Unfortunately, it caught Lucas right at the back of the neck, dropping him like a stone.

When he didn't move, two players from another court ran forward. Dr. Julian Harper was a friend of Irma's and someone I'd gotten to know a bit during my visit, and his tennis-mate was another doctor at the island clinic, Dr. Angelique Harris.

"Anj," Julian said to her, "Can you please help roll him over?"

Angelique nodded briskly and supported Lucas's head as they turned him. She checked the hollow of his neck with two fingers. "Strong pulse," she said.

Tiffanni was standing beside me, her hands slack at her sides. "Did you see that?" she said breathlessly.

"I think half the Club saw it."

She made a horrified squeaking noise and clapped a hand over her mouth, before running back to her little clique.

Lucas groaned, and Angelique fanned him. I stood, semi-frozen, hoping he was all right, and after a few minutes he pulled himself into a seated position. Julian helped him to his feet.

Irma'd abandoned her tea and sidled up to me. "What's going on?"

"The blonde says Lucas is going to pay for what he's done to her."

"Oh, righto, then."

Lucas was on his feet now, sweat rolling off his face, which was red with embarrassment. Tiffanni sobbed to her entourage, who patted her on the back, casting frowny glances at Lucas.

In unison, they picked up their pastel designer purses, slung them in the crooks of their elbows in a way that reminded me of a bunch of storks, and marched off the court, although it would have had a bit more impact if the redhead hadn't mouthed *call me* at Lucas as they left. I saw Irma's head slide into a tilt at that, which was never a good sign. But it sure seemed like there was more going on with her favourite tennis coach than a good backhand.

Three — Irma

I awoke at six thirty a.m. to another perfectly perfect Beaver Island day and went for my usual five-mile jog before making tea on my back deck.

As I sipped my tea, I looked out at Lake Ontario, at the deep, endless blue, while I tried to sort through the day's plans. I was an expert on many things—small arms, explosives, impersonating Scandinavian hotel staff—but I was decidedly a beginner at this retirement thing, so every day was different from the last.

Today's main task was to attend the ground-breaking at Beaver Brooke to support Stu, and another friend, Roger Patel, whose bank was underwriting the project. Later, I hoped to get some work done on my flowerbeds, which seemed to be criticizing me with their drooping marigolds. I told myself again that a lobbing a flash-bang in their direction was not going to convince them to do otherwise.

Eventually, Violet emerged from the house and we hopped in my boat. Almost immediately she was tugging on my sleeve, which was somewhat surprising, as she was most definitely not the touchy-feely type.

"Yes, dear?"

After a deep inhale, she said, "Can you please slow dooooown?" The last word was picked up by the wind and echoed out over the water.

I had to admit I was going a little fast, even for me. I throttled my sixteen-foot vintage Cris Craft speedboat down. She was a city slicker, the poor thing. Hadn't found her sea legs yet.

"Sorry, Violet," I said. "Is this better?"

She nodded, and I made sure to keep at that speed for the duration. We passed the ferry and waved at the ferry master, Asif, who waved back. It was the only way on or off the island without a boat or a plane, and it was always best to keep in the good books of folks responsible for hard-to-obtain-on-your-own transportation. Plus, he was a lovely man. Took part in competitive duck herding in his spare time.

We arrived at the ground-breaking site a few minutes later. I'd been worried we'd be late, but in fact we were ten minutes early, which was a nice surprise. Violet staggered a bit when she flung herself off the boat, but less than usual. I was heartened to see she was making progress.

"Irma!" My good friend, Roger Patel, strode toward us. "How lovely to see you!" His East

London accent was as strong as ever, even though he'd left home over thirty years ago and relocated to our tiny Lake Ontario island to run the local credit union.

"Roger!" I called out in return. For some reason my own English accent was always sharper around him, although it had been pounded down by a childhood growing up all over—military families, always on the run—and summers here.

He was wearing one of his signature high street suits, spiffy Italian dress shoes, and a meticulously folded pocket square in his breast pocket. White. He kissed me on each cheek, leaning down gracefully to do so. I liked that he never made any comments about my height, especially since it was such a long trip down for him.

"Violet," he said warmly, leaning forward to kiss her left cheek. She didn't flinch like she would with most people, which meant she liked Roger at least a little.

"Is Nelson coming, dear?" I asked.

Roger sighed, then lifted his shoulders in a tiny shrug. "He's with his mother."

That was pretty much enough said. Nelson, Roger's husband, had a mother who maintained a vice grip on him and his time. He wasn't particularly adept at wriggling out of it, poor thing. I'd told Roger I would put a bomb under her car—not to blow her up, just the car—to keep her out of his hair for a bit if he wanted. He was still thinking about it.

As we walked, I looked around. It was a gorgeous site, I had to admit. That was the problem. The condos were going to be built on a piece of land that jutted out into the lake, a beautiful little spot tucked into a natural bay. It had been owned by a prominent summer family who'd lost it in a high stakes poker hand in Idaho a while back. If I'd known it was going to be sold, I would have bought it myself.

Roger went off to schmooze for a bit. A gorgeous table of goodies was located at one side of the site, and people were milling about, partaking. In the distance, a huge red tractor was poised over a patch of dirt that looked like it had been cleared for the occasion.

There were two structures on the scene: a beautifully architected sales office with an earthy flowerbed snugged up to it that looked freshly mulched, and a sleek trailer on the other side of the site, where all the real office work probably happened. The two structures were located on opposite sides of what used to be the main house's croquet pitch, where the crowd was munching and milling.

But it was hard to be happy. Mother and I used to ride out here on our bicycles and sit and watch the water hit the natural beach in the bay. It was a beautiful spot, even with the gaping hole where the house used to stand taking up the far edge of the property.

Carlton Campbell, whose family owned the company in charge of the build, popped out from behind a waiter who was serving sandwiches shaped like tiny beavers. Much of the island's finger food revolved around this theme; our collective enthusiasm for beavers was unstoppable. "Irma," he said, his voice booming out over the crowd. "How wonderful to see you!"

Carlton had run over my bicycle last month, claiming he hadn't seen it. To be fair, his enormous gas-guzzling red Hummer was so high off the ground he might have even been telling the truth.

"Carlton," I said flatly.

"I'm thrilled you could make it," he said, grinning broadly. He had generic I'm-from-a-moneyed-family looks; freshly trimmed dark blond hair, tall, big-shouldered, nifty clothes. No tattoos or distinguishing marks except for his weak chin and soft hands. He'd recently turned thirty, I'd heard.

"Roger made me come."

Behind me, Violet made a strangled noise that I decided to take as supportive.

"Wonderful. Have you had anything to eat?"

A good friend of mine had been poisoned at a public event recently, and I was reluctant to partake of communal food for a while. "I'm full, thank you," I said.

He wrapped his arm around me, and I was proud of myself for not immediately stabbing him in the liver. I wasn't as averse to human touch as Violet, but I didn't really care for people putting their paws all over me. Especially newly thirty-year-old men who thought women of my age—and their bicycles—were no more than irritating inconveniences.

I extricated myself from his grip and put some distance between us. He started walking, motioned for me to follow. I fell in step beside him to get whatever he wanted to say to me over with.

"Irma, I know we haven't always seen eye to eye on things," he said, his way of glossing over my recently squashed bicycle, and the time he yelled at Mr. Pugglesworth, my neighbour's delightful fawn pug, who I'd been holding at the time. So, I suppose he'd really been yelling at both of us.

"That's very true," I said cheerily. I'd had to deal with some quite unpleasant people in my very long career, and I'd decided at a young age not to let any of them ruin my day.

He paused, seemingly unsure about how to proceed. Good. I hoped he'd—

"I have an investment opportunity I'm not going to let you say no to."

I looked at the shiny new tractor, the impressive-looking signage. Not cheap, I was sure. And then a bad feeling burst over me. If Carlton was in financial trouble already, the project might fail. Which meant Stu would be financially ruined, since he'd paid for his condo in cash. Probably his entire life savings. I took a breath to lessen the squeeze in my chest.

"Yes?" I said.

"You could get in on an amazing opportunity here, Irma," he said, his mouth arranging itself in an overly toothy smile. "One of my buyers has dropped out, and—"

How interesting.

"—I know you're very set up financially. Your father was rolling in it, wasn't he?" His laugh was too loud. I weighed what would happen if I gave him a quick larynx punch. I swept my eyes around the site, and saw a reporter from our local paper, a few businessmen in hard hats, and an Easter-egg-hued bunch of islanders. I might get away with it if Violet distracted the reporter. I kicked myself for not progressing further with our sign language lessons.

"As was yours," I murmured. For some reason we were halfway into a corn field by now. The previous owners had dabbled in hobby farming as well as losing at cards, and the strip of land between the festivities and the main road had been turned into crops, bordered by a stand of trees that blocked the view of the site. The heads for the field's sprinkler system were comically oversized and industrial, the type of thing people who knew nothing about farming would buy. Maybe I could trip Carlton out here without anyone seeing us, and blame it on an enormous sprinkler head. I might even get away with it.

"My father worked for a living."

"As did mine," I said softly, taking a breath to centre myself. I really hoped he wasn't going to insult Father.

He held his arms out. "My dad was the last of a dying breed. He built half this island with his bare hands."

His father had been a real estate developer who sat in a very nice air-conditioned office every single day of his life, and paid his staff a pittance.

"He'd be so proud of me with this project, I just know it. And I can't wait to get started. We'll have a whole thriving community here in no time. And," he lowered his voice meaningfully, "it would be an excellent place for you to move to. You're not getting any younger, you know."

A small shock bloomed in my chest. As if I would ever leave my beloved house. And nobody was ever getting any younger, so what kind of point did he think he was making?

"Women your age break hips all the time, and—"

I tried not to shudder.

"—a single floor penthouse is exactly what you need! Rent it out until you need to move in."

Interesting. His penthouse buyer had weaselled out of their purchase agreement.

He gave me a look that someone must have once told him was charming. "Whadya say, Irma? Doesn't it sound like a great idea? You can walk in the front door and out to your boat."

I tilted my head. I already had the exact same setup, only with my family's Victorian house.

"You can think about it," he said, like he was doing me a favour. But was that sweat gathering on his brow? Was perspiration darkening the back of his hair?

"Thank you for thinking of me, but I don't think so," I said, no emotion whatsoever in my voice.

"I'm not sure if you really understand the opportunity here, Irma." He brushed some hair off his forehead and swung around so he could take in the panoramic view: a natural beach, a hooked slip of land that protected the bay, a perfect place for a boat. Walk in the front door and out the back to a dock, sail all your troubles away.

"I'm quite sure I do, dear. I wouldn't mind tickets to your poker tournament next Friday, though," I said slyly. The tournament was an annual charity game held on his family's superyacht. It always attracted some intriguing characters, and I was someone who liked to know when interesting people were in town. I'd given my reserved tickets away to a friend of mine a few months back, thinking it would be easy to get more. Tragically, this had not been the case.

"The tournament is sold out, Irma," he said with a shrug. "Sorry. Well, think about that penthouse, all right? It's a beautiful investment opportunity."

"Carlton?" The CEO of Carlton's company, a rotundly pregnant woman named Elsa Lee, was trailing behind us. "We have to get started soon." A young woman with two-inch-long dark roots and blonde hair hovered beside Elsa, wearing formal office wear, her lavender shirt so buttoned-up I was impressed she could still breathe.

Carlton made an irritated noise, but nodded. I murmured a goodbye and walked back to the crowd with Elsa. The buttoned-up blonde flitted along behind Carlton.

"How are you doing, dear?" I asked Elsa. "And my goodness, does that young lady realize her roots are showing and—"

"It's called an ombré, Irma."

"I see." It was no beehive, but I supposed one must move with the times. "Who is she?"

"Our new office coordinator." Elsa was puffing a bit, so we slowed down.

"When are you due?"

"Three weeks," she said with no small amount of drama, pushing a lock of damp hair off her forehead. She was somewhere in her late thirties, with a shock of dark brown hair that fell to her shoulders. She was average height and build—or was when she wasn't hosting a little one inside her, with a lovely smile she wasn't shy about showing off. Her outfit today was pretty snazzy, but her shoes appeared to be orthopedic. Well, I'd always been a fan of sensible shoes. "I used to ski black diamond hills! And scuba dive, and... Soon they'll be able to roll me right down a hill."

I laughed. I didn't know her well—she'd only been in town a few years—but I was glad she'd come on board at Carlton's company—Carlton's *family's* company, really. Elsa had apparently despaired of ever finding a mate and had conceived her child with a donor. I liked that kind of moxie.

"You here for the pastry?"

"Stu bought a condo," I said.

"What a character he is," she said, grinning widely. She put a hand on her hip and winced.

"You all right, dear?"

"I seem to throw my back out almost every night these days. I just can't find a comfortable position to sleep in." She hitched a heavy-looking handbag up her shoulder and blew out a sigh.

"Have you spoken to anyone at the island clinic about it?"

She shook her head. "My obstetrician is on the mainland. She says this is all normal. At least it'll be over soon. Anyway, I'm going to go sit down in the construction office." She inclined her head toward the fancy trailer at the edge of the site. "Don't narc on me, please."

"My lips are sealed."

She waved, then waddled off. Some women barely looked pregnant right up until giving birth, but Elsa looked like she was about to have triplets. But when she reached the trailer, she dashed up the stairs and into the little structure like a schoolgirl. She *must* be intent on sitting down, the poor thing, and who could blame her? It was going to be a scorcher out today.

I walked back to the crowd. I knew Violet would be at the snack table and that's exactly where I found her. I bit my tongue instead of telling her how predictable routines made one susceptible to assassins and bill collectors. She knew I was a retired intelligence agent, but thus far, I'd kept mum on the details, which was really better for everyone concerned. Only a handful of people on the island knew anything about my colourful—and classified—past. My cover story was supply chain management, which luckily most people perceived as so dull they never asked me any questions about it.

"Hello there," I said, "and what on earth is that?"

Violet was holding a beaver-sized pastry with sprinkles and sky-high icing. "Cupckhk," she said, sounding like a teenager on a drinking binge. "Try one!"

I could smell the sugar from where I was standing. "Thank you, dear. Maybe later." Although perhaps never. "Are you having fun?"

She nodded her head fiercely. "Have you tried the beavers-in-a-blanket?"

"What on earth are they?"

"Pigs-in-a-blanket, but *fancier*."

I stifled my shudder. I wasn't still alive at seventy-one because I had bad situational awareness, and that extended to beaver-shaped foods, no matter how much I adored beavers, those majestic, hard-working little critters.

"This is a fascinating setup," she said, swallowing. I cast my eyes around, looking for tea, but saw only wine, champagne, and soft drinks. Bother.

"Why? And please note how I'm not reminding you I knew you'd have fun."

"Yeah, you have real restraint." She grinned. "First of all, they *also* have a sprinkler system here that's open to attack. The IOT scanner app on my phone has been going off like crazy."

"Didn't you mention something about that when we were at the Club?"

"Yeah. Can you hook up with someone there and let them know it's an issue?"

I nodded. I was on the Club's board and liked to stay on top of issues, especially security ones, although a compromised irrigation system wasn't exactly an all-hands-on-deck situation. "Thank you, dear."

"No problemo. Oh, and I forgot to tell you Lucas wanted to talk to you yesterday. I guess he went home after the whole Tiffanni thing."

"Did he say what about?"

"Something to do with letters he's been getting? He didn't want to go to Club management about it."

"Huh. Well, thank you. I'll give him a call later."

"Right on. Anyway," she pointed at the shiny new tractor, a *LEBLANC INDUSTRIES* logo stamped to its flank. "I've been reading about these. Remotely operated, and automated."

"Automated? Like robots?"

"Yeah, kind of. They're used for repetitive tasks, like if you were digging a ditch or something like that, you just program them and go for lunch."

"What if there are other people working on the site? Isn't that dangerous?"

"They have sensors just like automatic cars. Pretty cool, eh?"

I knew she was serious because she smiled the way she did when she saw cupcakes: thrilled, toothy, drooling a little. She was the Chief Technical Officer of a Toronto startup and was perpetually enraptured by machines. Myself, I preferred good, old-fashioned fieldwork and brain power, but I couldn't deny she knew her computer systems.

"The sign makes more sense, then," I said, gesturing at the oversized lettering announcing the site: *Beaver Brooke, A Green Technology Project.*

She shrugged. "They could be talking about the actual build. Or it could be a digitally connected community."

"I don't even want to know what that means."

"It means you're a technophobe. A Luddite, a—"

"That's quite enough, thanks."

"An analoguer, a—"

"That's not even a word."

"It could be. You deliberately leave your cell phone at home every chance you get. Who does that?"

I decided to let her win the point, mostly because she was completely correct. Cellular telephones were handy in some circumstances—if a sniper was trying to put a slug in your brain while you were crouched behind your car in the parking lot of a karaoke bar at three in the morning in Oklahoma, not that that specific example had happened to me and two friends last August—but were so noisy and annoying it was hard to justify it all.

Rose Campbell approached us, a smile almost as big as Carlton's on her face.

"Hello, dear." I turned to introduce her to Violet, but she'd already escaped back to the buffet table.

"Hello," Rose said, air-kissing me. She looked worlds better than she had yesterday. I examined her more closely. She was medium-sized, with delicate hands and long brown hair that was cinched into a bun. Her skin was plump with youth, probably courtesy of her spa.

"How are you?"

"Wonderful. I'm sorry I was so distracted yesterday when I saw you. I'm just not sleeping well these days."

I patted her on the arm. "I'm glad you're feeling better. You must be excited about the ground-breaking. Do you know when construction will be finished?"

"Should be move-in ready in the fall. I've been helping with the accounting a bit, and I don't think I can work two jobs longer than that." She had a flute of champagne in one hand, and after swallowing a huge gulp, she added, "What's wrong with your friend?"

"What do you mean?"

"I mean—" she giggled into her glass, "—does she ever wear anything that's not black?"

I turned my head to her, slowly, so she could see the expression on my face coming. Violet was wearing a t-shirt and jeans, perfectly normal attire. And I did not approve of clothing snobbishness whatsoever.

Rose turned to see Carlton gesturing at her. "There's my cue," she said. "See you later."

I nodded. Hopefully, all this wouldn't take too much time. I had another beautiful summer day in front of me. My retirement was going swimmingly. It was true I'd gotten pulled into a small operation recently that required some quick thinking, a bit of nerd herding, and a well-timed larynx punch, but surely now I could focus on my retirement goals: being on the water as much as humanly possible, getting periodic revenge on Snookie, helping Violet enjoy her vacation, sailing with Stu, training for the next island marathon, working on my tennis swing, tending my garden, and wrangling tickets for the poker tournament next Friday. I had no intention of being left ashore for that particular event. A European cat burglar had showed up one year and tried to walk off with the Campbell family jewels. Another year, the yacht had run aground. I simply couldn't take any chances with it.

A moment later, Carlton called us all over and the crowd gathered in a clutch in front of a modest podium that had been erected, the tractor gleaming in the sun behind it. I chose to stand at the back so I could have a full view of the crowd, and nobody standing behind me could stab me in one of my kidneys.

Rose joined him briefly on the little platform. He beamed a look at her that was full of youthful adoration. It had always amazed me how semi-rotten people could bloom in some circumstances.

I nodded at Violet, and she joined me at the back of the crowd. Her hands were empty, but I wouldn't put it past her to have stashed a cupcake in her underpants.

Carlton mounted the podium and held his hands up for silence. The crowd was carbohydrate-stuffed and compliant. Wind picked up from the lake and ruffled everyone's clothes, reminding me of how much I'd rather be out on the water.

"Irma." Ronnie Thomas had been inching her way over to me for some time now and had finally arrived. She was one of two reporters for the town paper and enjoyed trying to startle me. I liked her enough to not want to kill her over it. Across the pitch, Carlton started his speech.

"Ronnie," I said quietly. Her trim twenty-something figure was tucked into a faded pair of jeans, a t-shirt, and a stylish blazer, a tiny gold hoop through her nose, her ebony complexion glowing in the sun. She'd always had a smile that lit up the room. "This is my friend, Violet."

Violet looked at Ronnie's outstretched hand like she'd forgotten what to do with it. She finally stuck her hand out, overshooting Ronnie's a little. Ronnie smiled at her as they shook. "Nice to meet you."

Violet smiled briefly, then turned around to watch Carlton speak.

"Got roped into this, huh?" Ronnie said out of one side of her mouth.

"Roger asked me to come. And Stu."

"I heard Carlton's having financial difficulty. But you didn't hear it from me."

I raised my eyebrows. "Please go on."

"I'm not sure of the specifics, but someone somewhere will want to spill that tea. I'll do a little digging."

I gave her a meaningful look and she nodded. Ronnie and I had always worked well together. I generally liked people who asked questions that were none of their business, as long as they didn't pester me with any.

Carlton seemed to be winding his speech up, and scattered applause rippled over the crowd. I wondered if they were investors or just here for the free sweets from Luna's Café, an island treasure. I'd even convinced Luna to carry bran-protein muffins recently, which was an exciting contribution to our island's gastrointestinal health. None were here today, unfortunately.

Then, Carlton signalled to one of the men standing off to the side, who was wearing a hard hat and looked like the only person here who'd ever actually spent time on a construction site. He nodded and walked toward the dais.

Four — Violet

To our left, Irma's buddy Stu emerged from his battered blue pickup and loped toward us, grinning, his Gandalf-length grey beard flapping in the wind. He was wearing faded Levis and a t-shirt that said, *The Rodfather,* a happy-looking catfish holding a fishing rod stamped on his chest. I liked him. He was a jokester with a kind heart. I'd never had a grandfather, but if I had, I would have wanted him to be like Stu.

I waved while eyeballing another cupcake, hoping Stu could distract Irma long enough for me to grab it. Of course, after a moment of focusing on that, I tried to reason through how Irma had talked me into attending a groundbreaking for a construction project that had nothing to do with me instead of letting me sleep in and play video games.

Maybe it was Irma's cult-leader charm or her Jedi mind tricks. Maybe it was the fact that she cared about the state of my cardiovascular fitness and served me undrinkably strong tea and healthy—yet inedible—snacks on trays full of doilies. Maybe it was because my business life had recently exploded when I'd discovered my long-time friend and one of my two business partners had hollowed out our company's bank accounts, and visiting Irma had turned out to be a delightful distraction from all that. Getting shot at really helped you focus on the important things in life.

"Howdy, ya'll," Stu drawled, hugging Irma. He nudged me with his shoulder. "Hey, kiddo."

I grinned. "What's up, Stu?"

"I'm going to have a party at my place to celebrate my new place," he said. "Hey, that rhymed."

"When?" I asked.

"Soon," he said. "We'll BBQ a pig, do a potluck. You guys in?"

"Of course, Stuart," Irma said, her tiny cheeks rosy. "I'm so proud of you."

I turned away to give them a moment of privacy. That was when I noticed the hard-hatted guy's frown. He was trying to say something to the preppy-looking dude who seemed to be in charge of everything.

I looked out at the lake. The wind had picked up, and waves were crashing around the breakwater. When the project was completed, the bay would be full of boats at anchor and docked behind the townhouses. Piers would jut out into the lake, if you believed the brochure I'd just picked up from a pile beside the canapés. Plus, it was an eco-friendly project, which was cool. My own company had been built around renewables.

The hard hat-wearer on the dais looked to be in his thirties, and had a long ponytail that snaked down his back, wide shoulders and a scraggly chinstrap beard. He towered over Carlton as he gestured at the tractor. I cast another glance at the buffet table. I just wanted one more cupcake, and—

"Ladies and gentlemen," the preppy guy said into his mic, which squawked with feedback, "I'm Carlton Campbell, and we're about to break ground for our Beaver Brooke dig! Please stay tuned."

He switched the mic off and stomped over to Ponytail, who held a thick, boxy tablet computer he was swiping to try to accomplish something important enough to get yelled at about. Carlton seemed to be getting madder and madder. I'd worked for a few bosses who'd turned that particular shade of red every so often. It wasn't a great sign.

Stu and I chatted while Ponytail and Carlton argued. Finally, Ponytail pointed at something on the tablet, pulling it out of Carlton's hand. Carlton turned to the crowd, all smiles. Thirty feet away, the tractor stirred. Carlton slapped Ponytail on the shoulder. It looked like whatever problem they'd been arguing about was solved.

Carlton tapped the mic a few times. "Thanks for your patience, everyone, you know how technology can be."

I wondered if the people who made those kinds of announcements, especially to crowds, ever thought about the feelings of the people who maintained these systems and made them work in the first place.

Ponytail handed the tablet to Carlton and took a few steps back. Carlton hoisted the tablet above his head like it was the Stanley Cup, then held it out in front of him.

The large, red machine had a front-end loader, a bucket on arms that attached to the tractor. The bucket tilted up, down, down, up, until Carlton finally found the right angle of attack. Slowly, so slowly, it swung toward the ground. If this was the future of construction, no houses were actually going to be built ever again.

The bucket hit the ground with a muffled clang and grabbed a bit of land. Then it stopped. The crowd looked at each other hesitantly, and a faint smattering of applause broke out. I clapped my hands together twice and felt like I'd offered a reasonable level of support for the project.

Remembering the cupcakes made me start clapping again.

"Thank you, everyone!" Carlton said, beaming. "We have more drinks and refreshments and food and all that. Please help yourselves. And if you have any questions about the units, please find me!"

Beside me, Irma and Stu were chatting about a trip they'd taken in the nineties, which had somehow ended up with Stu sleeping in a tractor.

I was trying to figure out a way to get another cupcake. I took a step away from Irma, then another.

Carlton was chatting with Ponytail Guy and eventually handed the tablet back to Carlton. It was zipped in a briefcase before I could blink. It looked like Ponytail Guy had about enough of Carlton.

Another step toward the buffet table. But I stopped. The tablet they'd been using to control the shiny red tractor was still tucked away in Ponytail Guy's briefcase.

So why was the tractor moving?

I squinted. Maybe I was wrong. Maybe I was still nauseous from being in Irma's boat.

The crowd was noisy, all of them jostling for free champagne and beaveriffic finger foods. Carlton and ponytail were still on the dais, and behind them was the tractor.

The front end loader moved first; the bucket raising, then tucking itself, so it was off the ground but still in front of the wheels. Then it backed up and did a better three-point turn than I did most days in my little Honda, which I'd driven to the island, but had been sitting in Irma's driveway, unstartable, ever since I got here, probably because she'd secretly yanked its spark plugs so we'd have to spend more time together. And I wasn't even mad about it, more proof of Irma's hypnotic personality.

I glanced around. Irma and Stu were behind me, on the left, the rest of the crowd and the buffet tables on my right. A few of the spectators were glued to their phones, most of them carrying on a conversation with the people around them at the same time. Sometimes I thought Irma might have a point with all her cell phone negativity.

I looked at the tractor again. It was facing us now, still about thirty feet away. After a minute, I decided the strange movements had been a sign-off sequence of some kind. Then I took another step toward the cupcakes. I really wanted to try a red velvet; they were shaped like carrots and decorated with enormous beaver teeth.

While I contemplated the best way to do that, I heard a funny noise coming from the tractor. At first, I couldn't figure out what it was.

"Irma?"

"Yes, dear?" Irma answered. To Stu, she said, "And then the goat started eating your beard!"

Stu guffawed like the salty old sailor he was.

"Irma?"

"Yes, dear? Remember those ducks! They were definitely up to something."

"Irmaaaaaa!"

I had figured out what the problem was. The tractor was getting bigger.

On the dais, Ponytail Guy's arm flung out and he tried to grab a handful of Carlton's shirt, to pull him out of the tractor's path. Ponytail missed, and fell off the stage. Irma's friend Roger was in the corn field and ran to help but tripped on a gigantic sprinkler head instead, face-planting in the dirt.

The tractor bore down on the dais. Panic jolted me. My legs were suddenly frozen to the earth, my lungs iced into my chest. The crowd was silent, all of them equally immobile, except for a woman who'd been speaking to Irma earlier. She had her phone up, recording.

Then, to my left, a flash of pastels and tiny feet.

Irma was running, her arms out in front of her. She sprinted to the stage and was beside Carlton in a flash. She got down into a crouch and used her momentum to push him out of the path of the tractor.

But he fell the wrong way.

I could almost feel Irma's exasperation from where I was. Then she reached down and started dragging him to the side of the stage. It was slow going. The tractor ground to a halt about five feet away from them.

"Thank goodness that's over," I breathed. My heart was pounding in my chest. "That was very exciting."

"Oh, it's not over," Stu said cheerfully. "Not if Irma's around."

"Excellent point. Cupcake?"

Stu grinned. "Don't mind if I do."

But Stu was right. Suddenly, the tractor came back to life and started rolling toward the dais, which it crushed under its bulky wheels. Carlton had grabbed Ponytail's bag and pulled out the remote, which he swiped at wildly. Nothing seemed to be working.

"Oh no!" Stu said.

"What?"

"It's headed toward the buffet table."

"Not the buffet table!"

But it was true. The tractor's bucket was just the right height to scoop away all the goodies. Its huge wheels chewed up the table and kept going.

Then it turned, the crowd bursting away from it. Some people were headed for the parking area, some of them splashed with red wine, others with fists full of beavers-in-a-blanket. One guy had cheeks so full, he looked like a squirrel. He chewed and ran.

The machine started bearing down on the crowd, most of whom were crashing into each other trying to get out of the way. I felt my breath coming ragged in my chest. I didn't like crowds, and I definitely did not want to be trampled to death. Not while there were still cupcakes to be eaten, video games to play—

Irma sprinted to the tractor and leaped into the air, landing on the stairs. The tractor kept on going, but she grabbed onto a handhold on the side of the stairs and, one step at a time, ascended to the driver's seat. Immediately, she wrenched the steering wheel to the right, then pressed down on the brakes. But the tractor didn't even slow down.

By now it had rampaged the dais, the food services, and the circle of land the crowd had been standing on.

But a figure had become separated from the crowd. I squinted. Uh-oh. It was Snookie Smith, standing directly in the tractor's path, hands on her hips. And she wasn't moving.

Then Ponytail Guy was running beside the tractor. Irma held out a tiny arm for him to grasp, and he held onto it as he jumped up to the platform holding the operator's seat.

Irma gestured at Snookie to get out of the way. But Snookie didn't move. Then it was the tractor, Snookie, and fifteen feet between them. Irma motioned at Snookie to get out of the way, and yelled (I thought), "Move, you muppet!" but Snookie crossed her arms instead of finding safety. Then it was ten feet, then three. Snookie finally came to her senses and started her getaway, but it was too little, too late. The tractor bumped into her—well, her butt, actually—and kept going. Snookie screamed and fell to the ground, curling into a fetal position.

And the tractor rolled on. The bucket was now aimed at the sales office, a modern Scandinavian design with a flat roof covered in Titan 3000 solar panels, an excellent brand. The sales office was probably a thousand square feet, the lake-facing edge of the building made of wall-to-ceiling glass. It looked cute, I thought; great view, too.

The windows were what made the most noise when the tractor crashed into the office. They popped like explosions, glass flying through the air. The sales office hadn't been built to last. It was just a slapped-together thing that looked good and would have been gone soon anyway.

Irma hunched over the wheel, and so did Ponytail Guy. The tractor stopped, then backed up, and for a moment I thought Irma'd gotten control of it all. But the bucket had gone crazy; it raised and dove into the ground.

Finally, after part of the sales office roof was folded over the tractor like an umbrella on a sunny day, the tractor stopped.

It took me a minute to catch my breath. "Is she okay?" I asked Stu. But he was already running toward the building. My feet finally started working, and I followed behind him.

Dust rose from the building and was whipped away by the wind. The front of the sales office was destroyed, the back section still somewhat intact. But the building was creaking in a way that made me nervous.

"Irmie!" Stu called.

Ponytail lurched out of the building, crouched over, coughing. He was bleeding on the side of his head and looked woozy.

"Hey, you okay?" His eyes met mine—ocean blue—and he blinked. I led him from the wreckage of the structure.

Inside, Stu was calling for Irma. And then he was carrying her like she was a small child. My chest hurt. I'd never seen Irma actually affected by normal life things that were so bothersome for everyone else. Like the space-time continuum. And gravity. But I was worried.

"Put me down, Stuart!" Irma hollered, and the squeeze in my heart let go.

Until I saw the jean jacket that had been uncovered when the tractor had dug into the flower bed. And the body it was attached to.

Five — Irma

The island clinic was so cold it made my nose hurt.

"Hold still, Irma," Dr. Julian Harper said. He was sterilising a tiny wound on my left calf. Tiny!

"Honestly, dear, you worry too much."

"I don't, actually," he said, pushing back the wavy hair that always flopped across his forehead. He was tall and lean, just like his grandfather had been, with sharp blue-green eyes and a lovely smile. "You should not be hopping on remote controlled tractors at your—"

"At my *what*?"

He pressed his lips together like he was trying not to laugh. On the chair opposite me, Violet was making no such efforts. She jiggled with mirth, even though I could kill her with my thumb. Not that I would, I mean how impolite would it be to murder one's own house guest? But, still.

"You're all set, Irma," Julian said, pressing a bandage on my calf. He snapped off his gloves, smiled, and left us alone.

"Why don't you ask him out for dinner?" I said.

Violet made a noncommittal noise. "We're just friends, Irma."

I sashayed to the door and opened it with a flourish. "I could tell you about how I was just friends with husband number two, as well."

"Wasn't he the one you married twice?"

"Yes," I answered, "But the first time really didn't count."

She laughed. "Are we going home now?"

"No," I said. "We're going to thank that nice young man for his help."

"Cool."

I made my way down the hallway, avoiding Snookie's room. I knew she had been brought here as well. Three doors down, I found the heroic young man. He was lying in bed, a bandage on his head. His eyes were closed. I knocked gently on the door. If he was sleeping, I'd just leave him a thank-you note.

But he opened his eyes and smiled at us. He was in his thirties, his long brown hair loose on the pillow behind him. He had unusual facial hair, electric blue eyes, and a nice smile. "Hey there."

"Hello, dear." I introduced myself and Violet, and he told us his name was David Bell. "I just wanted to thank you for your help, David. That was very exciting, wasn't it!"

"Yeah," he said, looking sombre, "except for the dead body and all."

"I know. That was a surprise, definitely, but try not to focus on that part. You're a hero, Mr. Bell."

He drank some water from the pitcher beside his bed and didn't look convinced. "Do you know who it was?"

I shook my head. "The police will release the name once the family has been informed. But you just try to rest. You're a very brave young man. Someone could have been hurt."

"Someone *was* hurt," Violet pointed out.

"Eh," I said with a shrug. "Snookie deliberately put herself in harm's way. It couldn't be helped."

"Yeah, that lady's crazy," David said.

"You're absolutely correct on that point, dear."

He closed his eyes for a minute. When he opened them, he said, "Is Elsa here, do you know?"

"I haven't seen her. It was quite chaotic. And she wasn't feeling particularly well earlier."

A nod. "I'll call her later."

"Sounds good, David. We're going to go now, but I appreciate your help very much. If you ever need anything, please let me know."

"You're welcome," he said with a half-grin. "Let's not ever do it again."

I smiled and ushered Violet out of the room, closing it behind me softly. To Violet, I said, "I certainly hope Carlton gives me tickets to the poker tournament next Friday, after all that."

"What poker tournament?"

I sketched in the details for her, leaving out how I wanted to make sure that no miscreants drifted into town and joined the festivities. One year a con artist from Canarsie had almost an entire deck of cards up her sleeve before I relieved her of them.

"I'm sure he will," she said when I was done. "Are we going home now?"

"Oh, I think we need some tea, don't you?" I paused for a minute to take a breath. I was more bothered by the events of the morning than I wanted to let on. It was a particular worry of mine that people would let technology take over every aspect of our lives. It was part of the reason I was so bothered by cellular telephones. And an hour ago, I'd seen that reality face to face. I had no intention of dying at the hands of a killer robot. I planned on popping off while scaling Everest or trying out base jumping. You know, the usual.

"I'm going to have to delay your teatime a bit, I'm afraid," a woman's voice said.

Our town's brand-new police chief was standing in the hallway, legs at shoulder distance, hands clasped behind her back. She was somewhere in her late forties, olive-complected and sturdily built but with a feminine flair. Her dark brown eyes didn't miss much, and her long brown hair was cinched in a bun so tight it probably explained her cranky nature. I kept the disappointment from showing on my face. "Chief Mavis Pickle."

"Mrs. Irma Abercrombie." A stern nod. "It'll only take a minute."

Violet melted away from me. She was no huge fan of law enforcement, and she'd already given her statement about what had happened. The Pickle led me out the front door of the clinic, straight into a waiting police car, its engine still running.

"Oh, dear," I said, "That's terrible for the environment. And against one of the town bylaws, is it not?"

"Not sure, Mrs. Abercrombie."

We paused, her at the driver's side door, me on the passenger side. "Bylaw 187, paragraph two, I believe," I said.

"I can't transport you in the passenger side, Mrs. Abercrombie, I'm so sorry to say. Bylaw nine, paragraph five. Can you sit in the back, please?"

"Like a common criminal? I'm terribly sorry, dear." I smiled. "I couldn't possibly." The back doors of police cruisers did not open from the inside. I'd been trapped in such a way during a riot back in '91, and let me tell you, I did not enjoy it one bit.

The Pickle grit her teeth, but said nothing.

"I'll walk," I said sweetly. Of course, I planned on snatching Violet up and slipping away to my boat, but the new chief couldn't possibly know that.

"I'll join you," she said, turning the car off and extracting her keys from the ignition.

Was it wrong that I felt proud of her suspiciousness? Plus, it helped me feel like I still hadn't lost my touch. Chief Pickle was a smart girl. I wished we could get along better. Life had been so much easier before Chief Klein had retired four months ago.

When I stepped beside her, she acknowledged my presence with a military-style nod, then started a brisk walk toward the police station, which bumped my heart rate up and was actually quite lovely.

When we arrived, she ushered me into a meeting room, not one of the station's interrogation rooms, and I appreciated that. My chair had no squeaks, all four legs were the same length, there were no lights so bright they could cause brain damage, and she even got me a cup of tea, albeit a weak one. As far as interrogations went, this was the Ritz Carlton.

"Thank you for coming in, Mrs. Abercrombie," she said after handing me a battered mug. She was drinking coffee. Black.

"I didn't think I had a choice. *Did* I have a choice?"

"You're a big fan of doing your civic duty," she said with no inflection whatsoever, which was impressive. She must have been working on that in her spare time.

But I said nothing. It was always easier that way.

She pressed her lips together like she was trying not to smile. "In your own words, Mrs. Abercrombie, what happened this morning at the Beaver Brooke construction site?"

I blinked a few times to make it look like I was thinking. "I've already given a statement, you know. And I'm really not quite sure. Carlton and David would understand the technology issues in play far better than I."

"Not the computer part, just what happened, what you did." She took a long, hard swallow of coffee. She probably needed it. The poor thing had moved to Beaver Island to get away from big-city violence. "Please."

The *please* was a nice touch, and I appreciated her making the effort. She wasn't my biggest fan, to be sure, but I was hoping one day we'd reach some kind of détente. It would make things so much easier.

I took a sip of my own drink and set it down. Then I remembered how the Pickle had gotten the best of me recently, and that it would not do for me to be smug in her presence. *Then* I realized I hadn't actually done anything wrong, currently, and I had nothing to hide, even if that particular thought conflicted with all my training.

I took a deep breath. "Carlton was remote-controlling the tractor to do the first dig, the ground-breaking. And the machine went haywire. Almost ran down Carlton, destroyed the buffet table. And the sales office, obviously."

"And ran over Snookie Smith."

"Hardly," I said. "She wouldn't get out of the way. I believe only her, er, buttocks were involved in the collision."

"Yes, her posterior *is* bruised," the Pickle said, then added under her breath, "Slightly."

"A very unfortunate occurrence, to be sure."

"Any chance you hit her on purpose? I've heard there's some bad blood between the two of you."

"Have you?" I said lightly, before adding, "I am quite sorry about her, er, heinie, but all she had to do was take three steps to the left. Plus, I was not in control of that tractor. I believe Mr. Bell will confirm that fact."

There was a silence that could have been awkward if I was the kind of person who was nervous about law enforcement's perception of me. I mean, the average person would be. I had a friend who used to burst into tears if she got a speeding ticket. A few sessions with a cult deprogrammer acquaintance of mine had fixed her right up.

"Go on, Mrs. Abercrombie."

"I believe I was finished."

She took a deep, calming, breath before saying, "What happened when you jumped on the tractor?"

I blinked again. Just for effect. "I tried to shut down the machine. To turn it off, to get it to stop. I tried to put it into neutral, I tried to steer it away from the crowd. Nothing worked."

"Until the end."

"Which was completely due to the quick thinking of Mr. Bell."

"And what did he do?"

"He pulled a small, red lever under the right side of the steering column. I was working under the assumption that if I touched any of the controls, I'd be able to assume command of the tractor. Which was not the case, unfortunately."

"So, nothing you did worked."

I swallowed some more tea as I shook my head. "Not a bloody thing."

"And Mr. Bell just...what? How did he assume control?"

"He reached over and pulled the lever. It took a few tries because we were zig-zagging around quite unpleasantly. Plus, we were already in the sales office by that point. Well not, 'in,' but you know what I mean. The tractor had already crushed the front part of the building. It was perched on the roll bar, but quite a bit of it was on me."

"What's a roll bar?"

I smiled. City slicker. I'd heard one of the island farmers was offering a scenic 'package' where city folk could come in and walk the farm's alpacas, feed them, and muck out their stalls. For $250! She was a genius and I should probably invest in her. I made a mental note.

"It's a literal bar that's constructed over the driver's area. In case the tractor rolls, it stops it from going over completely and crushing the driver." Now that I said it out loud, it sounded like a wonderful way to get rid of—

"Go on."

I sighed. "He pulled the lever. I was already on the brakes. I was standing on them, actually, and we stopped."

"And what did you see at that time?"

I closed my eyes. The sales office had been a shambles, the floor collapsed, furniture askew, a desk calendar of *Far Side* cartoons ruffling in the breeze, an intricate diorama of the proposed build accordioned in the corner. On my left, the floor had been pulled back, the ground chewed up. Then the flowerbed and its pink daisies, the jean jacket. The arm.

"Jean jacket," I said. "In one piece. Between medium and large, more on the large side, buried in the flowerbed, but not very deeply." I opened my eyes. "Who was it?"

The Pickle looked down as if she had some papers on her desk she was consulting. Then she looked up, met me square in my eyes. I liked that. "Is there anything else you can tell me about the body?"

I took a moment. "It was mostly obscured. I really just saw the back of the jacket and the arm. The rest of the body was still buried."

"Anything stick out to you about it?"

"Who was it, Chief Pickle?" I asked softly. I wasn't telling her anything else until she revealed who'd been buried in the flowerbed. Something was bothering her about the body. I could smell it on her.

She thrummed the table with her fingers. "We're not releasing the name of the victim as yet," she said finally.

"And I'm afraid I can't remember anything else."

We sat there, each of us just a little bit irritated with the other. No matter. Everyone being annoyed was the sign of a good negotiation, Mother always said.

"If I told you, you couldn't communicate this information to anyone else until we made a formal statement. Which means no snooping around—"

"I have never snooped a day in my life," I said tartly. *Spied*, certainly. I mean, I'd done that a lot. *Snooped*, never.

"Of course." The Pickle looked down at her nails, frowned. "Do we have a deal?" she asked, examining her left index cuticle like it was going to give her this week's lottery numbers.

"When will you release the information?"

She met my eyes in one smooth movement. "Tomorrow morning."

I felt something ease inside me. This would be the first time the new chief had taken me into her confidence. "Yes, certainly."

Her face twisted into a grim look. "Another thing: The victim's living quarters have been sealed. The crime lab has done a preliminary search, but they're going to be doing another pass tomorrow. So I don't want to hear the seal there has been disturbed. Or the sales office. *Especially* the sales office. The building is not safe."

The Pickle had a blabbermouth uncle in MI6 who'd ratted me out, which was part of the reason she was so suspicious of me. But then I wondered: was she tacitly giving me permission to search the victim's home after her team finished up tomorrow? It sure sounded like it to me. "Is the home a crime scene?"

A pause. "We don't think so. We'll luminol later on today."

"Why hasn't that been done already?"

"Mrs. Abercrombie, these are police matters, and—"

"I'm just asking because I'm a taxpayer."

"We'll take care of it shortly. Not to worry."

I crossed my arms in front of me.

"What else did you see at the scene?"

"Who is the victim?"

"Mrs. Abercrombie," she leaned closer and said, "you have a responsibility as a witness to share what you saw at the scene."

"I mean, I think that's debatable, dear." I was starting to get worried about Chief Pickle's reluctance to share the information. Maybe our cold war was going to continue.

"The family hasn't been notified yet, Ir-Irma."

I'd asked her to call me Irma in the past and she'd always refused. I wasn't quite sure why she was offering me up this little compromise now. Progress?

"I understand, dear," I said, even though I did not. "I didn't see any other significant details. The roof was collapsed on us, with broken glass everywhere. And Stuart picked me up and carried me out, which I did not particularly appreciate, I must say."

"Was the flowerbed beside the building disturbed in any way before all this?"

I sat back in my chair. "Well, it was chewed up by the tractor. But when I arrived at the site this morning, I noticed the bed looked freshly maintained. I'm assuming someone dug into the flowerbed and buried the body there before arranging the flowers. Or re-arranging, I suppose."

"It's a possibility."

"The body wasn't buried very deeply."

She said nothing.

"I didn't notice anything unusual. It just looked like someone had laid out fresh mulch. It's quite a small flowerbed, not much to notice about it."

"Thank you, Mrs. Abercrombie. That's all we need for now."

I nodded. It was unfortunate she'd decided not to like me. I'd had a lovely relationship with the last police chief. But change is eternal as they say, and being adaptable was what had kept me alive all these years.

"Thank you, Chief Pickle," I said as I stood.

When I was halfway to the door, she sighed. "This is off the record."

I spun on my heel and was back in my chair before you could say *dingleberries*. "Yes?"

"It was Lucas García. The tennis pro at the Beaver Island Country Club."

I was so shocked, all the breath evaporated from my lungs.

"I understand you had a tennis session with him yesterday."

I struggled to regain my composure. Lucas was only twenty-seven. "I'm…I'm assuming you heard about the altercation between him and Tiffanni Morgan."

A nod. "Were you there for that?"

"Yes."

"What was your impression of the incident?"

"I…I couldn't say. She was very angry, and he was trying to calm her down." The pressure in my chest was making me uncomfortable.

"Were you aware of any…romantic relationship between Lucas and Tiffanni?"

I shook my head.

"Were you close to him?"

I took a minute to collect myself, then said, "I liked him. He was a good boy. I'd been playing with him since he came to the Club. About five years ago. What a waste."

"Sorry?"

"I hate it when it's young people."

A nod. "Did it seem to you that Tiffanni was a threat to Lucas?"

"I mean, really, Tiffanni doesn't seem like the type of person who could figure out how to use a can opener. But it's been my experience that anything is possible. Truly. People are…" I lifted my arms out beside me. "Unknowable."

"That's a strange thing to say."

"Probably. I've had a bit of a strange life."

She flashed me a lopsided grin that quickly faded. "I'll expect you to keep this confidential until the word goes out. I don't want Lucas's family to hear anything until we get ahold of them. We've been able to find contact information for his aunt, but she's not answering the phone and has no voicemail. And we can't find his parents."

"His parents are dead, dear. But of course, I won't say anything," I added. And I actually even meant it.

I was troubled on the way home. I adored fast machines: souped-up boats, good cars, revved-up motorcycles. But I took it slow and steady. Normally I was an optimist, but there was little worse than a nice young person's spirit being snuffed out prematurely.

I'd liked Lucas. I'd especially liked that he didn't treat me like a little old lady. We'd been sparring on the court for years, like I'd told the police chief. But we'd also developed some kind of friendship. I enjoyed his company, had drinks with him at the Club sometimes after practice, and he'd even picked me up and dropped me off occasionally when I wanted more than one adult beverage after my lesson. It was a service he offered only some of his clients. And he'd been an interesting fellow; had played tennis professionally until an injury had taken him out of the game some time back.

Eventually, my house loomed, a sprawling red brick Victorian with gingerbread trim, a boat house, a dock, and a basement with more than a few hidey holes. It had been a single-family home when it was built, but after my parents passed away, I had it renovated into three apartments so guests could have privacy and be self-sufficient, making their own food and the like. My flat was on the first floor, the other two on the second level. The third had a widow's walk, dropped on top of the house like a muffin top. Violet was my only current houseguest, but she wouldn't be home for a while, if she'd walked from town.

I could see the two wide-backed Muskoka chairs set out on my dock, optimally configured for sunset-watching. One of which was currently occupied by a very uninvited guest.

Six — Violet

I walked to Irma's home from the clinic, letting the sun and the wind blow away some of the craziness of the past few hours.

The front door was locked. After letting myself in, I pulled my shoes off in the entranceway, wowed by it yet again. Irma's home was spectacular; a gargantuan Victorian with sky-high ceilings, oak flooring, deep baseboards, and a majestic staircase that split in two and led to a balconied second floor. Every time I saw that staircase, I expected a Von Trapp child to pop out of nowhere and start singing.

The downstairs was Irma's domain, mostly; her apartment, packed full of mementos from all over the world, but still elegant and comfortable. She had a cosy wood-burning fireplace in her flat, with an easy chair in front of it that had an excellent view of the street. The rest of the main floor was taken up with a formal dining room, a sitting room, a massive kitchen, and a bunch of nooks and crannies. It was the kind of home that made you feel like you had room to breathe. And then some.

The second floor had two large apartments with top-of-the-line appliances and shabby chic coastal décor. I didn't know what was on the third floor; I hadn't had the nerve to go up there yet. Sniper's post?

After I'd trudged up the stairs to my apartment, I did what any reasonable engineer in my shoes would have done. I started researching driverless construction equipment. I liked to understand how things worked, a habit Irma had been mercilessly exploiting on my vacation. I also liked to *not* think about dead bodies in shallow graves under a summer sky and pale pink Gerbera daisies.

I took a few deep breaths and put my thoughts about the corpse in the flowerbed away so I could focus on my engineering problem. The research made it seem like there was a push to automate older equipment, which was then re-purposed for new projects. But that hadn't been the case with the oversized tractor at the groundbreaking. It was shiny, never used. I googled *Leblanc Industries*, the brand name of this morning's equipment. It was a fairly new company, building computerised and robotic construction gear. Their goal was efficiency and safety; apparently construction work was a deadlier profession than being a police officer.

I pictured Irma trying to tame the out-of-control tractor from this morning and didn't see anything safe. Most machines were built to fail in a passive way if there was a fault somewhere in their inner workings. Elevators should freeze instead of plunging its occupants to their screaming deaths, that kind of thing. She should have been able to stop the rampage just by touching the controls, which hadn't happened. I had a bad feeling about it.

But even though all this had taken place only a few hours ago, I could barely remember any details. Shock, maybe. I pulled up the town's website, which contained a forum for islanders to post pictures of the wild rabbits that chewed away their backyards, the endless beavers and beaver-shaped items.

First, I posted a thread asking if anyone had extra tickets to the poker tournament Irma was all fired up about, then looked for comment threads about this morning's tractor rampage. Someone named Ronnie Thomas had posted a video. I watched it a few times.

In the melee of this morning, the tractor's actions had seemed somewhat random; there were people all over the flat, grassy pitch where the buffet spread had been laid out. But looking at it from Ronnie's angle, the tractor's actions didn't seem random at all. First it had aimed at the dais, then it had chewed up the buffet table, where most of the crowd was gathered, before making a run at the sales office, with a stop to nudge Snookie Smith in the butt on the way. But it felt like more than a malfunction.

It felt deliberate. It felt like a hack.

And from what I'd been reading earlier, it was a hack that had already been created by a nerdy American duo who were trying to raise awareness of the safety issues attached to using automated construction machinery.

All that was required was some ingenuity, and enough know-how to clone the transmitters used to control the equipment. Unlike the radio messages sent when opening a garage door with a remote, the messages between construction equipment and their remote controls were often unencrypted.

It was interesting. I didn't want to consider what the ultimate goal had been this morning. Disrupt the event? Squash Carlton like a bug? Frame Irma for running Snookie over? It was impossible to tell, and human behaviour had always been a tricky thing for me to grok. But the mechanics, that I could understand.

I opened up an Internet Relay Chat window—a text-based messaging system—on an encrypted server I kept overseas, and poked one of my good friends, The Brain. I'd never actually seen him IRL, didn't even know what he looked like. But we'd met in the late eighties on a BBS message board, before the Internet was common and easily accessible. And we'd been friends ever since. He had a finger in a lot of different technologies and was always good to bounce ideas off of.

You there? I typed out.

The cursor blinked in the window. I wasn't worried. I didn't know what time zone The Brain was hanging out in these days, but he'd show up eventually.

If having an apocalyptic level hangover is "here," then yes lol.

I smiled. *Weird thing happened here today.*

Tell me while I get an icepack.

I smiled again. I'd always liked how nerdy folk could dispense with conversational formalities without getting offended. It just made everything so much easier.

A construction vehicle—an industrial tractor—went haywire. It was remote-controlled. Almost ran over a few people, took out some very delicious cupcakes.

Lol. Ow, don't make me laugh.

You heard anything about Leblanc Industries?

Naw. It's not my area, Vi, sorry.

Arg. I sighed in frustration. If The Brain hadn't dealt with anything like this before, that meant I was on my own.

How's the business stuff going?

I let out a sigh, ran my hands through my hair before answering.

The bank has given us an extension on our line of credit to cover our expenses for now, but the payments and interest on that are gonna suck.

Sorry, Vi. Any word on you-know-who?

You-know-who was Shane O'Meara, one of my former business partners. Our Chief Financial Officer, in fact. Which was how he'd been able to empty out all those juicy bank accounts.

I'm too embarrassed to even think about it.

Why? You did nothing wrong.

I trusted Shane. That's what I did wrong.

No answer. I knew The Brain was trying to think up a tactful response. There was no reason to. I didn't deserve any. I'd trusted the wrong person, me who had a con artist of a mother who'd made up pretty much everything that had ever come out of her mouth. Somehow I'd trusted another liar. And my company—my dream, the one I'd dreamed with my best friend, Max—was hanging in the balance.

Not your fault, Vi. I gotta go, but good luck.

After The Brain signed off, I felt agitated, restless. So, I logged into the monitoring app at my office in Toronto. The Solar Shoppe had almost five thousand clients now, residential and commercial customers who used the energy management system I'd developed in my spare time while working at a startup that built glorified large-scale arcades. We installed and maintained high-efficiency solar roofs and panels for buildings and homes, and they all integrated into a secure home management system that we built and controlled.

All the tiny dots were green, meaning everything was online and working the way it was supposed to. It always calmed me down to look at my monitoring system when I was stressed out. After watching it for a while, I sighed with relief and turned my attention back to that tractor hack, so I could recreate it myself.

This was going to be fun.

Seven — Irma

I docked easily; there was no wind. But there *was* someone on my pier, looking much too comfortable in one of my nice Muskoka chairs.

I threw one of the lines, and Carlton Campbell slipped it inexpertly around a cleat. It was good enough. I stepped onto the dock. The ground always felt strange under my feet after being on the water.

"Carlton," I said, my voice flat.

Carlton looked like he was going to reach out and hug me, but decided better of it.

"Drink?"

"Please," he said, relief in his voice.

I went into the house and fixed us two scotches, neat. Big ones. I brought them out and he accepted his glass with a grateful nod. I sat down beside him, placing the bottle at my feet. A breeze was coming off the lake, and the edges were blurred by a heat haze. I liked that you couldn't see the end of the water.

Carlton threw back half his drink. "How would you rate that ground-breaking, against others you've been to?"

"I'm not much of a ground-breaking aficionado, dear."

He shot me a look I couldn't quite place. "If you say so." Another sip. His glass was empty and I handed him the bottle, which he took with a smile. I'd have to call him a cab home. "Thank you for what you did earlier."

"I actually didn't do anything, Carlton. It was that young man—"

"David Bell."

"David. I had no clue about that little switch."

"He couldn't have gotten on the tractor without you."

I shrugged. "Do you know what happened, why the equipment went crazy?"

He shrugged his shoulders. "Some kind of malfunction. Just one of those things. Leblanc Industries says they'll do a post-mortem and fix the problem."

"I see." This did not assuage my killer robot worries whatsoever.

"I need your help," Carlton said. He was still looking out at the water. I understood it. There was something mesmerising about watching Mother Nature do her work, something beguiling about all that blue. But then he said, "I really need you to buy that penthouse."

I almost spit my drink out, which would have been a shame for two reasons; one, it was a twelve-year-old Oban, and two, I'd had all of those types of emotional responses trained out of me long ago. It would be a shame to pick up bad habits just because I'd retired from active duty.

He looked like he was going to speak again, but didn't. That happened to people who were in shock sometimes.

I let the silence lengthen and focused on my drink. Somehow, my next sip went down the wrong way, blazing a path through my innards. I coughed.

Carlton made a motion like he was going to whack me on the back, but I moved away from him. I did not like having people's hands come at me. Occupational hazard.

"Thank you." I coughed again. "I'm fine."

He sat back in his chair, a calculating look on his face. "I have some documentation here for you to look at." He pulled a bag out from under his chair. A sheaf of papers peeked out.

"Carlton, I'm not interested in any real estate right now."

"If you're not liquid, you could—"

"Or any financial advice, thank you very much."

Carlton's mouth pressed together.

"I'm sorry about your issues, dear. Can you push off your start date?"

He shook his head.

"Well, there are many people on the island who might be looking for an investment. I'm sure if you reach out—"

"Sure," he said. "Right." He bit off every syllable while pouring himself another few fingers of scotch—*my* scotch—and belted it down. "You didn't mention what I said to you at the groundbreaking to anyone, did you? About the penthouse?"

"Why would you think I had?"

"Because we have a second buyer who's trying to back out now." Bitterness underpinned his words.

"It might have been the dead body, and a killer on the loose, dear."

"Are you sure?"

"Am I sure about what?"

Another sip. "That you didn't tell anybody."

I gave him a look, which begat a moment of silence.

"I'm sorry about your bike," he said finally.

Something eased inside me. I'd always been a sucker for apologies, and he actually sounded contrite.

"I hate that car. I'm going to stop driving it." He looked into his glass, then met my eyes. "It was the last thing my dad ever gave me before he died. I'm sorry I ran over your bike, a hundred percent. I was having a bad day. I'll replace it."

"Ah. I see." I took a sip of my own. "Happens to the best of us, dear. Thank you for your apology. I appreciate it. But Stuart has fixed my bicycle already."

He nodded, flashed a relieved smile.

"Why are you so desperate to offload that penthouse?"

"Optics," he said, grim again. "We're ninety percent sold and that's how we're marketing the project. If we have a run on our units, the whole build might collapse."

"Ah." It didn't quite answer my question, but it didn't *not* answer my question, either.

"Do you know who it was?" he asked eventually. "The body?"

"I couldn't say, dear."

He scowled.

"A question, if you will," I said. "Why did you think of me as an investor in the first place?"

"Rose said you were nice. And…a woman of the world. Well, Rose told me that Lucas told her that."

Something crackled in my sternum. "Lucas García, the Club's tennis pro?"

"Yeah. He's been giving Rose lessons. I can barely get her to myself these days." He smiled, but his tone wasn't quite right and neither was that smile. I wondered what game he was playing with me. Was he really sorry about my bicycle? He'd seemed sincere about it, and most civilians were terrible liars, but sociopaths and psychopaths, who looked as normal as anyone else, unfortunately, made up about five percent of the population and they were all *excellent* liars. Which didn't sound like a large percentage if you looked at the big picture. But if you were trying to find the person who'd assassinated poor Lucas and jammed him under a flowerbed, it was a lot.

"Anyway," he said, picking up the brochures. "I can see it was a bad idea. I'll leave you alone." He said goodbye with a smile, but he seemed…deflated?

I decided it wasn't the right time to ask about tickets to the poker tournament and made sure he called a cab. After he was gone, I poured myself another finger of scotch. It sounded to me like the Beaver Brooke build might very well be in financial trouble, which made me worried for Stu's investment. Then I remembered Snookie's nasty words from the previous day, about how Rose was cheating on Carlton already. Surely if she was, it couldn't have been with Lucas…could it? Jealousy was the world's very oldest motive for bumping off a spouse's paramours.

Oh, dear.

Had someone intentionally buried Lucas, only to unearth him hours later in front of an audience? Was he a pawn in a larger scheme? Tiffanni Morgan didn't look capable of such a thing, but I was well aware that appearances could be deceiving. She'd clocked him once in the head in public—what might she have done in private? Why had Rose *really* been so distressed the morning of Lucas's death? And what had been hidden in Carlton's recent words? Jealousy?

I hadn't retired to rain on local law enforcement's parade. I'd come home to live a simpler life. And honestly, I had no choice but to do exactly that. I no longer had a team to help me slip over international borders, or any of the brainy back-room researchers who'd shuttled intel to me over the course of my career.

I sighed, looked out at the water, but it didn't make me feel any better for once. Lucas's parents had died when he was only eighteen. His surviving aunt was elderly, and he had no one to look out for him at all, the poor thing. I'd cared about him. Still did.

I tried to tamp down on my feelings. Bad for business. Lucas had been a lovely boy, but he was gone. He couldn't be saved. But there was a murderer on the loose, and the other islanders *could* be. I needed to focus on the living.

So, it was probably time for me to ask a few questions.

Eight — Irma

The news of Lucas's untimely demise ran through the town like a hot knife through butter. I heard it officially while breakfasting at the Club the next morning. To be fair, I'd specifically organised my morning meal there with Violet in order to be in the centre of things when the news broke.

I was at my usual table, my back to the wall, all points of ingress and egress in my eyeline so I could respond to any potential attack. It was highly unlikely that such an incursion would happen at my club, but a former co-worker of mine had been decapitated by a child's squeaky toy in Paris last year so really, anything was possible. I planned on living to a hundred, so I had twenty-nine more years to safeguard myself and the town of Beaver Island against rubber children's playthings and rogue assassins.

"More tea?" Theresa, a long-time Club employee and excellent source of intel, asked after Violet scooted to the ladies' room.

"Yes, please, dear," I asked. "What's new?"

And that was all it took, really. Apparently, the Club's management had gathered the staff this morning to break the news and put some messaging around how the information should be conveyed to guests, particularly the tennis-playing ones. And they'd also announced that they somehow had a new club pro waiting in the wings.

"That's right," Theresa said, drifting closer so no one could hear her. She pretended to pour me more tea. "He works in Toronto but has been trying to get hired here for the last two years, from what I hear. And—" Theresa looked up and smiled when the head of Maintenance walked past us. We all waved at each other cheerily, but as soon as she disappeared around the side of the club building, we went back to our huddle. "—he was here already. So, the club management felt like it was kismet."

"What do you mean, he was here already?" I asked, inhaling sharply.

"He was on the island. He's staying in someone's pool house for the summer, apparently."

"Wait, didn't you just say he works in Toronto?"

"I hear," she lowered her voice, "he quit to come here."

"I see." I glanced around. We were having a late breakfast, but that was the price you paid when you had a house guest who went to bed at three in the morning after killing computerized zombies. On the bright side, I'd had a wonderful run this morning that was making me feel invigorated. I just loved how I felt when I started the day with some cardiovascular exercise. Plus, the patio was deserted, so no one could hear us. "Do you know anything else about him?"

Theresa adjusted some of the condiments on the table. Without moving her face, she said, "No, but I'll try and find out."

"Thank you, dear." I slipped a few bills into her palm.

She nodded and turned to leave.

"One more thing," I said. "Did anyone not get along with Lucas? Did he ever get any complaints?"

"You know Lucas, Irma. He's nice to everyone, even that lunatic Tiffanni who hit him on the head the other day. I actually saw him training Elsa Lee—you know that lady who's so pregnant she looks like she's about to explode? The two of them basically had to stand at the net to practice, but he did it anyway. And did you know he sometimes picked up his clients and dropped them off after their lessons? All just because he's a great guy. Was," she corrected herself. Then she leaned closer. "I even saw him being nice to Snookie Smith. And that takes something out of you."

"You're quite right, dear, thank you."

"Oh, another thing?" She glanced over her shoulder. "Apparently the new guy and Lucas knew each other. Lucas was injured at a tournament years ago and had to pull out. The other guy ended up winning, and it was the end of Lucas's career."

"Good heavens."

She nodded. "He was a good guy, Irma." I put a hand on her arm. She nodded, taking a shaky breath. When she'd pulled herself together, she nodded stiffly and left just as Violet returned from the ladies'.

"May I please borrow your cellular telephone, dear?" I asked after she plopped into her chair. I saw something that could have been a nod and fumbled in her backpack until I found it. Then I dialled.

"Hello, Beaver Island Country Club," Imogene Flores, the general manager, sing-songed.

"Imogene, darling, what are you doing answering the phone?"

"Oh, Irma," she said, "Bina had to leave this morning, she was so upset."

"Oh, no," I said, trying to infuse an appropriate amount of distress into my voice. "What has happened?"

Violet looked up, but swiftly returned to her sausages. I couldn't deny they smelled delicious. Plus, they were low fat and made of organic, free-range pork. Which was why my fork was inching over to her side of the table. Seeing that, she pushed her plate toward me. *What's up*? she mouthed.

I held off on the sausages for now. I hadn't told Violet the news yesterday; she'd closed herself up in her apartment after the ground-breaking, and I hadn't wanted to disturb her. Plus, I'd promised the Pickle I wouldn't tell anyone, and an Abercrombie always kept her word. In my ear, Imogene rambled. She was a twitchy woman in the first place, and did not cope well even when things were going swimmingly.

I wondered, briefly, where Lucas had been killed. And how. If I called the chief, would she tell me what the cause of death had been? I didn't think the recent thaw in our relations would go quite that far. Dr. Julian might know, though.

Over Violet's shoulder, I saw two uniformed police officers walk toward the docks. Radio chatter drifted over.

"Are you at the Club?" Imogene asked.

"Yes."

"What was that noise?"

"One of the marine radios," I lied smoothly. "What on earth has happened, Imogene?"

"I'm so…sorry to say, but Lucas García has passed away."

"Oh my goodness, how? Was it an accident?"

"Er, yes. Yes, it was."

Well, that's what you got for trying to prompt people for responses. "What kind of accident?"

"I'm not sure of the details yet, Irma. Was there something I could do for you?"

"I wanted to book a tennis lesson, but I guess—"

"No, no, everything is well in hand. We have a guest pro with us right now. His name is Tate Hurst, and he's just wonderful. When did you want your lesson for?"

"I was hoping to play today sometime. I've just had a lovely breakfast and wanted to work some of it off."

"Of course. How smart of you, just like always, Irma." She was laying it on a bit thick, even for her.

"Any chance there's an opening?"

I could hear paper being shuffled. One of the things I liked about the Club was that it was still so analogue, as Violet would say. I liked tradition; it helped give life structure and meaning.

"We have something at noon, actually. That's in…thirty-three minutes. Does that work?"

"Yes, perfect. Thanks so much, Imogene."

We rang off, and I handed the phone back to Violet, who was finishing her waffles. It was nice to see a young person with such a hearty appetite. I just wished some of that energy could be devoted to pursuits that took place out of doors so she could keep her vitamin D levels up and not die of rickets. Although we were currently outside, so perhaps today's battle had already been won.

"You going to play tennis?" She frowned.

"Yes."

"What's the big thing that's happened?"

"I'm very sorry to say Lucas has passed away."

"Oh, no!" Violet sat up in her chair.

"Yes, it's a tragedy."

"What happened?"

There was a pause. "Lucas was the one who was found under the flowerbed yesterday."

"*What*?"

"Shhh." I glanced over at the couple who was currently being seated. Theresa, bless her heart, had deposited them on the other side of the patio, but one never knew when one was being eavesdropped on.

"Sorry."

"It's all right." I put my hand on hers and squeezed.

"He was only...like...thirty or something."

"Twenty-seven."

"Wow. Is that why there are police here?"

"Probably, although I'm not sure."

"Wow, Irma, just...wow."

"I know, it's terrible." I was feeling more rotten the more I talked about it. I really hated it when it was young people, especially since so many horrible people lived well into old age.

"And who are you playing tennis with at noon, then?"

I took a good look at Violet. Her voice sounded terrible. She wasn't looking too sprightly, either. "Are you all right, dear?"

She took a deep breath, then another.

"Do you want to lie down while I have my lesson?"

"What? This place even has nap rooms? Is there anything you guys don't—"

"There's a nurse's room."

"Is there a nurse?"

"Used to be. Now we just call someone in from the island clinic."

"Yeah, I think I might want to lie down. I'm feeling a little dizzy."

"Good idea." I motioned to Theresa to put our bill on my tab, and helped Violet hoist herself out of her chair. She was, to put it diplomatically, a little legless. But we managed to get her inside and to the nurse's office, which was beside the administrative offices. I thought Imogene might have a stroke when she saw us.

"Did she fall down? Is she injured? What can I—"

"Violet just needs to lie down in a quiet room for a mo'. Can we commandeer the nurse's room?"

"Of course," Imogene said, her hands fluttering. She was so tall and lean that she always reminded me of Olive Oyl with better hair and more neuroses. I tucked Violet in, then closed the door behind me. The poor thing. I kicked myself for not telling her the news at home. I hadn't realized it would hit her so hard.

Imogene stopped me in the hallway. "Irma, I wanted you to meet our new…er, acting, uh, guest pro, Tate Hurst. Tate, this is Irma Abercrombie. Her family were founding members of the Club, and she's on the board."

I stuck my hand out. Like Lucas, Tate was in his twenties. He had dark, wavy hair that was almost messy but not quite. He was muscled but still lean, probably five foot ten, and was wearing a skin-tight Izod shirt with white tennis shorts. His shoes were new-white, and his smile was lopsided as he met my hand with his.

"Hiya, Irma," he said.

"We don't say hiya here," Imogene said nervously. "We use the Queen's English. Correct, Irma?"

Lucas and I had once done an entire lesson in pig Latin, so I didn't know about all that, but I smiled at Tate. "Nice to meet you."

"Thanks, Irma." Tate glanced over at Imogene. "We're a little early, but do you want to walk over to the court after you change?"

"Certainly."

"Lucas had a lot of notes about your game. I guess you're a ringer, eh?"

"We don't say *eh* at the Club, Tate." Imogene looked like she was going to twitch herself right out of her dress.

"I'll be five minutes," I said, and Tate nodded and smiled. My feet took me toward the changing room without me even thinking about where I was going. Lucas used to say *eh* all the time.

That's when I realised I was really going to miss him. And it sat like a stone in my belly. So I turned away from the locker room and down a hallway full of offices. I dashed into Lucas's office, locking the door behind me just as I heard a staffer coming around the corner.

Luckily, Lucas's office was small and spare. An erasable monthly calendar hung on one wall, with Club events and reminders. I'd always liked his handwriting: loopy, beautiful script. I scanned the calendar: nothing of interest.

I sat at the desk and started opening drawers with a pen so as not to disturb any prints the police might find, if they hadn't already tossed the office. The desk was unlocked, the drawers containing sports equipment, tennis balls, and the like. I sighed and sat back in the chair, realizing Lucas's daily schedule was tucked into the corner of an ink blotter.

Radio chatter in the hallway.

Bloody hell. I rifled through this week's schedule, landing on yesterday. His afternoon had been blocked off after Violet's lesson—until nine at night, when he'd had a lesson booked with Rose Campbell. Nothing after that.

Voices outside the door. A rattling doorknob.

I held my breath.

When I heard footsteps going back down the hallway, I bolted to the door. Unlocking and opening it a crack, I pined for the little telescoping mirror I usually kept in my handbag but had somehow forgotten to bring with me today. But the hallway was clear. I locked the door behind me and fast-walked back to the changeroom.

I took a seat in front of my locker, feeling a bit fluttery. Why would Rose take a lesson so late at night, especially since she was at the Club earlier in the day? And what had been lurking in Carlton's tone yesterday when he'd mentioned her lessons with Lucas? Could Snookie's mean-spirited gossip be right after all?

Eventually I roused myself and opened my locker. All the storage in the changeroom was for day use only, but I preferred to keep some necessities at the Club instead of dragging them back and forth all the time. Obtaining a permanent locker had been a gruelling, off-the-books operation that had cost me a pretty penny and dented my dignity a little. If the head of Maintenance ever retired, I was doomed.

I turned my attention to the brace Julian had recently recommended for my left knee. I was in excellent shape, but I couldn't deny I'd picked up a few aches and pains recently. Although I'd originally injured that knee when I was only in my fifties. I'd been scaling a fence in Bosnia into a—

Well, no matter. I had an excellent pain threshold. We'd discovered when I was quite young that I didn't have very strong pain receptors, which wasn't always great news—certainly if you put your hand on a lit burner, you wanted to know about it fairly promptly—but with my particular career it had worked out swimmingly. And if I wore the brace to my first lesson, it might signal weakness to Tate. Of course, if my goal was to win a set with him, that might work.

I finished dressing, ignoring all the posters for the upcoming poker tournament on Carlton's boat, which I'd been thus far unable to procure an invite for. I left the brace behind; it did not feel like a coincidence that a former competitor of Lucas's had scooped up his job the day after he was found murdered, and I aimed to find out what was behind it.

Tate's first serve went down the court so hard I was surprised it didn't damage the clay. I had to jump to the left to get out of its path, my eyes following as it slammed against the back of the court.

Out," I called to him, and readied myself for his next serve.

"That was in," he corrected, a twist to his mouth that I didn't particularly appreciate.

The next serve was exactly the same; low and hard with some spin. "Out," I said.

"You sure you don't need to get your glasses checked?"

"I don't wear glasses, dear. And I thought we were going to rally to warm up," I said.

"Sure, Mrs. A, if that's how you want it."

I had a ball in my pocket and bounced it a few times before windmilling my arms to get the kinks out. I was starting to regret the extra hard route I'd taken this morning on my run—uphill both ways—and there was a clutch of club members who were gathered at the umbrellaed tables between the courts. A few more people had drifted outside and were watching us.

I bounced the ball again from centre court, and gave it a gentle volley over the net. Tate, who I'd suddenly realised had unnaturally long arms, reached out from his perch at the back corner of the court and sent it back to me. It was a nice, slow exchange, the two of us politely hitting the little yellow dot back and forth.

I tried to shrug off an annoyance I couldn't quite explain. There was no reason to be emotionally engaged in this situation whatsoever. The voice of one of my former mentors rang in my ears: *Show no emotion.* He was the kind of person who wanted robots working for him. He'd had a bad end, though, which cheered me up a bit. And he wasn't wrong. Getting emotionally involved in other people's problems was always a mistake. It could get you killed.

"So, did you want to grab lunch, bro?" Tate said.

"Sorry?" I whacked the ball straight to him. He casually flicked his racquet out and tapped it back.

"I was thinking at the Club. What do you want to do?"

"Oh, I just had breakfast, thanks."

"Okay, I'll see you in a half hour."

I was starting to wonder if Tate was hearing voices. I looked for the tell-tale bulge of an earpiece embedded in one of his ears. But I saw nothing.

"So, Irma, you need some work on your grip," he called to me.

I stepped closer to the net so I could hear him better. Not that I was having age-related hearing problems whatsoever; the man was a mumbler. Tate took the opportunity to smash the ball to the far corner of my side of the court. I looked at it as it bounced.

"Pretty sure that one was in, Mrs. A." Tate chuckled the way men do when they're humouring a woman and want everyone to know it.

I gritted my teeth. "Let's play," I said.

"If that's what you want."

There was a challenge in his voice, which was just perfect. I so enjoyed being underestimated, and I just loved proving people wrong. Especially the tall ones.

"Why don't you serve?" he offered.

I had a few smiles. In my former line of work it had been imperative to become all sorts of people, and each persona had its own smile. But the one on my face right now, I knew, was the same one that had been periodically described as *wolfish.*

I pulled my sunglasses off so he could see my eyes and stepped toward the court's mid-line, my hand out. We shook over the net. He tried to crush my hand with his, but I pinched a nerve under his index finger, which stopped that nonsense right away. I enjoyed the surprised look he threw my way immensely.

I almost skipped to the corner for my serve. I did some more stretches, and heard a few titters from the cluster of tables to my left. A few millennials were seated with blender drinks, two of them barefoot, one of them wearing a tennis skirt so short I could almost see her fine china.

Then I served. And the chatter quieted. The ball whizzed past Tate's knees and bounced before hitting the fence at the back of the court. He looked up, bewilderment in his eyes.

"Fifteen-love," he called.

And he sounded piqued about it. Good. I'd been raised in a family of vertically challenged folks and we were not sorry about it at all. I loved being petite. I could hide in the most wonderful of locations: closets, car boots, once in the ceiling of a particularly unpleasant South American dictator's office. And the thing about all that was that I could serve low and lean, with a nice little spin I'd spent most of my teen years perfecting.

I grinned at him. Then served again. The ball flung itself just out of his reach. I supposed he was expecting the same serve again. Pity.

It was all over in a few minutes, and after I won the game I walked forward, my hand stuck out. Tate was now firetruck red, sweat dotting his brow. "Great game, Irma. Let's do a set."

"Oh, I couldn't possibly. I have a friend with me, and she's not feeling well. I'll have to go check on her. But thank you ever so much for the game. I thoroughly enjoyed myself. And I learned a lot."

"Oh?"

I leaned forward. He still hadn't taken my hand, which was terrible manners. "I certainly did," I said. "You have very big shoes to fill."

"Do I?" He grinned lazily.

"Yes," I said sharply. After wishing him a lovely day, I walked off the court past the millennials, one of whom held a hand out for a high five. I tapped her hand smartly and continued on my way.

I didn't look back the entire way across the courts. It was only when I'd turned the corner and was shielded by one of the Club's over-trimmed hedges that I started limping.

Bloody hell. I'd really buggered up that knee now. Plus, the combination of my jog this morning and all the running I'd just done on the court was making my gluteus maximus throb mightily, which was most embarrassing. I hop-limped to the side of the clubhouse, then tried to walk normally. I'd been in less pain from being waterboarded.

I went to find Violet. She wasn't the only one who needed the nurse's office.

Nine — Violet

I'd never seen Irma look so terrible. Actually, I'd never even seen her with a hair out of place, other than during Tractorgate, and she'd had a whole building on her head at the time.

Irma was a grand dame with a unique style; crisp, stylish summer-wear featuring a lot of pastel pedal pushers and white, collared shirts, tiny colour coordinated tracksuits, more than a few Chanel ensembles, and the occasional groovy dress she'd picked up in London in the sixties. Which all still fit her.

"Did you get into a fight?" I asked finally. "And did you, like, lose?" It was inconceivable to me that Irma might not prevail in a conflict.

She carefully lowered herself into the chair beside the nurse's cot. Since my dizziness had lifted, I'd been playing games on my phone.

"I've lost plenty of fights, dear," Irma said, her voice heavy.

"I find that seriously hard to believe."

"Believe it." Irma tipped her head back and added, "Do you mind getting me an icepack, please?"

I made my way to the little bar fridge in the corner. "Okay...do you want the adorable bear-shaped icepack?" In a sing-songy voice I added, "It has scrunchy earsss." The soft teddy bear form held a pocket to slip the icepack in. "Or do you want the kangaroo?" The kangaroo was much bigger, its ears flopping eagerly over my hand. I assumed the ice packs were child-friendly because they were intended for that particular demographic, but with this crazy island it was always hard to tell.

"Kangaroo, please."

"You got it." I handed it to over and Irma settled it on her knee, securing the icepack around her leg with its built-in strap. The Velcro had worn off, so she knotted it like the sailor she was. "How was your lesson?" I asked.

Irma groaned.

"That good, huh?"

"I miss Lucas."

"Yeah, he was a nice guy."

"His replacement?" Irma met my eyes. "Not so nice."

"Why? What happened?"

"He was quite unpleasant during our game."

"How badly did he beat you?"

Irma gave me a look. "I won. Forty-love."

"Is that good?"

"He didn't get a point."

"How is that bad? You know, you have to ease up on yourself a bit."

"I like being…un-eased. Uneasy? Yes, I excel at uneasiness, I do believe. In any case, it was luck only. He let me take the first serve."

"Right. Yeah. I grew up with a hotplate for a kitchen. So, I really don't know the ins and outs of country club tennis, Irma."

"The server controls the game. Had he served first, I'm quite sure he would have won. He's very competitive. I mean, he almost hit me with the ball."

"You hit Lucas with the ball last week. Twice!"

"Yes, but it's funny when I do it."

I grinned. Irma was obviously not as banged up as she'd seemed at first, and some of the worry hardening in my chest eased itself.

"May I please borrow your cellular telephone, dear?" Irma threw me a grin when I handed it to her, then dialled. "Yes, hello, there. It's Irma." After a pause, she said, "Is Julian at the clinic? Lovely. Can you please tell him I'm on my way? Thank you very much."

I frowned. "Is it that bad?"

She moved the icepack so the kangaroo's grinning face was pointing at me. I tried not to snicker.

"No, I'm fine. Julian has been talking to me lately about starting cortisone shots anyway. I have a little issue with my left knee, which seems to be slightly more irritated as a result of my recent…activities."

I sighed. "Well, was it worth it? To beat a twenty-year-old tennis pro?"

"Yes."

I tried not to roll my eyes. "Seriously? You're half crippled."

"Normally I enjoy melodrama as much as the next girl, dear, but in this instance, I think you're overreacting a little."

"You don't look awesome."

"Thank you."

"I mean, normally you do. Just not right now."

She moved the kangaroo to a new location. So far, she'd iced five different spots on her knee, which didn't seem awesome. "And it was worth it. I think he made a lunch date while we were rallying! Very rude young man. And he's a liar."

"What did he lie about?"

"He claimed that a number of balls that were clearly out were in. Can you believe it? In any case, how are you feeling?"

"Fine." I shrugged. "I felt dizzy, but now I'm okay."

"The shock from the news about Lucas's death must have done it."

I frowned. "I don't think so. I don't normally have emotional reactions that make me sick." And definitely not in front of others. I didn't like to show emotion in public. In this way, Irma and I were exactly alike.

She looked contemplative. "I wonder if you have vertigo."

"Why?"

"Well, you're always so…green when we're on the water. It might be vertigo."

"I'm green when we're in the boat because you drive like a maniac. I mean, a maniac with excellent evasive driving skills, but you can see something's wrong with you when you're driving. Whether it's a boat or a car. Can you fly a plane?"

"Yes."

I groaned.

"And a helicopter! I think you'd really like flying, Violet. It's very nerdy. Lots of checklists."

"I do love a good checklist."

Irma shrugged as if to say *and there you have it*. She adjusted the kangaroo again.

"All right, dear, we need to hobble me out of here without anyone noticing I'm gimpy."

"Does it matter if someone notices?"

"Do you want armed mercenaries to break into the house in the middle of the night and murder us in our beds?"

"Does that question really have more than one answer? And why would that happen? Is that something that could happen?" Alarm ran through me.

"Not if you help me look like I can actually walk. Never let people see your weaknesses, dear."

"Yes ma'am." I pretend-saluted, which Irma took surprisingly well. Normally she was a stickler about military form.

Of course, she knew of a secret shortcut to the docks, and we hobbled her all the way there. Once out in plain sight, Irma walked like she had bionic legs, with long—for her—and steady strides. Her boat was docked close to the clubhouse, thankfully, and it didn't take long for us to get there. I clambered aboard and cast off.

"Wouldn't it be fun if you learned how to captain the boat?" Irma asked.

"I don't think so, no."

"Don't you find it odd you've spent your entire life in Toronto, a city located essentially on top of a lake—this very lake—and until you came here, you'd never been on the water?"

"I've just been very busy for the past forty-three years. And I *have* been on the water. Just on really, really big boats. How big is your boat?"

"Sixteen feet."

"See? That seems unbelievably small."

Irma didn't say anything to that. She was waving at the inhabitants of a superyacht who were blaring the radio. As soon as they saw Irma, they turned the volume down. That was the kind of creepy skill-set I was hoping to learn from her on my vacation.

Irma sat in the driver's seat as we travelled, which meant she really must be in pain. Normally she stood at the wheel, her tiny form regimented and focused.

At the dock, I tied the boat up as well as possible, then put out my arm so she could hobble a little more efficiently to the clinic, which was on Main Street, a road that ran parallel to the pier.

If we'd walked up to Main Street, it would have been picture-perfect, with overstuffed baskets of flowers hanging from real gas lampposts, upscale pastel boutiques, and hip restaurant patios spilling out onto sidewalks, one with fusion cuisine so good it always made me believe that world peace was actually possible.

Since the Club's early regatta had recently kicked off, all the businesses on Main Street would have some sort of beaver-shaped, nautically-inspired decoration on display.

I had yet to locate a single pothole in the town, even though there was one in front of the Toronto parking lot where I kept my car that was so big, small children had actually disappeared into it.

Instead of taking Main, we made our way up the little path behind the clinic. A more challenging route, but fewer witnesses.

"Hello!" Kendelle Chang, the receptionist, called out when we entered. She was obviously expecting us. Kendelle was in her early twenties, her long black hair perfectly blown out, cats-eye makeup and deep red lipstick carefully applied. Her nails were on point and so was her stylish ensemble. She was a good kid, although not the best in a crisis. On the wall behind her was an illustrated poster of a sailboat with a toothy all-beaver crew, including the captain, who had an eyepatch.

"Hello, dear," Irma said.

"Let's get you in the back. Hey, Violet."

The three of us hobbled down a long hallway and Kendelle deposited us in an exam room. It took two tries to get Irma up on the table. She winced.

"I'm sorry, Irma. I'm trying to—"

"It's not you, dear. I'm perfectly fine."

Julian strode in. He looked particularly charming today, his wavy brown hair flopping over his forehead more than usual. He needed a haircut. I looked away before he could notice my eyes on him.

"What have you done to yourself this time?" he asked Irma after greeting me warmly.

"I think Violet has vertigo, actually."

"Huh?" I exclaimed.

"Really?" Julian walked toward me.

"No, we're here because Irma—"

"First things first, dear," Irma said sweetly.

"Unbelievable."

"What's the problem?" Julian asked.

"Irma drives like a lunatic on uppers, that's the problem."

"She got dizzy this morning and needed to lie down at the Club," Irma said.

Concern bloomed on Julian's face. "What happened?"

I explained my earlier dizziness as dispassionately as possible. It *had* been odd, but I was fine now.

"Was it right after being on the water?" he asked.

"Yeah. We docked behind the Club, and I went to the ladies' room to splash water on my face, but it didn't help."

Julian took my cheeks in his hands. For a minute, I couldn't breathe. He was looking in my eyes and I was looking at his and we were looking at each other and it was probably the highlight of my vacation so far, except for all the cupcakes.

Then he yanked my head to the side, in a brisk, sharp movement. It didn't hurt, but the world turned fuzzy.

Irma sprang to her feet and almost launched herself into the air. But she couldn't; she was jumping on her right leg, tiny little hops that barely got her across the room. "What in the name of all that is holy are you doing to Violet?"

"Sorry, Irma," Julian said, his eyes still focused on me.

"Almost gave me a heart attack," she grumbled.

"Just doing a test to see if Violet has vertigo."

"If I was less incapacitated—"

"Yeah, yeah, I get that. I'm looking at you next."

Chastened, Irma hopped back to her perch on the examining table.

Julian did a few more tests. "I think Irma's right," he said finally. "There are some exercises you can do to help treat vertigo. I'll email them to you." He snapped off his gloves. For some reason, even though I absolutely had no time for men whatsoever, and Julian and I were just friends, I wanted his hands on my face again. I could still smell his cologne, crisp and clean and sporty.

He changed into some new gloves, then rounded on Irma, and the moment passed, thankfully. He examined her knee, probing a few spots, putting pressure on others. Irma's face stayed immobile throughout. It was a little creepy.

"Does this hurt?"

"Yes," she said, her voice almost cheerful.

"If you had to describe the pain out of ten, with ten being—"

"Six."

He nodded to himself. "All right. I know we've talked about this before, but now is the time to—"

Irma was looking at me.

"Do you want me to leave?" I asked. I didn't want to make her uncomfortable.

"No," Irma said, "please stay, dear."

I had the impression of something shifting in the room, although I wasn't quite sure what. But a sense of pleasure that Irma trusted me lodged itself in my chest.

"Okey dokey," Julian said, popping off the second set of gloves and disposing of them. He pulled up a wheeled stool and sat down. "I think it's time to start cortisone shots. The muscles around your knee joint are inflamed, and I'm worried your kneecap might dislocate. You do not want that, Irma, I promise you. And on top of that, if you're quantifying your pain at a six, it's probably a seven or eight. Your mobility has been impacted, and—"

"I see your points, Julian. Excellent as usual. Let us proceed."

He shot me a look before leaving the room.

"I'm sorry, Irma," I said.

"It's all right. I've had problems with that knee ever since an incident back in Istanbul in the eighties."

"Not even gonna ask."

"Or was it Bosnia in the nineties?"

"I'd feel happier if we didn't go down that particular memory lane."

Irma continued, "I'm quite sure I'll be right as rain as soon as the good doctor gives me a little jab with a needle."

Julian came back, a pair of tiny crutches under one arm, carrying a tray of instruments and the biggest syringe I'd ever seen in my entire life. I tried to turn my gasp into a cough.

"Has Lucas's autopsy been completed yet?" Irma asked. She'd told me before that the clinic functioned as a temporary morgue on top of seeing patients, which meant Lucas's body must be tucked away in the basement somewhere.

Julian pressed his lips together while getting everything ready. "It's going to be completed today. Preliminary blood work has been sent to the lab already and a cursory examination's been done."

"Did it show anything? Do you know what the cause of death was? Have you seen the body? Can I see the body?"

I glanced at Irma. Her face was completely neutral, like she was asking what the weather was going to be like tomorrow.

Julian cleared his throat. "Irma, you know how I feel about—"

"Well, he's dead," she said matter-of-factly. "So, there's no need for patient confidentiality."

"Irma, we've talked about this before, and—"

"There's a lot of wiggle room in the regulations, dear. The goal of patient confidentiality is to protect the patient. Do you feel like that applies here? Especially since there's a cold-blooded killer currently running around the island, probably looking for another victim?" Irma said all of this so pleasantly and reasonably, it was obvious to anyone who had a brain that she was totally, completely correct in what she was saying and what she wanted. This was another one of the Jedi mind tricks I was hoping to learn from her.

Julian sighed and ran his hand through his hair. "Single penetrating gunshot wound to the base of the skull, large calibre."

"Close contact?"

Julian nodded as he gloved up again and prepped the injection site on Irma's tiny knee. "But we don't have all the results back yet. Don't get ahead of yourself."

"What does your gut tell you?" Irma pressed.

"Wait for the reports, Irma."

"They could take weeks!" she exclaimed, like the system had been set up just to vex her.

"Yes, they could," he said carefully. "And that's a good thing. Slow, thorough investigations mean less mistakes are made. You know that."

"Any clue about time of death?"

"Around midnight, based on his liver temp. But again, Irma, we'll know more later."

"So, someone murdered him, then drove to the work site and buried him, replanting those flowers exactly the right way," she said doubtfully.

"They might have taken a picture first," I said.

"They might have just killed him there," Julian added.

"True," Irma said. "It's not a bad plan. They would have felt confident he'd just fertilise those flowers and no one would be the wiser. They couldn't have known a robot tractor would go berserk and dig him up."

There was a pause. Julian plunged the needle into Irma's leg. She didn't flinch, but goosepimples broke out all over my arms anyway.

"I don't know about all that," I said finally.

Irma looked at me, pain swimming in her eyes. "What do you mean?" It came out sharper than she normally spoke.

"I think the tractor might have been hacked."

"Why do you think that?" Irma said, her eyes laser-focused now.

"Well, the tractor *was* remotely operated. Someone could have easily—and I mean easily—assumed control and set it on its little rampage. And if someone knew there was a body there, and wanted that to come to light, it would be the perfect cover for…er, uncovering it."

"How easily?" Irma asked.

"There's less security on most construction equipment than on your garage door opener."

"I don't have one." Irma sniffed. "I like the exercise of opening the door myself."

"Of course you do," I said with a grin, then added, "It also has less security than the key fob for any modern-day car."

Irma gasped.

"Seriously?" Julian looked sceptical.

I nodded. "There's been a push to update the technology, but the focus on construction equipment—and most electronic devices, frankly—is functionality and safety. Not security."

"How do you know the tractor at the site was even hackable?" Julian asked.

I smiled. "I have a few deliveries coming. I'm going to build a remote device and test to see if I can assume control of that tractor. Once I do that, I can take a look at the logs and see what happened during the ground-breaking brouhaha."

"Wow." Julian was smiling at me.

"Carlton told me the company—Leblanc Industries—says it was just a malfunction of some kind," Irma said.

"Companies sometimes say that when they think they've been hacked," I replied.

"Good point," Julian said. The smart IV stands the clinic had been using before Irma and I had recently unravelled a mystery attached to them were now in storage because they'd been hacked and the manufacturer refused to admit it.

"So, someone in the crowd might have been piloting the tractor remotely," Irma said.

"Not necessarily," I answered. "The code could have been uploaded beforehand. Or it could have been done via drone. It was a cloudy enough day that we might not have even seen it.

Plus, nobody looked up to see if there was a drone, I'm guessing. I didn't."

"Me neither," Irma said, and it sounded like she was taking it as a personal failure.

"A few people are having a get-together for Lucas this week," Julian said, changing the subject. "Sort of like a wake."

"Yes, I heard about that," Irma said.

How? The news about Lucas's death had only been released this morning and Irma didn't have a phone with her. Had her brain just pulled the information out of the wireless communications that flowed past her on a daily basis? Was that why she didn't need a cell phone?

"What?" Irma said, looking at me like she could read my thoughts. "I ran into Mrs. Sepp on my run this morning and she told me. Which reminds me, she needs us to mind Mr. P later on today."

"No problemo."

"Violet should be the one to go pick him up," Julian said firmly. "You need to stay off that knee for the rest of the day."

"But it'll be right as rain tomorrow, correct?"

"Not correct, Irma, geez, I've told you a million times it'll take a while to get back to normal. Three to seven days for the initial improvement, and it can take up to six weeks to re-attain full functionality. Plus, you're going to need to maintain a reasonable injection schedule."

"All right, dear, no reason to be crabby."

Julian threw me a look while the two of us helped Irma off the exam table.

"I have some crutches for you," he said, once she was back on terra firma.

"Of course. Thank you."

"You could also use a cane," he said.

"I have one at home that's perfect."

"Sounds good," Julian said, even though he seemed to very much not believe a word Irma was saying. Trying to get her to do things she didn't want to was always a theatre of sorts.

Julian adjusted the child-sized crutches for her, and after a round of hugs, we left the clinic via the back exit. Irma had me go down first to see if anyone was there. After my recon, Irma crutched herself down to the pier so fast, I had to run to keep up with her.

"I can't wait until you start learning how to pilot the boat," Irma said, daintily taking a seat behind the wheel while I untied all the ropes. "I'm very excited about this vertigo discovery!"

I didn't want to admit I was excited too. Maybe she had a point about me spending more time on the water, and that I should try to experience some *vitamin sea*, as she referred to it, while I was here. There was something…

weightless about the waves and the sun and the quiet sounds of the lake propelling us places. I liked looking out and seeing nothing but water. It felt like anything was possible.

Of course, Irma hit the gas once we were away from the pier. Being half-crippled wasn't going to slow her down whatsoever. Especially since there was a murderous hacker on the loose in her little town.

Ten — Irma

I put some ice on my knee when I got home. While I sat on my back porch with my knee elevated and my temper short, I tried to think of where I'd stowed my cane. It was a miracle of 1980s technology: a single-shot pistol on one end, a stiletto in the other. I was almost looking forward to using it, if I had to. Which, really, I didn't think I would. I planned on being totally recovered by Lucas's wake.

While my icepack slowly glacierized my knee, I noodled on when I was going to take a look at Lucas's place. The Pickle had mentioned they'd be done looking at his abode today. Tonight was free, so it certainly felt like fate to me.

Then I heard grunting noises and cast my gaze around. The little snorts sounded like Mr. Pugglesworth, my next-door neighbour's fawn pug. I had two neighbours in my little cul-de-sac; Mrs. Sepp was the good one. I hadn't seen the other yet this summer. She was probably still in Transylvania with her family, but it was only

June. She'd show up eventually, the little vampire.

Mr. P burst around the side of the house. He was wearing a fitted checked coat—blue, black, and white, the colour of the Estonian flag—and tiny booties, also patriotically hued. The leash attached to his harness was trailing on the grass behind him. I frowned. I needed to mow the grass, that's what I needed to do. And my flowerbeds, oh, dear...

Mr. P fixed his beady eyes on me. He snorted while his tiny legs pumped: right, left, then right again. Then he stumbled and fell on his face, but corrected and came in a straight line at me—well, straight-ish—his focus and concentration so complete I was mesmerised. He pumped and pumped his little legs. He was halfway across the lawn now.

Mrs. Sepp shot around the corner of the house and stopped, her hand on the brick. She was bent over, heaving. Mr. P made a squeaking noise and kept barrelling at me, his enormously sad eyes bulging, his plump sides heaving. He was going to do it.

He can't. He just can't.

But he could and did: He ran up one of the patio chairs and launched all nine pounds of himself into the air. All nine point seven, completely non-aerodynamic pounds. His ears flattened, his legs tucked away like a set of miniature landing gear, his face an expression of unbridled joy.

Horror consumed me. He wasn't going to make it. He'd tried this particular move a few times before, and normally I was able to catch him, but this time—

I hopped toward him, my arms out in front of me.

Still, he came, all ears and eyes and unrestrained excitement, as pure and uncomplicated as emotion got. He was like a sausage-shaped, cuddle-seeking missile.

He slammed into my chest like a sledgehammer. And immediately started wiggling. I got my hand under his jacket and held on while he slurped his unbelievably long tongue right up my left arm. His legs wiggled like a bag of leeches. But I had him. Even gimpy and injured, I'd done it. I let out a huge sigh of relief.

"Irma!" Mrs. Sepp yelled.

"Mrs. Sepp!" I set Mr. P down and he started running in a circle around me. I hopped back to my chair and my tea, which was still steeping.

"I am so sorry, Irma! I told him he was coming over here tonight and he ran away from me, the naughty little thing." She walked toward me, one hand still on her side. "Mr. P!"

Mr. P sneezed on my right foot. I tried not to shudder. Mrs. Sepp was a grandmotherly woman with too many cats plus Mr. P, and treated the whole lot almost the same as she did her actual grandchildren. Mr. P looked at me adoringly, his mouth open, his tongue sliding out of it until it dangled on the ground. A ladybug started to traverse it.

"Do you want some tea, Mrs. Sepp?"

She looked like she was trying to suppress a shudder for some reason. "Oh, no thank you, but I will sit with you for a moment if you don't mind."

"Not at all."

She sat and Mr. P started a waddling circuit around the two of us, before getting distracted by a tulip he seemed to think was attacking him.

"I'm so sorry, Irma. He just gets so excited when he sees you."

"I wish he could get excited about our hikes in the woods," I said ruefully.

"It is not in his nature," she said, a hint of an Estonian accent in her words.

I sighed. It was true. I had tried my very best to get him to actually *walk* on our walks, but I'd started bringing the little knapsack Mrs. Sepp had given me to carry him in. It was like a baby Bjorn, but for small, lazy dogs. And I'd been trying to train him as a guard dog, but I was growing ever more suspicious *he* was training *me*.

Thank goodness none of my old co-workers could see it.

"What are you off to tonight?"

"Actually," she said, with a sheepish lift of her shoulders, "I was hoping you could take him now."

"Of course."

"I am having a meeting for the project I'm working on. Mr. P is not allowed to come." She looked affronted at this injustice.

"Oh, dear."

There was a silence. Mrs. Sepp was excellent at not talking through them, probably some sort of vexing Estonian cultural habit.

Finally, I prodded, "And what project is that?"

She looked at me, full on. Her eyes were the lightest blue, her hair still white-blonde, even though she was somewhere in her sixties. At least. She was rotund in a pleasant way, with strong peasant's arms and hands that could crush a beer can or sculpt a tiny arrangement of flowers. To be fair, she often used tweezers when doing her floral art. But nobody knew or cared. Her face was round and kind and beautiful. She'd moved in year-round ages ago, and we'd hit it off immediately.

She looked sad, I realised.

I poured my tea. It was really unfortunate she didn't want any. Tea brought such comfort in these moments.

She took in a deep breath and put her hand over her mouth. Mr. P made a sorrowful noise and she tried to pick him up. But his leash was entwined around us so completely, I briefly wondered if he had been trained by someone to—

Mr. P belched, then rolled on the ground, ending with all four legs thrust into the air.

Perhaps that was just my paranoia talking.

"I'm working on the flowers for the poker tournament for the Campbell Group," Mrs. Sepp said eventually, before adding, "But I am missing my husband."

I could feel my eyes widen. I'd never met him, and she didn't talk about him much. "I'm so sorry," I said. "Do you want something a bit stronger than tea? I'm a little indisposed, but there's some—"

She pulled a flask out of the pocket of her floral housedress in one easy movement and took a swig. Then another. Eventually, she held it out to me.

I gave her a quizzical look.

"Vodka," she said simply.

"Thank you," I said. It had been my habit when among people of other cultures to partake of their customs. I finished my tea and poured a healthy glug of vodka into the cup. "Delicious," I pronounced after a sip. And I meant it. This was no off-the-shelf discount vodka. I'd always been a fan of people who insisted on quality liquor. "Do you want to talk about it?"

She picked up Mr. P and snuggled him to her ample bosom. He made keening noises and slurped at her shoulder. I sipped my vodka and waited. I had time. There were benefits to being retired, I was learning.

"It's just..." She looked away, at the water, blue swells we couldn't see the end of. The water surged to the shore, hitting my dock in waves. We could get big weather on the lake, but today it was calm, almost no wind. Not a sailing day.

She cleared her throat. "I just had a meeting about another project, the flowers for a wedding. Doing weddings is sometimes very difficult. We had such a wonderful wedding..." Mrs. Sepp was semi-retired and had to be coaxed to practice her trade. She was particularly known for her wedding arrangements, had made it into the paper and been interviewed in the glossy magazine one of the island daughters published about our little piece of heaven.

Mr. P tried to scale her shoulder, but couldn't get any purchase.

"I'm very sorry to hear that."

She met my eyes. Hers were shiny. The fingers of her left hand, holding Mr. P's rump, were trembling. He dropped his chin onto her shoulder, so he was now facing backwards and his bottom was staring directly at me.

She sniffed and I looked away. I knew, instinctively, she would be unhappy if I saw her cry.

A sailboat appeared about a hundred feet off shore. It looked like it was an older model, maybe thirty feet long. A Grampian, perhaps. A sturdy, inexpensive boat. Two people on board. Stuart had a Grampian, but those were not his sails. For a moment I worried someone was prepping for an aquatic attack. I reached under my chair, where a pair of binoculars was taped to its undercarriage. I adjusted the focus, then returned the binos to their hidey hole. It was Lorraine Santos, the island postmistress. I'd heard she had bought a new boat. Good for her.

Mrs. Sepp sniffed again and I returned my attention to her. "Whose wedding were you working on?" I asked, not to be nosy. Just because I liked to know what was going on.

"Cynthia Leblanc," she said. "Such a lovely girl."

I didn't know about all that. Cynthia Leblanc had kicked me in the shin once when she was a toddler. Not that I held a grudge, but—

"And Tony Romano."

"Aren't the Leblanc and Romano families feuding?"

Her raised left eyebrow perfectly conveyed how correct my intel was.

Mr. P hung his front legs over her shoulders so he was wrapped around her neck like a good fur. I waved at him and he snorted happily in response. "I'm too much of a bother," she said. "Thank you so much for taking Mr. P off my hands today."

"No bother at all. That's what neighbours are for."

"Oh," she said, looking confused. "You don't help our other neighbour."

"I help her all the time," I said cheerily. And it was true. I helped her stay alive by not killing her.

"I just worry about Mr. P. He gets so sad when he's lonely. And if I leave him at home, the cats gang up on him."

Mrs. Sepp had six cats at my last count. Briefly, I wondered if I could train them to—

No, they were cats, after all. I was barely able to make Mr. P use his God-given legs to get from point A to point B. I tried to pry him off her shoulders, but he was reluctant. It took Mrs. Sepp five minutes of baby talk to make him release his iron grip on her. As soon as he let go, he flung himself at my face like one of those little creatures from that horrible movie, *Alien*, Violet had made me watch last week. Only cuter, of course.

"Yoo-hoo!"

Mr. P took off across the lawn toward Elsa Lee, who was laboriously walking toward us.

"Elsa, dear!" I said, jumping up. Immediately, I regretted it when pain knifed through my left knee. I gritted my teeth and smiled.

Elsa put a hand on her round belly, squared her shoulders, and kept coming. I organized a chair for her.

"Can I get you some water or juice, dear?" I asked.

"I have a water bottle in my purse," she said. "I'm sorry to intrude like this, Irma, but Carlton dropped me off at Mrs. Sepp's, and nobody was answering the door."

"I am so sorry," Mrs. Sepp said, frowning. "I thought our meeting was in an hour? At the boat?"

She sighed. "Carlton had…other plans."

Mrs. Sepp made an annoyed noise. "Other plans, like golfing the entire afternoon while you do all the work again?"

"I've learned when you're working with a family-owned company, some rules are..." Elsa trailed off with a shrug, then rooted around in her bag for a water bottle and drank half of it down.

"Yes, but you should not be doing everything in your condition," Mrs. Sepp tut-tutted.

"Thank you," Elsa said. "But I feel fine. Pregnancy is not an ailment."

"If you say so," Mrs. Sepp said dubiously. "When I was pregnant, Mr. Sepp always used to go to the grocer's when I wanted pickles."

"I'm quite happy without a mister," Elsa said with a grin. "I don't like being told what to do."

"Me neither," I said, and we all laughed.

"Shall we?" Mrs. Sepp said to Elsa. "I will drive us."

After the two of them left, Mr. P jumped in my lap, and turned over so I could rub his belly. I felt sorry for Elsa, who was working while Carlton spent his office hours on the links. What other activities had he gotten up to with all his spare time?

Mr. P sneezed on me, then took off across the lawn. I sighed and went to retrieve him. It was going to be a long afternoon.

Eleven — Irma

I was not enjoying my evening activities as much as usual. Possibly because I was sitting in a ditch wearing night vision binoculars and had somehow forgotten my little ditch seat at home. It wasn't anything fancy; a gardening kneeling pad that fit perfectly under my bottom and kept me dry in difficult circumstances.

I always kept a pair of latex gloves in my handbag—you know, just in case—and I'd been contemplating knitting the gloves together to make a fanny protector, but I needed them for what was going to happen next, so it was impossible. I tried not to be cranky about it.

I'd snuck out of the house so Violet wouldn't worry about me. Hopefully she was glued to her screens and wouldn't notice when I came home.

The sun had been down for a while, but people were still out and about at the trailer park that hosted Lucas's Airstream at the edge of town.

I tried to think about the optimal line of attack for what I had planned next. The Pickle had heavily implied—or I'd heavily inferred, hard to tell, really—that the police would be done with Lucas's abode by now, so I was going to take a little look-see to determine if anyone had been threatening or blackmailing, or just generally being unpleasant to him. He'd been upset about some letters, and I was hoping to find them tonight.

I frowned in the dark, in my little ditch. Lucas had always been so friendly to me, so helpful. It was hard for me to see him as someone with enemies. Or someone who'd partaken in extramarital shenanigans. But recently, I'd been completely fooled by someone I thought I knew, so perhaps my own judgement couldn't be trusted. If someone was determined to lie about their life, they were unstoppable. That, I knew for sure.

I could see the crime scene tape coiled around Lucas's trailer from where I was sitting. I'd tried crouching, but my left knee—which was already feeling quite a bit better, thank you very much Dr. Julian Harper—wasn't going to let me. Thus, the sitting.

I wasn't quite sure how I was going to explain myself if one of the young folks from the trailer park stumbled upon me, but I was sure I'd think of something. I'd once talked myself out of being arrested in the North Korean DMZ, which, believe you me, is no easy task.

A bonfire roared a few doors down from Julian's trailer, which, mercifully, was at the edge of the parking lot. It looked shiny and well-maintained.

A young woman in a striped sundress walked her little scruff of a dog past Lucas's trailer, toward me. She hovered while he did his business. I was glad I'd left Mr. P with Violet; he had a number of odd habits, and fixating on strange dogs with his big googley eyes was one of his worst. Other members of the canine family did not seem to care for his enormous-eyeballed stares whatsoever.

My left knee was starting to ache. I did some deep breathing to centre myself, and visualised squishing the pain into a ball so small it didn't exist anymore. Calm rippled over me.

The girl and her little fluffball finished up, and she wandered back to the bonfire. I waited. When the group around the fire started up an off-tune, guitar-accompanied version of "American Pie," I knew I'd have eight minutes and forty-two seconds of off-key folk music to block the noise of my efforts, if they were following the song's LP edition, which one could only pray they were.

I stowed the night vision goggles in my knapsack and got up, ignoring the cracking in both knees as I made my way to the edge of the ditch. I looked around, then gently made my way to the Airstream, happy I was wearing all black for once. Violet would be proud.

I considered the windows as a possible entry point but eventually rejected them: they were all closed and presumably locked, with more crime scene tape across them. I had convinced myself that the Pickle had given me permission to take a gander at Lucas's trailer, but I didn't want to test her good humour. The front door was also out of the question for similar reasons.

I was going to have to go up. Luckily, I had everything I needed in my knapsack, and—

Voices came around the side of the trailer.

I froze, dropped to the ground, and rolled under the Airstream. The voices drifted closer.

"I literally ate the entire lasagna," one said. I wished I had my night vision goggles on, but they were in the knapsack and I didn't want to make any noise. It really would not do to be found under Lucas's trailer. I focused on the voice. It sounded local, no regional accent I could determine. I closed my eyes and listened.

"It looked good," the other one responded with a flat Toronto-area cadence. Both eventually stubbed out their cigarettes and melted away.

I waited a few more minutes before rummaging in my bag and pulling out the little suction-cup climbing tools that a good friend had given me for my seventieth birthday. Frankly, I didn't know how I'd managed without them before. I didn't know the specific details—something about stored kinetic energy—but I did know I could climb up the Statue of Liberty with these little suckers and not break a sweat.

I took in three deep breaths and peered out from under the trailer. The coast seemed clear, so I rolled out, got my feet under me, and snugged up to the side of the Airstream. I held my breath.

Nothing.

I pressed the suction cups on the front of my shoes and grasped the other two in my hands. I attached one against the side of the trailer. I let out a sigh, then fastened the second a little higher. It held.

"What was that noise?"

I went back to holding my breath, which really was a terrible habit. It was one of the smokers again, and I was hoping *his* terrible habit had decreased his lung capacity enough that he wouldn't be able to move very fast.

I placed the right suction cup higher up, then the left, and got going.

"I don't hear anything." The second man sounded reluctant, but footsteps were coming in my direction anyway.

Left, right, left, right. I was at the top of the trailer. I just had to swing my legs up and over.

The young men's sneakers made dragging noises against the pavement, and I felt annoyance clutter my throat. Why couldn't young people just pick their feet up? I mean, honestly.

All I had to do was swing my legs and—

I bloody well missed. My left foot met metal, jarring my knee. I gritted my teeth as the pain whooshed through me. My legs dangled under me like dead trout.

"You're gonna tell me you didn't hear that?" the sloucher asked.

"Yeah," his friend said, his voice bored. "I think you're hearing things, bruh."

The sneakers schlepped around the other side of the trailer.

I breathed out, hooked my left foot over an antenna of some kind, and pulled my right leg up—silently, so silently I could barely hear it myself—and rolled onto the top of the trailer.

I didn't move, didn't breathe. I could see the moon hanging over me, suddenly thrust out from behind a cloud. If anyone had higher ground, they'd be able to see me perfectly. If a sniper was in the neighbourhood, I was doomed.

I could hear the feet drag themselves around one side of Lucas's trailer, then back around the other way. I focused on my current conundrum while one of the little snoops sparked up another cigarette. The smoke wafted directly into my lungs' cilia. I put my hand over my nose so I wouldn't sneeze. Terrible habit, smoking.

It went on forever, my lungs yearning to be free. On the one hand, I liked the young man's suspiciousness. On the other, I really wanted a nice cup of tea and to watch *Matlock* with Stu.

I tried to calm my heart rate and focus on something else. I was lying flat on my back under the stars. Not such a terrible place to be. Then I asked myself: Who wanted Lucas dead? Tate Hurst, who wanted his job? What had been in Carlton's voice when he spoke about his wife's lessons with Lucas? And why had Rose *really* been so unkempt that morning? Rose, who'd had a lesson just before his death. There were so many possibilities. I tried to focus on the Airstream and the little snoops on the ground under me, but being distrustful of people was second nature to me, like a comfortable old suit. I couldn't turn it off if I tried.

A young woman broke off from the bonfire and wandered over. Then one of the young gentleman smokers started flirting with her. My goodness, this was going to take forever. I contemplated how this would have played out when I was still in active duty: I would have had a compatriot provide a lovely little distraction—explosions had always been my diversions of choice—then I'd be able to slip into the target. Not for the first time, I thought about how different my life was now. I was on my own out here. No backup, no intel, no nothing. My breath quickened.

Then the two started snogging. Slurpily. This was a nightmare.

I closed my eyes and tried to turn my focus back to problem-solving my current situation. Had Tate bumped off Lucas to get his job? Would it have been worth it? I made a mental note to find out how much tennis pros made. On the other hand, it might just be proximity Tate was after: The Club was a great place to sniff out unmarried heiresses and attach yourself to a meal ticket.

Plus, Tate was a hyper-competitive little liar. In my twenties, I'd known a tennis player who sabotaged every single ball at a tournament he'd been axed from. That kind of revenge required a level of competitiveness that the general population simply didn't contain.

After approximately ten thousand years, the two young lovers moved off. It was like a miracle. I breathed warm summer air in and out for another few minutes. I wanted to get my search over with, but I knew from experience that if I moved too soon, I'd get caught. Possibly by a pair of lip-locked twenty-somethings.

I let five minutes go by, then ten. The gloves slid on. I pulled a pair of booties over my shoes. Then I popped the skylight open and slipped into the Airstream.

TWELVE — VIOLET

I finally finished my online game with Hubert, a friend in Bora Bora who worked at an upscale resort and blew off steam by helping me kill zombies. That was when I realised Mr. P had waddled into the room and made his way to my lap while I'd been playing. Irma'd once told me I'd never see an assassin coming if I didn't take my eyes off my screens, and I was beginning to think she might be right.

I rubbed Mr. P's tummy while trying to visualise the project I was about to start. I now had all the pieces I needed for my remote-controlled-tractor project.

Mr. P tilted his head and made a sorrowful noise. I didn't want to build the remote if he was here—I was worried he'd eat one of the pieces. Or get one lodged in his face folds.

My phone *binged* with a notification for my personal mailbox, and I tried to pick it up, but Mr. P suddenly decided to become best friends with my phone. It took some effort to separate them.

But then I saw the email. And cursed.

The message was from Shane, the jerk who'd run off with all the money my company had in the bank, except for a small emergency fund. He would have needed all of our signatures for that one. I was secretly pleased Max and I had been smart enough to accomplish at least that much.

Of course, why would we have suspected Shane of anything? He was from a wealthy Toronto family, had lots of money. They'd summered in the Hamptons, jetted off to Paris to celebrate New Year's Eve.

I'd practically grown up with Max—we'd lived in the same dumpy rooming house downtown as kids—and we'd met Shane at U of T. It didn't matter. I should never have been stupid enough to trust him. What had happened was all my fault.

I pursed my lips, read the email:

Vi, I'm sorry. I ran into a little gambling snafu. Had to get out of town. I know you'll land on your feet. You always do.
Shane.

Icy cold rippled through my body. I hadn't realised it was possible to be even more angry with Shane. I'd worked and saved for years to be in a position to start my own company. So had Max. And even worse, some of the money Shane had taken was out of our line of credit, so it wasn't even really money at all.

Last week, Max had been able to sweet talk the bank into increasing the limit on that line of credit so we could pay our operating costs, but the payments were going to come due every month just like clockwork.

I let my head fall on my chest. What was I going to do? It felt hopeless. But suddenly my face was wet from my chin to my forehead. Mr. P was licking my face, and he was panting, his little sides heaving, his mouth hanging open like he was smiling.

"Thanks, Mr. P."

He curled up in my arms and rested his head on my shoulder with a squeaky yawn. I called Max.

"Vi?" he said, and he sounded anxious. "Everything all right?"

"Yeah, Maxy. You?"

"Just went for a run. I feel like death."

"I told you exercise was for the birds."

"Didn't you used to be some fancy prima ballerina?"

"I gave it up for Lent. Look, I got an email from Shane." I tried to forward it to him, but Mr.

P's legs were suddenly twined around my arms like an octopus. Eventually, I succeeded, although I was newly convinced Mr. P was craftier than we gave him credit for.

"Wow," Max said. Then he cursed for a while. I understood the temptation. "He doesn't even feel bad about it."

"I know. It's almost unbelievable."

Max let out a heavy sigh. "Is it bad I was still holding out hope he'd just...give it back?"

"Nope." I'd been hanging on to the exact same tiny, stupid hope.

"Still don't want to go to the police?"

"They don't care about white collar crime, Max. And Shane could be anywhere. He could be at the family's summer home in the Hamptons. He could be in Ecuador. And I don't think anyone's gonna extradite someone who took money out of a bank account he had legitimate access to. His family's lawyers would eat us alive."

He sighed again. "I hear ya, Vi."

I cocked my head. Mr. P copied me, his two front legs curled up in front of him. *Family.* Max and I had no family—no functional family, at least—except for each other.

"Maxy," I said slowly. "What if we go to Shane's family?"

Silence.

"Or," I said, "What if we post the evidence of what he did on social media? The family won't want any negative publicity. At all. Aren't they doing a big merger with—"

"That Irish company. Yeah…" Max said. It sounded like gears were turning in his head. "But everyone will know we're almost insolvent if we go public."

"Do we have anything to lose?"

"I don't like it," he said finally. "I don't like the idea of airing our dirty laundry, Vi."

"What about talking to the family?"

There was another pause. I could hear him bouncing his tennis ball off the wall like he usually did when he was trying to solve a problem. Probably drove the neighbours nuts, but Max was suave enough to smooth anything like that over. My neighbours—ironically, the same people, since Max lived down the hall from me—would come for me with pitchforks and a pre-assembled noose. "Maybe," he said finally.

I laughed. "We're quite the pair. I don't want to go to the police; you don't want to go to the family. What do we *actually* want to do?"

"Great question, Vi."

"Thanks, Maxy. Got an answer?"

"Nope," he said. "We have enough money in the bank and enough brains in our heads to make it work, Vi. I'm sure of it."

"I should come home."

"Forget about it," he said firmly. "You haven't had a vacation in, like, ever. If you come home, I'm gonna be very unhappy with you. Everything's under control. Your staff are doing their jobs, and we have a solution to our financial issues, now that we have that extension on our line of credit. There's nothing you can do about the money situation anyway. It's literally not your department. You come back early and everyone is going to know something's wrong. Stay where you are, have some fun, and stop worrying. Please. For me."

I rubbed my forehead. "All right, all right. But I wonder, what if we asked the family to pay his debt…"

"No way, Vi. They'll claim we're blackmailers."

"What about filing a missing persons report?" I asked. "That way there's no public fuss about anything he's done. We're just concerned friends and business partners."

"That could work," Max said slowly.

A missing person's report could even involve the family a bit too. It could definitely work.

"I wonder who he was gambling with," Max said, "And if he still owes any money to anyone."

"I wonder if a missing persons report will pull them out of the woodwork."

"It might. Geez, Vi, you're really becoming ruthless."

"I have an excellent teacher," I said, thinking of Irma. "When are you coming for a visit? There's awesome food, drinks, sailing, power boating, patios, bunch of other things."

"Can we sit by a pool with umbrella drinks?"

"We can sit *in* a pool with umbrella drinks. And check this out—there's some kind of charity poker tournament next Friday on a megayacht. This place is crazy."

"You should enter."

"Enter the pool? You got it."

"No, the poker tournament. You paid for half your living expenses that way when you were in uni."

I laughed. "I played Blackjack, which is very different."

"Counting cards is counting cards, Vi."

"Poker is about people. Not my area, Maxy, you know that."

He laughed. "Alright, that, I'll give ya." He was sounding better than he had at the start of the conversation, which made me happy. I loved Max like he was a brother.

And I was going to get our money back, even though I was sure Shane expected to get away with it. Which would make it even more satisfying.

"Maybe," he said finally.

"Maybe you're coming here, or maybe we should go to Shane's family?"

"Maybe both. I just wanna be sure we're doing the right thing."

I didn't push it. Nothing was going to get done until I got home anyway, and Max always needed time to sort through data and come to a decision. It was one of his best qualities. But I could feel him almost agreeing with me. I could wait.

He hung up to go take a shower, and I looked at my desk; covered with monitors and computer equipment, and one oversized pug, who'd wiggled up on top of my desk, stretched himself out over my keyboard, and gone to sleep.

I collected the equipment that had been delivered and set myself up on the kitchen table. I was going to build my remote and prove that the tractor had been hacked. I was sick and tired of evil people ruining everything for everybody else.

THIRTEEN — IRMA

The Airstream smelled aggressively clean and fresh. I wondered if it was some new, hip law enforcement scent they were trying out, then let the thought go. It was important to focus. I didn't have a lot of time, especially if those bloody snoggers came back.

I left the lights off. Luckily, the shades facing the bonfire and the off-key folk singers were already lowered. I pulled the other ones closed as well and took a headlamp out of my knapsack, slipping it over my forehead. Instantly, I could see the police had been here, and they'd been thorough. Black fingerprint dust covered half the trailer: the kitchen counters, the door, the breakfast bar.

The Airstream was laid out beautifully, with a full bedroom and ensuite bathroom designed just like a boat. Every inch was used; every nook was purposeful. At the opposite end of the trailer was a lounge area with an enormous television.

The middle section contained a nicely appointed kitchen and dining area, as well as a second bathroom. A small office nook was tucked beside the lounge. Black powder dusted the desk, which contained exactly zero office equipment. There was a small filing cabinet attached to the desk. Empty.

The police had probably taken everything of value, but I had to try anyway. I started in the bedroom, then moved to the bathroom. Everything had a home, and everything was neat and tidy except for the mess the police had left. I made a mental note to clean it up after they released the trailer.

The floor was intact. The Pickle had said they were going to luminol, which meant that none of the floor had been evidentiary. Nothing had been chopped up and ferried to the police lab; the walls were all still in place. This hadn't been where Lucas was murdered.

I wondered for a minute if Lucas had been lured to the construction site and killed there. It would be the easiest play. It also meant that Lucas had probably known his killer. Or killers.

But it would be difficult to determine after the carnage caused by the tractor. Had that been the point? Maybe, but I couldn't understand why Lucas's killer had buried him in the moonlight, only to dig him up the very next day. It felt like two different goals were being served by burying, then unearthing Lucas, and in my experience, that sometimes meant two different bad guys.

But in the intelligence world, operations often had many branches, little tendrils that reached out and tried to achieve the same goals using a variety of methods, and different teams. It often confused the people trying to work it all out or stop whatever nefarious plans were being organized, which was the point.

I'd once posed as a singing telegram worker to locate an operative who was trying to murder a member of the British aristocracy. The rest of my team had been casing his workplace for weeks. I found him my very first day. To be fair, the man we were looking for really liked petite women who could tap dance.

I kept searching: in the freezer, inside the light fixtures, the drain of the shower. I was quick but didn't rush. Things were missed when one rushed. I had to try to get into Lucas's head and see where he would hide something. He was a good boy, which made me think it would be somewhere pedestrian, like in an ice cream container.

I let out a sigh. I didn't want to be here, rooting through Lucas's things. I hinged my head from left to right until it cracked, forced myself to keep going.

I lay down on the floor and swept my gaze over the trailer. I liked taking a different angle of approach in these types of situations. But nothing was out of place.

A twinge of frustration ran through me, and I sat up, letting out a cranky sigh. I wondered if the police had found anything—or everything. I needed some solid evidence, or Lucas's murderer was going to go free, free to sit at the next table over at brunch and enjoy their waffles. Maybe even free to kill another islander. I could not let that happen.

After a sigh, I went into the bedroom and opened the door of Lucas's closet. Everything was neatly hung, all his Club shirts and the baggy shorts he favoured, his shoes. I poked around the floor with the end of a broom. Nothing.

Bollocks.

I wandered back into the living area and sat down at Lucas's office chair. My legs swung restlessly. Maybe there was nothing here. Maybe Lucas had been living a completely normal life and had been swept off the board by a sociopath who'd been passing through town and was now on their way to Tuktuyuktuk. It was possible.

And I was no murder investigator. If you wanted me to track down where—or whom—a shipment of illegal arms had come from, or to tap dance my way into a suspect's abode with a knife hidden in the heel of my shoe, I was your girl. But figuring out why civilian number one had bumped off civilian number two, no matter how nice he was, or how beautiful his backhand had been, was not my area, unfortunately. And I had no access to a law enforcement lab, or my former back-of-the-house buddies. I was on my own.

My right foot tapped the filing cabinet idly. The top of the cabinet sounded hollow—because it was. But the bottom sounded…different.

I got on my hands and knees, trying to ignore the twinge in my left knee that had become un-ignorable. I peered under the cabinet and spied a few printouts stuck under the desk leg. I sat down to take a look. It was a client schedule for Lucas, printed on Club letterhead. For the last three weeks on Tuesdays and Thursdays, Rose Campbell had been having her lessons at six p.m. in the evening. So, nine o'clock wasn't her usual time. Why had she scheduled a lesson at nine the night of Lucas's murder?

I put the papers down and looked at the desk. Then I realized the lower drawer was too high. Because it had a false bottom.

A little thrill ran through me. I *knew* Lucas was interesting enough to be up to something. I pressed down on the bottom of the drawer, and it released with a lovely little click.

But then I cursed under my breath. I'd finally found something, which was wonderful, except now I had a new problem. It was a safe. And I had absolutely no clue how to crack it.

FOURTEEN — VIOLET

I slept in until nine-thirty the next day and lay in bed with my phone for way too long. After catching up on my Instagram feed, I pulled myself together and made some coffee, giving the machine a little pat. It'd helped me and Irma solve a crime last week, and I was subsequently enamoured of it. I'd always thought machines made more sense than people, anyway.

I was on my second cup of coffee when Irma burst into my apartment. I was sitting on the couch, under a blanket with a mug in my hand, my computer in my lap, while I responded to a LinkedIn request from David Bell, the engineer who'd been at the ground-breaking the other day. I clicked *accept* just as Irma stopped, backtracked, then knocked on the door.

"Hellooo!" she said cheerfully.

I gave her a look.

"What? I knocked."

I stifled a sigh that somehow turned into a giggle. I was terrible at staying mad at Irma. It must be the British accent, which she wasn't above playing up if she wanted something. "Thanks?"

"You're welcome, dear. What are we up to today?"

I felt suspiciousness envelop me; Irma didn't normally believe I should have that much free will. "I have a delivery coming. I wanted to be here when it arrives."

"What is it?"

"I'm working on that remote I was telling you about. I'm still waiting on something, though. One of the parts I originally ordered isn't the right one."

"I'm impressed by your mistrust, dear. But can you show me why you think the tractor was hacked?"

I ran the footage I'd viewed the other day, and afterward, her eyes were the size of Frisbees.

"I do see your point, Violet, and well done on your suspiciousness, but do you really plan on sitting at home on a beautiful summer day waiting for a delivery truck? Is that something young people do these days?"

I nodded, took a sip of coffee. It was perfect; packed with cream and sugar.

"When you could be outside having fun?"

"I *am* having fun."

She pressed her fingers against her eyebrows in an attempt at looking hopeless. But her left eye was peering at me under her hand.

"I see you, Irma."

She massaged her forehead briefly. Then she seemed to get a second wind. "I was hoping we could go to Lucas's memorial later on today. Well, it's not really a memorial, it's a get-together for his friends. A wake. It'll be a good opportunity to ask a few questions."

"Oh, of course. No problem. And I'm so sorry about Lucas."

"Thank you, dear." Her voice wavered on the *dear*.

"Irma, are you okay?"

She seemed to deflate. "I'm sorry, dear. I've just been a little...off ever since Lucas died. It's not easy, losing someone you care about." She met my eyes. "Or being betrayed by someone you care about."

"I wonder who betrayed Lucas."

Her head tilted. "Well, we're going to find out, I promise you that. May I borrow your cellular, dear?"

I nudged it toward her and she dialled.

Fifteen — Irma

"Oui?" Camille Beaulieu answered the phone with her soothing French-Canadian accent. She had a security company in Toronto and helped me out from time to time. I'd worked with her father, a lovely chap.

"*Bonjour, Camille, ma chérie*," I singsonged. *Hello, my dear.*

"Irma! *Quelle plaisir*! *What a pleasure*! How can I help?"

"It's Violet and I, actually. You're on speakerphone. We wanted to see how you're doing." Camille had been on the island helping with a security issue recently, and she'd been drugged by a lunatic for her trouble. It had only been a small tranquiliser dart, but it had shaken her confidence. She'd been ambushed by a deranged criminal hiding behind a door, which, honestly, could happen to anyone. She was young, and it had all been good experience for her in the end, although she probably wasn't going to agree with me about that for a few years.

But anything that made her more vigilant when she was in the field was a good thing as far as I was concerned.

She made a small French sound. "Bonjour, Violet!" Violet waved in response, even though we were not on a video call. Camille continued, "Oui, Irma, I am okay. I am just upset I let you down."

"Not at all, chérie," I said. "You did your best, and you came out alive, and so did your team, not to mention the person you were protecting. And you learned something. That is a good outcome."

"Oui, if you say so."

"Trust me on this," I said firmly.

"So," she said, a smile in her voice, "Are we done talking now, or is there something else?" After a brief pause, she added, "We are very slow here these days. I was hoping to get a bit more work, but…"

I knew what she was doing. "Oh, well, I did have a small thing."

"Oui," she said briskly.

"I need background checks done on a few people, please: Tate Hurst, Lucas Waters, Tiffanni Morgan, Carlton Campbell, and his wife, Rose."

"*Bon.*" *Good.* "What is the situation?"

I caught her up on Lucas's untimely death, as well as Tate's suspicious appearance in town,

Tiffanni's tantrum the day of Lucas's death, and Carlton and Rose's odd behaviour.

"And Lucas was the victim?"

"Yes. And can you please check to see if he had any enemies or disputes with anyone? He was getting letters that concerned him."

"Do you know what was in the letters?"

"No, I haven't been able to locate any of them, and he died before we could discuss them. But he found them upsetting."

"I understand." A pause. "Why do you believe the tractor was hacked?"

Violet ran her through the observations she'd made about the tractor's trajectory, then emailed a copy of the video to Camille, who made tut-tutting noises while watching it.

"What are you thinking, Irma?" Camille asked.

"It sounds like two different assailants," I said. "And it feels like they might have been working together and turned on each other. I mean, who would know about Lucas pushing up daisies if they hadn't been there when he was murdered?"

"Coincidence?" Camille said.

"I don't believe in them," I said.

"Oui."

"And when I searched Lucas's office at the Club—"

"You searched his office? When?" Violet asked.

"The other day," I said vaguely. "The last lesson Lucas had that day was with Rose, Carlton's wife. Nine at night, and he was killed around midnight. She looked very upset that morning at the Club, very unhappy indeed."

"What if they were having an affair?" Camille asked. "That is an odd time of the day for a lesson."

Violet's eyes widened.

"Plus, the other young woman, Tiffanni, what was the nature of their relationship before this blow up?"

"Unclear," I said. "But Lucas was a very sensible young man. You think maybe Rose or Tiffanni killed him in some sort of crime of passion?"

"Possibly. What's security like on the construction site?" Camille asked.

"It's wide open, really. No fences or anything like that yet. Anyone could have done it."

"But why would someone have dug him up the next day?" Violet pointed out.

"Oh, this is so vexatious!" I said. "Camille, can you please take a look at the financial situation for the Beaver Brooke build? A local reporter mentioned they might be having issues. I'm also feeling uneasy about Carlton Campbell,

Rose's husband. It felt like he was hinting about something to do with Rose and Lucas."

"Perhaps because they were having an affair?" Camille repeated.

"Lucas was a nice boy," I said firmly. "He would have told me if he was in a relationship."

"Life is complicated," Camille said, as only a Frenchwoman could. "And it could be this Carlton Campbell *thought* they were having an affair, and then..."

"I know." I swallowed hard.

"What are you going to focus on next?" Camille asked.

"Violet and I are attending Lucas's wake tonight. I want to chat with Rose and Ms. Morgan."

"*Bien.*" *Good.* There was a pause. "Irma," Camille said hesitantly. "I do not want to mention this, but..."

"Go ahead, dear."

"Have you seen Boris Andropov again?"

I took a moment to collect my thoughts. Boris had been a Bulgarian secret service operative back when I was working, and we'd had a little cold war all to ourselves. His nephew was currently summering on the island—a data point I had to admit seemed suspicious—and Boris had recently popped up in town.

"Yes, he came to the BBQ we had after the half-marathon. You had to leave town early, remember?"

"I see."

The silence lengthened.

"It's just...." Camille hesitated. "I do not like him being so close to you."

I laughed. "Oh, Camille—"

"I am not laughing, Irma. He tried to kill you!"

"Just the once, chérie, and it was a long time ago." Good heavens, I needed tea. "And he even said sorry!"

Camille made an irritated noise.

"I'll be careful, I promise," I said. Camille pretended to accept that platitude, and we hung up. Then I turned to Violet and said, "I have a great idea."

SIXTEEN — VIOLET

After Irma shuttled me outside a few minutes later, I said, "Don't take this the wrong way, but are you trying to kill me?"

She cocked her head like she was considering my question.

"Why are you taking so long to answer?"

"I was just trying to see if I felt any unresolved conflict with you, dear," Irma said sweetly.

"I don't feel very safe right now."

"But I don't, so all's well."

"Yay?"

"Yay indeed, Violet. All right, old girl, let's get this show on the road. Metaphorically speaking, of course. It's been a challenging week, and I really need to get out on the water. So do you."

I looked around. We were standing on Irma's dock, beside her beloved speedboat, *Vitamin Sea*, which was still tied up. When she'd decided we needed some cheering up after recent events, I'd proposed a cheering-up nap. I'd lost. "Maybe today's lesson could be that we stay at the dock and I sit in the driver's seat."

"Did you write your personal watercraft test?"

I thought about lying for a minute, then rejected the idea. Irma could smell a lie like a truffle pig going after upscale mushrooms. "Yes, but—"

"Then it's legal for you to pilot a boat. How wonderful!"

"Yes, but I really don't think I should be punished for it."

"Who's punishing you?"

"I feel like it's you. I've read that using feeling words is important, so that's why I'm using feeling words to communicate my feelings to you."

"Nonsense, we're having a great time."

"I feel like that's not actually what's happening."

"You feel like that any time you're not playing video games and eating cupcakes."

"One," I said, holding up a finger, "Video games are awesome. Two, I never have time to play them when I'm not on vacation because I'm working, and—"

"We really must do something about your workaholic tendencies, dear."

"That's what the video games are for!"

She opened her mouth, but I kept going. "Three, cupcakes are also awesome. They're like tiny little individualized cakes, just for you! You don't even have to share! And up until coming here to visit you, I hadn't had a cupcake in, what, three years? I normally just drink meal replacements when I'm working."

"Have you thought about some of Luna's protein muffins? Lots of bran fibre and—"

I held up a hand. "Have you thought about decaf?"

She looked like she was trying not to smile.

"I like cupcakes, I like video games. I'm forty-three years old, and I know what I like."

Irma turned her neck until it cracked, a noise that did not help me feel any better. "Touché, my dear. But you like the water, I know you do. Have you been doing your vertigo exercises?"

I mumbled something un-hearable.

"Yes, and they're going very well?" she said, a glint in her eye.

"How do you *do* that?"

"Small ears filter sound more efficiently."

"Oh, you're making that up."

"Violet, I just want you to know I'm proud you're trying something new and letting me teach you how to captain a boat."

The remark moved me a little off-kilter, which I was sure was exactly her intent. "Uh-huh," I said, not bothering to stamp the scepticism out of my tone.

"So, can we progress to you sitting in the driver's seat?"

I made a noise.

"That's excellent, dear. Let's get in the boat, shall we? It's still tied up at the dock, so it's all very safe."

"Do you remember what I said about you trying to kill me?"

She pursed her lips. "Can you be more specific?"

"And how I told you not to?"

"Ah, I see. Yes. No, I'm not trying to kill you." She flashed her perfect teeth. "But I might if you don't get in the boat. We're burning daylight, dear."

"See, that makes me feel unsafe."

"Could you feel unsafe in the boat?"

I nodded grudgingly and picked one foot up off the dock and set it in the boat, which immediately tipped my way. I pulled back. Irma made a supportive noise, which I ignored.

I took a few deep breaths and tried again, even though my feet felt frozen to the dock. It was often better if I got right into the boat instead of crouching with one foot on the dock and the other in the boat, the two of them floating away from each other like something from a *Three's Company* episode.

I dragged my other leg with me and stood. My legs shivered and the boat jittered under me. *Being on the water will make Irma feel better*, I told myself. *Keep going.*

"Very good, dear!"

I inched over to the driver's seat. When I finally got there, it felt solid under me, like I could count on it. I let out a deep breath. Then another. I'd been on this boat many times, and had never had this kind of reaction before. It must be because I was suddenly responsible if anything went wrong. Would I have to go down with the ship? I decided not to ask. I didn't want to know the answer.

"You're doing very well! Can I cast the lines off now?" Irma asked sweetly.

All my senses pinged when I heard that tone. I could feel my face scrunching up like I'd just eaten a lemon.

"Oh, it's so very adorable when you're cross," Irma said with a faint smile. "But you're the captain, and I can't cast off until you say it's all right, although it would be helpful if you turned the engine on at some point."

"Are you saying when I'm the captain you have to do what I say?"

She tilted her head to the side and looked like she was contemplating what I'd said. But she said nothing. Because she was trying to figure a way around it.

"Like, everything is my way?"

She pressed her lips together. "Do you want me to untie the stern line, dear?"

I narrowed my eyes so she knew this discussion wasn't finished. In response, she smiled like she was a nice little old lady, which she was not. I gave her a look, then focused on the panel in front of me. After making sure we were in neutral, I turned the boat on. The engine hummed beautifully. I did like well-engineered machines, although I decided to keep the thought to myself. "Yes, please, untie the stern rope," I said to Irma, who gave me a wry nod and unlooped it from the cleat.

"It's a line, dear."

"A line?"

An emphatic nod. "There are no ropes on boats. There are lines and sheets."

"What's a sheet?"

"It's used in sailing. I do hope I can get you out sailing with Stu this week."

"Let's walk before we run."

"Indeed. Any instruction about the bow line, Captain Blackheart?"

"Is it wrong that I like the sound of that?"

"Not at all, my dear. Getting drunk on power is nothing to be ashamed of." She untied the line with a petite gracefulness that most of the population could only aspire to, before hopping in. "You can't stay like that forever, of course."

"Why not?" I put the engine into forward and eased away from the dock. All the blue in front of us was clear and calm and our propeller sliced up the lake up under us. It felt, just for a minute, like we were walking on water.

"Staying permanently drunk on power turns people into dictators. And they're simply no fun at all," Irma said sagely, untying the fenders from the side of the boat and stowing them in an ingenious little locker under some of the seats. One thing I did like about boating was how so much storage could be *Tetris*ed into such small spaces.

I turned the boat slowly to the right and started to follow the shoreline.

"Alright. So, you're doing very well, dear, but we really need to go out a bit further." She threw her arms out. "To the lake, Violet!"

"Am I still the captain?"

She sat down and put her feet up. "I suppose."

"You suppose or I am?"

She pulled her sunglasses down. "You are, dear. Although it feels like you might be a bossy one."

"I might."

"Carry on, then."

To make her a little happier, I turned us toward the lake again and putted us out a bit further. I couldn't see the bottom anymore; the water was blue but not clear, and Irma's fish finder was showing that the water was twenty feet deep here. I swallowed. I wasn't sure exactly what my worry was. I let out a few deep breaths. There was more wind the further out we went, and it ruffled my hair in a way I was discovering I liked.

"You're doing excellently, Captain Blackheart."

"Thanks, Irma."

"I like the sound of that, Captain Blackheart. Maybe I'll get you monogrammed towels for Christmas."

"You know, I've heard a rumour that you're some kind of Christmas fanatic."

"Fanatic?" She pressed her lips together again, her head on a tilt. "You can speed up just a tiny bit, dear. But only if you'd like to." Then she scooted closer and walked me through the instruments again, like she had earlier when we'd had a dock-only lesson. She directed me on the right angle to approach a wave so the boat *stayed stable*, another way of saying we didn't all die horribly, and reminded me of a few other boaty things, like port versus starboard and aft and bow.

And then she had me. I loved learning new things, new technologies. And boating was kind of like a programming language or a technology. Actually, it was both. I sped up a bit. The wind was in my hair, the sun was on my face, and it smelled like nothing I'd ever smelled before. After an hour or so, I felt more comfortable with the controls. As I was motoring us back to Irma's dock, I said, "You know, I don't even want to puke!"

"Well, that's wonderful, dear. It's often the case that if you're in control, you don't feel as…unsettled as when others are driving."

"Right on!"

"Of course, the way you drive, you'll never actually get anywhere, although that is up to you." But she smiled.

We were about a hundred feet out from Irma's doc, heading home. I felt like I was finally doing normal vacation stuff, that I was really relaxing. Of course, I should have known that those feelings would not last.

"Do you want to drive the car, dear?" Irma asked me a few hours later. "I was thinking about having a few drinks at the wake."

I did a double take. Irma, the queen of pastels, was standing in my doorway wearing a deep red pantsuit with a nifty silver clutch and stylishly thick-soled black sandals. Her hair was brushed back and she was wearing a single strand of pearls.

I had a light summer top and a pair of black dress pants on. With Converse.

"I'll drive back," I said. "How far away is it?"

"Not very," she said as I followed her downstairs. There was a blur at the front door and Irma's arm darted out. She pushed me into the wall beside the vestibule so quickly, the air whooshed out of my lungs.

"There's someone at the door," she said quietly.

"I think…I think that's, like, a normal thing that happens." I tried to regain my breath. Irma had a way about her that made it seem like mercenaries were going to crash through the windows. No matter where we were. I had no clue how I was going to go back to a desk job after a month of living with a retired spy.

"Stay there." She slipped something that looked like a small rod out of the potted Ficus near the front door. After an elegant flick of her wrist, it expanded. Irma kept a telescoping baton in her Ficus. Of course she did. I tried to calm my breathing.

She opened the door to the vestibule, pausing to look through the spy hole at the front door. The noise she made sounded vaguely happy.

"Boris!" she said as she pulled the door open.

Aha! I peeked out of the spot she'd shuttled me to. When Boris saw me, he lifted a hand in greeting. I waved back. He was sixty-something, wearing a bright Hawaiian shirt, with salt-and-pepper hair and a friendly smile that didn't quite seem to fit his face. Irma's was like that sometimes. I knew she'd met him during her former career, a job calling I tried not to think about too much, lest it keep me up at night.

"Violet, it's Boris!" she singsonged. I emerged from behind the Ficus and smiled at both of them.

"Nice to see you again," he said, with a hint of an Eastern European accent.

"We're just on our way to a wake," Irma said.

He raised an eyebrow.

"The local tennis pro has passed away."

The eyebrow went higher. "I have heard about this. A friend of yours?"

She nodded. His face became calm in a way that made my stomach hurt.

"This is very unfortunate," he said.

"I know." Irma pressed her lips together. Were there tears in her eyes?

Quietly, Boris said, "Would you like me to join you?"

She nodded.

"I cannot stay long, unfortunately. I have another obligation, but I can come for a little while. I shall drive ahead of you," he said, pulling the door back like an old-world gentleman.

She nodded, then looked down. When she lifted her head, she looked just like normal. A bit more refreshed, possibly. When I was upset, my face turned purple. "Thank you."

He murmured something comforting, put his hand on the small of her back. There was a closeness there that was kind of charming, if you ignored the fact that Irma could kill him with her thumb.

Irma let the rod fall out of her sleeve and onto the side table in the vestibule. He smiled knowingly, looking at it. I didn't even want to know what that might mean. Dealing with Irma was challenging enough. Dealing with two Irmas was out of the question.

Unlike Irma, Boris drove sensibly, which forced Irma to slow down behind him. It was a nice change. I felt a little like I was on a very strange family outing.

It wasn't a long drive; it couldn't be, on such a tiny island. We headed north, and Boris turned down a nicely paved road. A sign hung at the entrance said *Indian Runner Winery.* A duck adorned the sign. I spent longer than I should have looking at it. Why would a duck have anything to do with a vineyard? There was a lot about island living I didn't quite get. Maybe I never would. But I liked it here anyway. Maybe I even belonged a little.

The road was winding, trees dotting each side. The fields were wildflowers and grapes, the parking lot was enormous and the Cape Cod-styled manor house was oversized and imposing. It was a beautiful building.

A number of barns and sheds clustered around the house, all of them done in the same rustic but elegant style. It was the kind of place I'd like to come to for a wine tasting.

Not a wake.

Irma seemed to know where she was going, so I followed her and Boris. I tried to figure out what their history was. They had to have been on different sides during the cold war, so how had that worked?

Irma led us to one of the outbuildings. It was smaller than the main house, but inside was country-fabulous, all weathered wood and barnboard, the furniture hand-crafted and comfortable-looking. A massive bar made from a single piece of wood took up one side of the room. Wine was stored and displayed everywhere.

The place was packed, and I took a deep breath as we crossed the threshold. The crowd was a blur. And they were loud, noisy. This was no depressed death vigil. It was the celebration of someone's life. A laptop spun out images of Lucas and his friends on one of the walls. I took another deep breath before heading to the bar.

"Hey, Violet," Theresa, from the Club, said. She was moving cases of wine like a member of the merchant marine.

"Hey." I eased myself onto a stool. "How many different places do you work at?"

She grinned. "As many as possible. I have a college fund to finance for my first grandbaby. I only work part-time at the Club these days." She paused in her work and showed me some pictures of a peanut-shaped newborn. I made the appropriate cooing noises. "We're pouring a Chablis today. Interested?"

"Please." I looked around while I waited. It was an eclectic crowd, but more people looked like year-rounders than at the events that happened at Irma's private club.

Theresa pushed a good-sized wine glass toward me. She poured a slurp from the same bottle into a jelly jar and clinked her glass with mine.

"Did you ever meet him?" she asked.

"I played with him once. Briefly. Irma was close to him, I think. Nice guy."

She nodded. "I didn't know him well, myself."

"How's that possible on an island this size?" I felt bad as soon as the words were out. I didn't mean anything by them; I just didn't really understand how such a small place functioned. What happened when people wanted soup dumplings at three in the morning?

She chuckled. "It's not that small, actually, and people tend to keep to their own little groups. Lucas had been working here for a few years, but he only came in the summers."

"Ah."

Someone took a seat beside me. "Hello." It was David Bell, wearing a t-shirt that said, *There's No Place Like 127.0.0.1*, tucked into black jeans. In geekspeak, 127.0.0.1 meant *home.*

"Oh, hey," I said, relieved to see someone I knew.

"How're you?" He spoke out of the left side of his mouth.

"Good, you? Have you recovered from the other day?"

He looked at my chin, not my eyes. I was used to this kind of thing, though, and it didn't offend me. Occupational hazard. "Yeah, I bumped my head, but they said no concussion. I think I'm okay."

I looked around to make sure no one could hear me. Theresa was at the other end of the bar, chatting with Agnes O'Muffin, an eighty-seven-year-old librarian who, according to Irma, terrorised people who didn't return their books on time. It looked like she was challenging Theresa to an arm wrestle. They'd be tied up for a bit.

"I've been thinking about what happened at the ground-breaking," I said, hoping we could dispense with conversational niceties like most nerdy discussions did. His eyes met mine abruptly. Nice eyes. "What are your thoughts on what Leblanc Industries said about it? You know the system better than anyone else."

I'd read during my morning phone-fest that Leblanc Industries was adamant the equipment hadn't been hacked. They'd put out a press release and had started an aggressive social media campaign trumpeting their innocence. Which definitely made me more suspicious that it had, in fact, been hacked.

There was a silence. He wasn't drinking; his hands were jammed in his pockets. He glanced around. "I've looked at your LinkedIn profile," he said, "and I heard about you figuring out that IV stand hack last week. You seem to know what you're doing."

"Uh-huh," I said. "What can I do for you?"

He picked up my wine glass and downed what was left. "I need to tell you something."

Seventeen — Irma

My eyes ran over the crowd. Boris's did the same. Old habits. It looked like a good mix of people. Violet was at the bar with that nice long-haired fellow from the other day. I glanced away for just a moment, and when I looked back, they were both gone. I sincerely hoped he hadn't kidnapped her. I really just wanted to have a calm evening for once. I was retired, for heaven's sake.

"Penny for your thoughts," Boris said with a sly look.

"I'm thinking Lucas's killer is here somewhere." I really needed to speak to Rose and Tiffanni. And Carlton. And whoever else I could squeeze intel out of. But surely a few minutes with Boris wasn't too much to ask for, was it?

One of the servers popped by and took our order; red wine all around.

"Are you certain?" he asked.

I shrugged. "He or she might be long gone. I know I would be."

The server came back with our drinks and the two of us *cheers*ed each other. It was a full-bodied red with a beautiful nose. I was a big fan of this winery. To be honest, I'd invested some of my money in it a while back, after the master vintner put together a delightful pitch for me. Plus, let's face it, I liked wine.

"Who would have wanted him dead?" Boris asked.

"I don't know. He was a lovely boy. Killer backhand."

Boris smiled sadly. Then his hand was on mine and I tried to ignore how good it felt. My fourth marriage had been to my second husband. After he passed away ten years ago, I'd been alone.

"Will you excuse me for just a moment?" he said.

I nodded, and he made his way to the restroom just as Geraldine Greenwood approached my table. "May I?" she said, motioning at his chair.

"Of course, Geraldine, how are you?"

"Good. I got your voicemail this afternoon. What can I do for you?" She smiled pleasantly. Geraldine was somewhere in her sixties and looked like a stereotypical grandmother—little old lady curls, sensible shoes—which she was, except for a few small details.

"Thank you for coming."

Like the fact that she'd done sixteen years for dispatching her abusive husband to the sweet hereafter. And that she had the best hands in the safecracking business.

"Anything for you, Irma."

I smiled. "I have a safe I need some assistance with, please."

She looked around, then scuttled her chair closer to mine. "Where? What kind?"

"I took pictures." I'd actually even remembered to bring my cellular telephone with me tonight, so I was able to show them to her. I tried not to feel smug about it.

She pulled out a pair of reading glasses and took my phone, scrolling through the pictures, making small noises at each one. "This safe is a Werther," she said finally.

"Is that a good thing?" I asked in a hopeful voice.

Her lips pressed together, and she shook her head. "No, unfortunately. It has a glass plate that is very easy to break when someone is trying to liberate the contents. This is a very high-end safe, Irma. A speciality item. Where did you find it?"

I smiled at Jenny Obenbaum, who stopped to chat with Geraldine about some kitting project they were working on together. When she was finally gone, I whispered, "Lucas's trailer."

Her eyes met mine.

"He was a lovely boy," I said. "He didn't deserve to die. Not at twenty-seven."

"No." She shook her head, face down. She scrolled through the pictures again. "How did you get in?"

"Skylight."

She pressed her mouth together.

"Something funny?" I asked.

She let out a short laugh, then looked like she was trying to contain herself. "Do you know you're seventy?"

"Seventy-one."

She giggled. "Even better. How did you get up the side of the trailer?"

"I have some suction cup—"

She burst out laughing. "You went up the side of the trailer with suction cups?"

"What? It's not that high."

After taking a deep breath, she seemed to calm herself. "Aren't you worried about falling on your head? Breaking a few ribs?"

"I never have so far, so not really," I said, glad she hadn't mentioned anything about my hips. That particular worry was always with me, naturally.

She coughed into her sleeve. "Of course not. Well, Irma, I'll give the safe a shot. But only for you. I'll need a day or two to do some research. But no guarantees."

"Thank you, dear, that's lovely of you."

She threw me a lopsided grin, which faded rapidly. "Do we have permission from the next of kin? Have the police released his trailer yet?"

"I'll get it, and I'll find out."

"Okay, super, because I'm not going up the side of anything with suction cups unless it's Dwayne Johnson. I'll do some research and you give me a shout when we have access."

"Delightful to do business with you," I said, and she threw me a grin before heading to the bar.

Across the room, Tiffanni Morgan's raised voice made me turn my head. "Yes, you will!" She was wearing pink again, the same shade as the sparkly tennis racquet she'd bonked Lucas on the head with the other day. I wondered, for a minute, if she'd been the one who killed him and buried him in a flowerbed. It felt like too much effort for her, but when one was motivated, it'd been my experience that anything was possible. Plus, she seemed like a bit of a hothead. People with short tempers could sometimes be responsible for unexpectedly terrible things. I'd once known a taxi driver—a CIA asset—with the most atrocious, yet intermittent, road rage. He ran over his mother-in-law one afternoon just because she burned one of his chalupas.

Tiffanni's voice was getting louder, and I squinted to see what the commotion was about. Then she poked someone in the shoulder, and I felt a calmness descend over me as I got to my feet.

A small knot of people were gathered around two figures, loud voices and some gasps accompanying all the poking. Then a small head reared up, and hovered over most of the ensemble. It was Imogene Flores, the general manager of the Club. Her face looked puckered. I decided to make my way over, to see if she needed any assistance. I passed Boris on the way back to our table. He gave me a *need some help*? look and I replied with a *no, I'm fine* nod.

"You promised!" Tiffanni yell-whined.

"Young lady." Imogene sniffed. "I did no such thing."

"You did you did you did!"

Imogene took a step back and glanced around the crowd. "I'm so sorry about all this, Ms. Morgan," she continued, as I pushed myself forward. When I got to the edge of the circle, I stopped. Tiffanni was an energetic, spoiled young lady who *looked* like she could take Imogene in a fight. But I knew something about Imogene she didn't.

"If you were sorry, you'd do what you're told."

Imogene raised herself to her full six-foot-one height, pulling her shirt down with a sharp yank. "Ms. Morgan, I do not work for you."

"My father is going to hear about this."

"By all means." Imogene looked unflappable. My head tilted, all on its own. How interesting for Imogene to be so strong now but so emotionally squishy normally. Her refusal to be compliant had obviously stirred up some serious emotions in Tiffanni, because she took a step closer to Imogene. Then she raised her finger for another shoulder-poke.

Imogene's face didn't move. She looked placid and calm. Too calm, perhaps. "That's quite enough, young lady," she said quietly.

Someone stepped forward and put their hand on Tiffanni's arm, but she shrugged it off. "I'm going to get you fired," she said, a sneer in her voice. For the first time, she glanced around and took in the crowd. She looked buoyed by the attention, which was never a good sign. I put my weight on my toes in case I needed to step in. Adrenaline started to swirl inside me.

But then one of Tiffanni's friends stepped forward, and yanked her away from the crowd, which melted like ice cream on a hot sidewalk. I watched her go. I wanted to squeeze some intel out of her, but she was surrounded right now. And Imogene looked terrible.

"You all right, dear?" I asked her. Now that everyone had dispersed, two pink splotches had appeared on her cheeks. I led her back to my table and sat her down. After introducing her to Boris and procuring a drink for her—Jim Beam with a water back—she drank the whole thing down in one swallow, then sipped on the water.

"I'm fine, Irma," she said stiffly. "I'm sorry to have intruded on your evening."

"It's not a problem. Do you remember the forehead smash I showed you the other week?" I taught a weekly self-defence class at the local barre studio, and Imogene never missed a session. The nervous ones always really liked hitting people.

She nodded as she started on her second drink. She was looking unhealthily pale now.

"That's always good, even in a crowd situation. One little tap, and her eyes would water, and then you can—"

"Irma." She put out a hand. "You're very kind as always, but I don't think I can go around face-smashing the children of Club members."

"Well, of course not. But you can most certainly defend yourself."

She nodded.

"What was that all about?" I said.

She sighed heavily. "She seems to have gotten the idea in her head that she can have poor Lucas's personal belongings. Of course, we can do no such thing. His next of kin has to take them."

"Of course. But why would she want his belongings?" I said casually. Boris's eyebrows lifted, then retreated.

Imogene looked uneasy for a moment, before shaking herself out of it. "I really couldn't say."

"I see." I tapped my fingers on the table. "Where are they? His belongings, I mean."

"In his office, still."

"Of course." Bloody hell. I'd already searched the office and found nothing probative. Was a nice little sinister letter or mail bomb too much to ask for? "Imogene, I had a question for you."

She glanced around nervously.

"Do you know anything about the threatening letters Lucas was receiving?"

She drew back, looking horrified. "My goodness, no! Who on earth would want to do such a thing?"

"Excellent question."

"Everyone liked him! The poor boy. To die so young, and to be threatened before his death. It's just too much."

I put my hand on her arm. "Do you know if Lucas was seeing anyone? Socially, I mean."

She pressed her lips together. “He was a social person, Irma, I honestly didn’t keep track. But I thought he was single.”

From across the room, I saw Carlton, who was wearing a spiffy porkpie hat with a casual summer suit. Rose stood next to him, wearing a simple but stylish summer dress. I tried to think of scenarios to extract her from his company. I had a few things I wanted to ask her. After Imogene left, I’d be sure to ask Boris if he had a spare flash-bang in the car.

“I see,” I said, returning my attention to Imogene. “Tell me, did you ever receive any complaints about Lucas? Anyone unhappy with him?”

“Most certainly not! He was a wonderful boy,” she said.

“Hey, Mrs. A, Imogene.” Tate Hurst, temporary tennis pro, put his hand on the back of Imogene’s chair, and leaned into our conversation.

“Evening,” I said. Imogene nodded.

He looked from one of us to the other. In a low voice, he asked, “Are you okay, Ms. Flores? I saw—”

“I’m quite fine, thank you.”

A nod. “Okay, sorry to intrude. I was just worried.” He flashed a friendly smile and backed away.

Once the little suckup was gone, I said, "How's he working out?"

"People seem to like him." Then she nodded to me and Boris. "Thank you for the drink. I'm going to head home, I believe."

"Lovely to see you, Ms. Flores," Boris said.

"You as well, Irma, Mr. Andropov."

"Well," Boris said after she left, clinking his wineglass gently with mine before taking its last sip. "I'm sorry, but I must also be going."

I put my own glass down abruptly. I was surprised about my sudden swirl of emotions. It took me a minute to realise I'd been looking forward to spending some time with Boris.

"I'm sorry to hear that," I said, trying to keep my voice flat, but failing utterly.

"I have an early meeting tomorrow and I must get my beauty rest." He half-smiled.

"I understand," I said, trying to insert a note of cheeriness in my voice, but failing. There was an awkward moment of silence. Then, "Perhaps…perhaps we could go sailing later this week."

Boris pinked all the way to his ears. "I would like that very much," he said. "I shall call you."

"Wonderful."

He kissed me on both cheeks, then left. I tried not to watch him go. On his way out, he almost bumped into Elsa, who looked like she was searching around for a seat. He apologised to her like the gentleman he was and kept going.

I called out to her, "Elsa?"

She turned my way and I pointed at Boris's newly empty chair. She threw me a grateful smile and waddled over.

"How are you doing, dear?" I said.

Her grimace as she tried to mount the high-top chair answered my question.

"Need some help?" In a flash, I got up to assist her and put a hand on her arm. My elbow pressed into the soft swell of her stomach.

"No!" she snapped, shaking me off.

I stepped back. "I'm so sorry, dear. I wasn't thinking."

"Sorry, Irma. Sorry. I'm just so tired." She shook her head. "I'm going to be in this state for a while and I'm on my own. I have to figure this stuff out for myself."

I watched her settle in. It seemed like a major undertaking for the poor thing, but I respected her desire to be independent. I was the same way. "Do you have everything all ready?"

She nodded, blowing her bangs out of her face. "Since it's only me, I've been ready for months now."

"You'll do marvellously. I admire you for going it alone."

She grinned. "Yup, just me and donor 583468. Best relationship I ever had."

A server came around, and Elsa asked for a Shirley Temple. I ordered another glass of Malbec.

"I wish," she said longingly.

I chuckled. "I'll have one for you."

She grinned.

"I had a question for you, dear," I said.

"Shoot," she said, sipping on the drink the server brought her. But then she made a face and put it down.

"Something wrong?"

"Too sweet," she said. "I don't want the baby to be exposed to a lot of sugar."

"Do you know if it's a boy or a girl?"

"I'm waiting to find out."

"That's nice. Would you happen to know how late Carlton stayed at work the night before the ground-breaking?"

She cleared her throat carefully. "Why do you ask?"

It was a good question. "I was hoping to talk to him about that penthouse for sale, but I couldn't reach him." It wasn't the best phony baloney reason I'd ever come up with, but it would probably do.

She looked embarrassed at her suspiciousness. Good. If she'd been an intelligence agent, she'd have no such worries. Maybe civilian life was easier, in some ways, after all. "We're at the job site these days until ten-ish, most days. Well…most of us. But we all went home early that night—six or so. We were beat, and we wanted to be fresh for the next morning. I can easily get his assistant to set an appointment up for you, though."

"Thanks very much," I said. "I'll take a look at my schedule and give her a call."

My mind raced: If Carlton was the culprit in all this, and had finished work at six p.m., that left him more than enough time to bump off Lucas and shove him under a few daisies. But why wouldn't he just bury the body in the woods? Dump it over the side of his boat? Did Carlton think he'd be able to control access to the construction site forever?

Of course, if Carlton had killed Lucas at the site, burying him there did make a certain kind of sense, especially if he'd panicked, which was always a possibility after killing someone without a backup plan. Happened to the best of us. Maybe he'd intended on moving the body later. What a bother it was, trying to unravel the actions of civilians. The intelligence world had rules and mores and a certain understanding between agencies. So much more civilized.

"Well, Irma, nice to see you, but I think I'm going to head out," she said, pushing her drink away with a face. "I'm a little tired."

"Lovely to see you, dear."

She clambered down from her chair. Remembering her earlier words, I didn't offer to help her down.

"Hey, Irma." Violet was dragging the nerdy long-haired hero from the other day behind her.

"Good evening, David," I said.

He mumbled something and half-smiled, before ducking his head down and looking at the table.

Violet ushered David into a chair. "Irma," Violet said breathlessly. "David has something he wants to tell us."

"Does he? How wonderful," I said, craning my neck to look at the cluster of people around the exit. Carlton and Amelia, his new, ombré-ed assistant were talking. Rose stood off to the side. Elsa had stopped to chat, and Rose walked her out when they were done. Carlton and Amelia leaned in to speak to each other after she left, before leaving as well. I was annoyed with myself for not accosting Rose before her exit. I'd have to search her out tomorrow. I turned my face to David's. "What is it?"

He mumbled something.

"You can't...I'm sorry, David. You can't what?" I said.

"I can't talk about it here," he said, his voice suddenly loud.

I glanced around to make sure nobody was listening to us. "That's fine. Where would you like to talk about it?"

He mumbled something again.

"My house would work, yes," I said. Violet's eyes widened. I had a lot of experience with people who couldn't speak clearly. It was best not to dwell on why. "When would you like to do that?"

"Now," he said, almost audibly.

I looked around the room. I wondered if the killer was here somewhere, putting on a nice face and pretending to be sad, even though soil from the construction site still clung to the shoes they'd worn while popping poor Lucas into the garden for a dirt nap. Was the killer taking in the crowd right now, looking for their next victim?

I looked up at the slide show playing on the side of one of the walls. Lucas sailing, Lucas swimming, Lucas aiming a ball at my head.

I didn't want to leave the wake if the killer was skulking around. But I owed Mr. Bell for his quick thinking the other day. And so far, I had zero evidence whatsoever. I itched to know what he wanted to tell us.

"David is a structural engineer," Violet said excitedly.

"Your parents must be very proud," I said, leaning forward.

Violet met my eyes head-on. "They are. And he knows something about what happened at the ground-breaking."

Eighteen — Violet

Excitement was bouncing around inside me as we made our way to the door. Right as I opened it, Irma's friend, Roger, pulled her aside.

"I gotta go," David said. He was looking around nervously.

"Just hang on another sec," I said. "She won't be long."

He shoved his hands in his pockets. "I'm leaving town tonight. If she can't come now, then forget it. Maybe this was a mistake, anyway."

"Nonono, it's not a mistake. Why are you leaving town?"

"It's just for the best." He jammed his hands in his pockets. "Trust me."

I had no idea what he wanted to tell Irma. He'd hinted about knowing something more about the day of the ground-breaking, but would only tell her. Apparently, he'd heard about how she recently foiled a murder attempt and wanted to spill some juicy secrets. He didn't seem to be a huge fan of the police.

I tried to get Irma's attention. David was backing away from me. "Look," I said, hearing the desperation in my voice, "Why don't you take off and meet us at Irma's place? It's private and quiet. No one will see you there. Let me give you the address."

He looked relieved, jotting it down in his phone and stepping out the door before I could say another word.

Irma freed herself from Roger and re-joined me. "Have we lost young Mr. Bell?"

I put my hand on her arm and pulled her out of the barn.

"Good heavens, dear, where's the fire?"

"He's leaving town. Like, tonight. We need to go right now."

"Of course," she said, "I do appreciate your sense of urgency, I must say."

"Thanks."

"With a nice touch of paranoia."

"Yeah, that's awesome. Let's go."

I chucked her in the car and we drove out the long lane that attached the winery to the main road.

"So where's the fire?" she asked again once we were on the road. I took the tone of her voice to mean she was going to shiv me unless I told her soon.

"I don't know, exactly," I said. "We were talking about how he had something to tell me, when he suddenly asked if I knew you."

"What else did he say?"

"Not much. Just that he had some information about the ground-breaking. He'd heard about you solving that mystery last week and—"

"We solved that mystery. *We*, dear. One must take ownership of one's successes in life."

"Yeah, that's great. So, look, he's meeting us at your house and he's going to tell us something. Something big. That's all he said."

She sat back in her seat and looked pensive. I turned right and headed back to Irma's. The night wind was warm and hit the top of my head, which meant my hair probably looked like an octopus by now. I didn't care. David had been so nervous he'd been stuttering at one point. I wanted to know what he knew.

"Did he say it had to do with Carlton at all?"

I raised my shoulders. "No, he wouldn't tell me anything. Only you. We'll be at your place in like five minutes, so I'm not worried."

"Well, home, Jeeves." She threw me a grin. "You could step on it a little if you wanted to, you know."

"Alright."

"It's just that if you keep driving this slowly, we won't get to my place until the next thaw, dear."

"Irma," I said, "sometimes it's important to slow down and smell the flowers."

"That's very true," she said. "Of course, this isn't one of those times."

"Of course," I said dryly.

But then I saw the fire.

NINETEEN — IRMA

"Violet!" I yelled. "Stop!"

She hit the brakes so hard, my neck snapped back. After regaining my senses, I saw we were stopped in the middle of the road and Violet's hands were still on the wheel, her eyes glued to the car. She was in a fugue state.

"All right, dear, let's calm down now. That's a good girl." She let me peel her fingers off the steering wheel. And she seemed to rouse herself when she saw the wreck up ahead, flames licking the air.

"Stay here and dial 911, please, Violet." I got out of the car, jogged to the trunk, and retrieved my fire extinguisher and an old go bag I kept there for emergencies, before heading to the fire.

I surveyed the scene, adrenaline throbbing in my gut. It was highly unusual for cars to actually burst into flames on impact, but it did happen sometimes. A new-ish beige sedan sat almost sideways in the ditch, the passenger side of the hood crunched into an avant-garde art project, flames pluming out the windows, skid marks painted on the road behind it. I did not recognize the car.

I was five feet away, and I could already feel the heat in my pores. I pulled a towel and water bottle out of my bag, wet it, and placed it over my nose and mouth. I took a few deep breaths and walked forward.

The fire in the engine block wasn't huge yet, but a wind had kicked up, blowing the flames everywhere. I sprayed my extinguisher on the car's hood, my heartbeat thudding in my chest. Flames surged out of the engine. The passenger side of the car was mostly crushed, but the driver might still be okay. Hopefully only one person was in the car.

I peered in the window. It was David Bell. A pang of sadness jolted me. I tried to focus. The window was rolled down, and he was unconscious, his head thrown back, blood dripping down his ear. The air bag had deployed, and he was still buckled into his seatbelt.

"Smart boy," I muttered. I tried the door, but it wouldn't open. The flames were still confined to the hood, but the car was hot. We needed to move.

I took off my left shoe, expanded the blade secreted in the heel, and cut through the seatbelt, before spraying foam on the inside of the car and more on the hood, hoping it would slow the fire down if it reached the car's interior. The extinguisher stuttered. It was empty.

I took a deep breath and got ready for what would come next. Normally, I would never move a car crash victim, but the flames were on the move, and I couldn't hear any sirens. I wrapped part of my shirt tail around the door handle. I could feel the heat all the way through the cotton, and the fumes from the fire were making me dizzy.

And if the wind moved…

"Irma, you okay?" Violet called.

"Help," I said, but the wind took it away. I cleared my throat, tried again. "Come help!"

I could hear feet slapping against the pavement. On my third try, I had the driver's door open. We eased him out from behind the airbag. I pulled his shirt up and behind his head, keeping it there so it would hold his head up. I put my hand on one arm, and Violet took hold of the other.

"On three," I said.

Violet nodded, and on three we pulled him down to the grass, the shirt still supporting his head. I held my breath while I checked for a pulse.

He was alive, thank heavens.

"We gotta move, Irma." Violet grabbed his left arm, and I stuck with the right. It occurred to me that I'd been spending a lot of time in ditches lately, which wasn't exactly how I'd visualized my golden years.

"Quite right, dear." I got to my feet, and we pulled David along the ditch, stopping every few feet to recharge. He was getting heavier.

I could hear sirens in the distance. Thank heavens. The wind kept whipping the smoke into my lungs, and I had to pause because of my coughing.

A fire truck blazed down the road. I could see it coming for miles. They screeched to a halt and firefighters poured out. One of them yanked on my arm, which I had to say I didn't really appreciate. "I'm fine, I'm fine," I snapped.

"Let's get her to the truck," someone called out, someone I didn't know. My spine instantly zipped itself into a straight line, adrenaline pressing down on my chest.

This would be the perfect ambush scenario: someone in distress, uniforms meant to make you immediately trust whoever was wearing them, a lonely country road. If I'd learned anything from my career, it was that things weren't always what they seemed. And that misdirection could cost you your life.

"Please unhand me," I said stiffly. My extinguisher might be empty, but I could still use it to conk someone on the head if need be.

"Sorry, Irma," Rex Sapperstein said. He was a nice young man who worked as a chiropractor during the day but moonlighted as a firefighter. He pried the strange man's hands off me.

"It's no trouble at all, dear." I was suddenly, utterly exhausted. And my knee was throbbing in tune with my heartbeat.

David was having a brace Velcroed to his neck, and I made my way over to him. His eyes fluttered.

"David, what happened?" I asked.

He tried to look at me. I reached out to hold onto his hand, and he grasped mine fiercely. As he blinked, a tear ran down the left side of his face. He struggled to speak. "All I could…see was…red."

"Where?"

He closed his eyes again.

"Irma, we gotta work," Rex said.

"Just one more minute," I said, my heart fluttering in my chest. I had to know what David knew.

"Irma!" Rex said.

"Sorry." I stepped back. To David, I said, "You're going to be just fine, dear."

Rex and an EMT started to move David to a stretcher.

"Let's get you over here," Julian said. Violet was already beside the ambulance. She looked glassy-eyed, the poor thing.

"What on earth are you doing here?" I asked Julian.

"Filling in for Gabe," he said. "I lost a tennis game and this is my penance. Did you fall at all? Hit your head?" He walked me through a basic, *are-you-still-alive* questionnaire that I passed with flying colours, obviously.

"What's wrong with Violet?" I asked.

"I'm fine," she said, her eyes trained on the fire. A set of sirens abruptly stopped, mid-scream. The police were here.

"I think I've banged my knee a little," I admitted. "I'll come see you about it later, though."

"We're going to look at it now," he said firmly. Then he ran me through a series of tests which could only be described using a Medieval-era torture scale. I didn't make a sound. But it wasn't easy.

"Mrs. Abercrombie," Chief Pickle said.

"Evening, Chief." I might have squealed a little on the *chief* part. In my defence, Julian was trying to maim me at the time. He finished up, pronounced me alive, and went to help with David.

"What happened?"

Violet got up to stand closer to the fire. The Pickle and I were alone.

"I don't know," I said, irritated it was the truth. "We were just on our way home from Lucas's wake."

"Who's the victim here?" she asked.

"David Bell."

"Who's that?"

"He was the engineer in charge at the construction site when the tractor went berserk," I said with a heavy sigh. "He was at the wake."

"Was he drinking?" she asked.

"I didn't speak to him. Violet might know. They were chatting for a bit. I certainly hope not."

She nodded briskly. "Single car accident, could be impaired driving."

"Maybe. I only see one set of skid marks. Could have been a deer or another animal he was trying to avoid."

She examined the road.

"Mavis, you should know that Tiffanni Morgan threw a fit at the wake," I continued, my voice still low. "Imogene Flores told me that Tiffanni wants Lucas's personal effects from the Club."

The chief raised her eyebrows. She looked both grateful and confused. Of course, she had no way to know I was banking a favour. I wasn't sure how I was going to get Geraldine into Lucas's trailer, and I was going to have to do some serious sucking up to make it happen.

Julian and the EMT he was working with shuttled David into the ambulance and took off. At the main road, they turned left, which meant they were taking David to a hospital on the mainland. I felt conflicted; on the one hand, I wanted him to get hospital-level care. On the other hand, I wanted him nearby. Now that someone had—possibly—tried to send him to join Lucas in the afterworld, I was sure he knew something of interest.

Mavis had someone take Violet home. I made myself comfortable in one of the folding camping chairs I kept in the trunk of my car, and watched the buzz of activity that always manifested after a fire was put out. I watched until there was a heaviness in my chest that was going to keep me up all night.

I finished the water one of the nice young firefighters had given me and got ready to leave. I couldn't do anything more here. When I got into my car and turned on the headlights, light sprayed over the back of the wrecked car.

What was *that*?

I squinted. Then I turned off my engine, leaving the lights on. I walked toward the formerly-beige hunk of wreckage, my heart thumping in my chest. The front of the car was pretzelized and singed to a crisp, but the back was still recognizable as a vehicle. And then I saw it for sure: a red streak. The paint of another car. I registered that detail right before everything went black.

TWENTY — IRMA

The ceiling in the island clinic was unbelievably boring. I knew this because I'd been staring at it ever since I woke up this morning. They'd run a battery of tests on me last night, and now we were waiting on the results. Until the second coming, it looked like.

I hadn't exfiltrated the clinic yet, because the truth was that I was somewhat concerned about the dizziness that'd landed me on my caboose in the middle of the road in the middle of the night. To make matters worse, the Pickle had me kidnapped! Plopped me in a police cruiser so I could be dragged to the clinic. It had to be illegal, what she did.

On the other hand, my pelvis seemed to be fine, so at least I wasn't going to get an artificial hip stuffed into me when I wasn't looking. But I really wanted to close my eyes. I wanted to rest. It was an unusual feeling that I was not enjoying one bit.

"Irma," Julian said as he entered the room. He was holding a tablet computer but didn't seem to have any needles he was about to plunge into me, which was heartening.

"Hello, dear. I'd just like to remind you of the time I drove you to Toronto in the middle of a tornado—"

"There was no tornado, Irma," he said firmly, although the corner of his mouth was twitching.

I struggled to sit up. "Do you deny there was a tornado *warning* in effect that day? Perhaps it was a mistake for me to do such a nice favour for you. When can I go home?"

"It was not a mistake," he said. "I greatly appreciated it. Still do. And there was a tornado warning in effect for Ontario that day. But it's a big province, bigger than Texas, actually, and there was absolutely no warning for our area. Zero, zip, nada."

"There should have been."

"Okay, Irma, you win."

Normally, when I won a pointless argument, a little spurt of adrenaline ran through me. Tragically, that was not the case right now. "So, what's wrong with me?"

Julian placed the tablet on the bedside table. "Smoke inhalation." He placed the oxygen tube I'd plucked from my face back under my nose in one easy movement.

"You said earlier that my oxygen levels were perfectly fine."

"That's not actually even close to what I said." He pulled a wheeled stool beside my bed and sat. "You're being treated for smoke inhalation, which is very serious. Remember the form I made you sign that said, 'I understand I'm being treated for smoke inhalation, which is very serious'?"

"Yes, but it was just a note you hand-wrote. Honestly—"

"It's still a binding contract. And I'm your doctor. I want you to stay here for at least twenty-four hours for observation. And treatment."

"Oh, I couldn't possibly." I folded my arms over my chest.

"Why not?" He was pinching the bridge of his nose like he had a headache, the poor dear.

"Yeah, why not?" Violet said from the doorway.

"Hello, dear! How are you this beautiful morning?"

Violet threw a look at Julian, and he rolled his eyes at her. Then she plopped down in a chair beside my bed and handed me a tea in a biodegradable to-go cup from Luna's Café, with the bag still in. I sighed happily.

"What's wrong with her?" she asked Julian.

"I mean, if you ask me, a lot," he said with a grin.

"Yes, yes, you're both so witty and entertaining. I'd like to go home now," I repeated.

"And like I just said," Julian's tone had definitely darkened, "I'd like you to stay for observation for the full twenty-four hours."

"Why can't you stay?" Violet asked as she pulled the lid off her coffee. She appeared instantly enraptured.

"I have to go to a barre class," I said reasonably.

They gave each other another look.

"Why," Violet said slowly, "Would you have to do that?"

"Absolutely not," Julian said at the same time.

"Tiffanni Morgan, you know, the one who threw a fit at the memorial last night, was trying to weasel Lucas's belongings out of Imogene. She's hiding something, and I want to speak to her about it. She teaches a class that starts in twenty minutes, and I need to be there."

Julian sighed. "Irma, even before the smoke inhalation, your knee simply wasn't up to a barre class. There'd be too much strain on the joint."

"I don't know," I said. "I think I'll be fine."

"Do you want to lose the use of your knee?" He leaned forward. "If you lose the use of that knee and fall again, you might break a hip."

I gasped.

Violet looked like she was trying not to smile. After taking a few gulps of coffee, she said to Julian, "How's David?"

He rubbed his forehead. "Banged-up, but he'll live."

"Oh, good. Did he tell you anything last night?" I asked.

Julian frowned. "In the ambulance, he said he was run off the road. By a red car. He was in and out of consciousness, though, so we didn't push it."

"Understood. Well, I'll just get my things." I threw my leg over the side of the bed.

Julian put his hand on my shoulder and gently pressed down so I couldn't get up. "Irma, do I ever ask you for anything?"

I sat back, surprised. "No. But you're a very self-sufficient young man."

"Right. And how often do you ask me for things?"

"Er...sometimes?"

He nodded. "Actually, you ask me for things all the time. And I never ask you for anything." He took a breath. "You're as close to a crazy aunt as I'm ever going to get. And I'd like to make sure you stick around for a very long time."

I swallowed hard. I'd never even thought of having children—just not a possibility in my line of work—but I had often wished for a sibling so I could have some nieces and nephews to spoil rotten. Julian and a few other young people I knew were the closest I was ever going to get. Plus, he was right. I was constantly pestering him for information.

"Of course, dear," I said, pulling my leg back under the covers. "Can we play rummy later?"

He threw his head back and laughed. "You always win!"

"Just lucky."

"You've been winning for twenty years."

I waved a hand. "My luck will change soon, I'm quite sure. It has to."

"All right," he said, putting his hand on the rail of the bed and standing. "I'll come check on you in a bit."

Violet sipped her coffee happily while I mulled over what Julian had said. It was most unfortunate that he knew of my phobia about broken hips. He'd been trying to weaponize it lately, which was disconcerting.

"How are you feeling today?" I asked Violet.

She shrugged, put her coffee down. "I had some trouble sleeping. I was worried about you, and—"

"Violet, dear, I've told you not to worry about me. I am always fine."

"Yeah, that's awesome, but you're not the boss of me." She grinned and drained her coffee. "How does barre class help with talking to Tiffanni?"

"It can put people's guard down when you participate in shared activities with them."

"I'm not even gonna ask where you learned that." She dropped her cup in the recycling bin and sat back in her chair.

"What are your plans today, dear?" I asked sweetly.

"I don't have any. I can stay here with you if you want."

"Actually," I said, flashing my wolfish smile, "I had something else in mind."

Violet looked alarmed. "What—"

"Morning." It was Carlton Campbell, standing in the doorway. I felt a jolt of fear run through me. I hadn't even heard him coming. If he'd been an assassin, I'd be pushing up daisies right now.

I tried to shake it off. I wasn't actually feeling quite as fantastic as I'd intimated to Julian, but who could blame me for a little fib now and then? Julian worried too much for someone his age, although growing up with globe-trotting parents who barely paid attention to you could have that effect on someone.

"Morning, Carlton," I said. "Have you met my friend Violet?"

He nodded briskly and stepped into the room. "I was wondering if we could have a word. I—" He turned to close the door, when some little fingers stopped it. It was Mavis Pickle, who had the tiniest hands and feet I'd ever seen on a normal-sized person.

"Good morning, Mavis," I said warily.

She nodded briskly, then opened her mouth to speak.

"If you wouldn't mind," Carlton said, his tone somewhat less pleasant than was a good idea in these types of situations. "This is a private conversation."

Mavis quirked an eyebrow at that, glancing over at me. I gave her a *Who, me*? shrug in return.

"You're going to have to continue your conversation later, Mr. Campbell."

Uh-oh. She was going to arrest me for something. I searched my mind. What had I done recently?

"And why's that?" he said. His ears were flame red.

"I'd like you to come down to the station and answer some questions for me, please."

Oh, good. She isn't here for me.

Carlton looked gobsmacked. "About what?"

The Pickle glanced at me and Violet. "I think you'll want it to be a private discussion, Mr. Campbell."

"Well, I don't. And frankly, this is harassment. I've already answered all your questions and I don't have anything else to say."

I watched them with growing dismay.

A rookie officer who I'd never met before—and who looked about twelve—stuck his head in the room, then entered. He stood with his hands behind his back, his brown hair military-short, the back of his neck stiff and official. I could see he wanted to take over from Mavis, which I was quite sure she would not appreciate.

"Mr. Campbell," the chief said patiently, "we'd like to ask you some more questions about the incident at the Beaver Brooke site the other day."

"When are you going to release the sales office? We have to demo it and start building—"

"Sir, please don't raise your voice," the rookie said.

Mavis shot him an annoyed look.

"Is it illegal now to raise my voice? Are you going to *arrest* me for speaking loudly?" Carlton had pulled himself up to his full height and had his hands on his hips.

The rookie had his hand held out, palm to the ground. "Calm down, sir. You're coming down to the station one way or another."

"I'm doing no such thing," Carlton said, punctuating every word with a jab to the rookie's left shoulder. Which, if he had asked my opinion on, I would have said was a mistake. Alas.

"Over here," I said to Violet instead, so she could scramble to the other side of the bed just as the rookie unsnapped the clasp over the pepper spray on his belt.

Carlton, it had to be said, did not take this well. He took a swing that missed by a mile.

And they were off. The two of them banged against the far wall before starting a wrestling match on the floor, and the chief moved between them and my bed. It was very nice of her to want to protect us, and I made a mental note to thank her for it later. Although it occurred to me, she might be trying to block our view of any unprofessional shenanigans. After a minute or so, the Pickle took out her handcuffs and had Carlton trussed up before you could say *Christmas turkey.*

"Mr. Carlton Campbell," she said with a certain satisfaction, "you are under arrest for assaulting a police officer." And they led him right out the door.

Twenty-One — Violet

During the last few years of my ballet training, I'd taken class six days a week, on top of school. So that was probably why I walked over to the barre studio feeling so smug. Irma needed a favour, and I'd be able to knock it out easily before getting on with the rest of my day.

"Hey there!" the woman at the desk called out. She had lip-gloss as shiny as turtle wax, topping off a monochromatic ensemble of leggings and bra-top. Baby blue.

"Hi," I said, feeling awkward already. "I'd like to sign up for a class."

"For sure!" she said. "Just fill this out. Your first three classes are on the house!"

"Thanks." I scanned the forms. Lots of detail about things I couldn't sue them for later.

"Super!" the woman said when I was done. "There's a dressing room if you want to change, and here's a free water bottle." She shoved it across the desk at me. It said *BARRE BUDDIES* in a funky cursive script, with a happy face dotting the *I*. It was put together like a sippy cup, with a rigid lid and a straw jammed into it that looked like a unicorn's horn.

"Thanks," I said, picking it up and heading to the water fountain. I had nothing to change into, but I tried not to let it bother me; I was wearing a t-shirt with yoga capris and sneakers. I'd just do class barefoot and go home and take a shower afterwards.

I filled my purple unicorn water bottle while I waited for class to start. Geraldine, Irma's friend, plopped down beside me, and I felt better about things. She was sixty-something, a grandmother. If she could do this class, I was going to be fine.

"Hello, Violet," she said, smiling at me.

"Hey, Geraldine."

"I heard you and Irma discovered a burning car last night. Is that true?"

"Yeah, it was really terrible."

"Who was in the car?"

I paused. Geraldine *looked* a lot like somebody's granny, but the tone in her voice sounded like Irma's when she was trying to find out something she probably shouldn't know.

"The engineer from the Beaver Brooke ground-breaking," I said.

"Huh," she said, chewing on the side of her lip. "What did the police say?"

"I didn't really speak to them. Just gave a brief statement."

She seemed unperturbed by my reluctance to give her any details, which also reminded me of Irma. Exactly what kind of retirees populated this island, anyway? Was it some sort of old folks' getaway for spies?

"What did the car look like?" she persisted.

"Smashed," I said. Then turned to look at her.

She read something in my eyes and gave me a half-tilt of her head in response. "I heard Irma's at the clinic."

I nodded just as a gaggle of skinny spandexed women converged on the room, with perky bra-tops, bright NASA-designed leggings, and bare feet with toenails sporting pale pinks, probably this season's must-have colour. My nails hadn't been professionally manicured since that one time in the nineties.

Tiffanni was at the front of the room, putting a designer dance bag on the floor and flipping her long, blonde hair over her shoulder. She greeted three similarly skinny—but unexpectedly busty—students with a laugh and a smile. She looked pleasant and professional, which was a bit of a surprise. I was more used to seeing her tantruming like a child. After a few more minutes of chitchat, the gaggle went to claim a spot at the barre.

It moved something inside me, seeing that. Every ballet student had a regular place at the barre in their classes. There were a lot of old feelings tugging at me, but none of them made sense in this room. I tried to brush them off. Ballet was finished for me.

"Well, hi there," Tiffanni said. She was suddenly leaning over, right in my face. Her smile took up the whole room.

"Hi-i," I stuttered out.

"It's so nice to meet you," she said in that cutesy voice twenty-somethings sometimes used.

"We've already met," I said.

"Have you done barre before?"

"Yes."

"I'm only asking because this is an advanced class."

"Right." When she kept her face looming over me and didn't leave, I added, "Thank you." Was this the right time to ask her about Lucas? Probably not. The class was about to start. And Tiffanni's perfume was overwhelming all my senses. It smelled citrussy but with a metallic undertone that was making my eyes flood with tears.

"So, you're going to be able to keep up?" she asked, still in that voice. A flash of irritation ran through me.

"Yeah." My voice sounded harsh in the pastel-hued studio. I'd never raised my voice in a ballet studio before. Of course, this wasn't ballet, it was just barre.

She stood up, smiled faintly, and swaggered to the front of the room.

"She's a real peach," Geraldine said.

"Hmph." There was a dizzying array of leggings in the room. I was starting to feel a little faint, even though I'd been doing the vertigo exercises Julian had given me, and they seemed to be helping.

At the front, Tiffanni hooked a headset over her ears and tested the volume. I winced. Ear-shattering was apparently the noise level she preferred. "Everyone find their place at the barre, please," she singsonged.

I took a spot beside Geraldine. Everyone else in the room was in their twenties, or close to it.

"Ready!" Tiffanni screeched, as loud music blared into the room.

We started with a few easy stretches that I had to admit felt kind of good. Then we transitioned to some simple rises onto the balls of our feet: relevés. The movements woke up something inside me that had been asleep for a long time. I tried not to dwell on it, all those old ballet rhythms.

We moved to some core work, which didn't seem so bad.

I'd thought about going back to ballet someday. It was part of the reason I'd started my own business, so I could have a more flexible schedule. I'd been hoping that after we got up and running, I'd have a bit more time. Hadn't happened yet, but—

I moved into a plank position with the rest of the class. I was starting to emit a sheen of perspiration, which was odd, since I wasn't normally an overly sweaty person.

The planks became mobile: one hip dipping down and touching the mat, then the other. Then we moved on to plank step-outs, which were as awful as they sounded.

I looked to the right: Geraldine was planking like a pro. To the left: the rest of the stick-thin class was stepping out like they were at a disco.

I tried to breathe.

"Just two more minutes!"

Two more minutes was nothing when you were napping, but it was basically the entire history of the world when you were planking. And was that my imagination, or was Tiffanni grinning at me? She was so smiley it was hard to tell for sure. I mean, what had I ever done to her? No, seriously, I couldn't remember. Or feel my feet.

"To the barre!" Tiffanni said, looking cheerful. Of course she was; she wasn't actually doing anything, just standing in the middle of the room and yelling. I'd had evil teachers before—ballet sometimes attracted them—but none that were quite so perky.

Tiffanni rattled off a simple exercise. Was it wrong that I felt a sense of triumph when she demonstrated a plié in second position with terrible form? I didn't care. Being petty was the only thing keeping me alive. I felt like the class had been underway for twenty minutes or so. When I looked at my watch, it showed that six minutes had gone by.

I swallowed hard. It was possible I'd overestimated myself. I hadn't stood in front of a barre since I was sixteen. Which was, if I thought about it, almost thirty years ago.

Oh, crap.

"And plié!" Tiffanni yelled.

We turned out our legs, bent our knees, and pliéed. Somewhere deep inside me, the movement made perfect sense. Muscle memory clamoured to be heard. Suddenly I got a flash of my first ballet class—a free class at the Y I'd begged my mother, Phyllis, to let me take when I was a kid. I'd had to get my Nan involved to convince her. I'd loved it instantly. And I'd shown a little talent, apparently, even from a young age. Ballet had been like a language I was born speaking. Computers were like that for me too.

"Vio-let!" Tiffanni sing-songed. I glanced around and saw that everyone had moved on to another combination. I narrowed my eyes at her, and she did the exact same thing back to me.

I raised myself onto my metatarsals, pliéed, and pulsed along with the rest of the class.

"Pulse pulse pulse!" Tiffanni called out. "You're not pulsing, Violettttttttttttt!"

I looked at myself in the mirror as I pulsed. Geraldine was bopping along like a sixteen-year-old cheerleader. I looked like a dump truck in high heels. But I pulsed. I couldn't feel my legs anymore, but I pulsed.

I was also an odd colour.

"And lift lift lift!" Tiffanni yelled. She was boogying around the room to an edgy hip hop song I'd never heard before. I was distinctly feeling old. And nauseous.

Geraldine lifted. The twenty-year-old on my other side was lifting. I put my head down and fumbled around on the floor for my ridiculous unicorn water bottle. I sucked on that straw like I was a vacuum cleaner.

"No resting, now," Tiffanni said in a fake-pleasant voice. While looking directly at me. Irma's propensity towards punching people who annoyed her was suddenly making a lot more sense.

She was behind me. I pulled myself back up, a twinge of dizziness hitting me.

"Violet," Tiffanni said, "Do you need to leave the class?"

I turned and fixed her in my sights. "No. I need water. Which I'm drinking." I held the unicorn cup up and shook it.

"Alrighty!" she singsonged, then jogged into the middle of the room. "Let's do lunges!"

The rest of the class made a groaning noise, which wasn't the best sign in the world if you were trying to stay alive. We started lunging with a stretchy TheraBand around our knees and weights in both hands. I had a brief moment where I blacked out completely and time stood still. I felt horrible, I looked horrible, and I smelled horrible. And I kind of wanted to throw up.

The class finally, mercifully, moved into the cool-down. I almost cried, I was so thankful.

But then Tiffanni said, "Let's bridge!"

Soon my legs were burning, and I was pretty sure I'd pulled a muscle in my butt. But I raised my hips. When Tiffanni turned to another part of the room, I put my hips down, just for a second. I took in a few deep breaths, then raised my torso. I wasn't going to let her get to me. I'd once done sixteen clean pirouettes for a diabolical pointe teacher from the Bolshoi who probably kidnapped poodles in her spare time. I was tough. I could take it.

"Now, let's lift your right leg into tabletop!"

I couldn't take it.

"Tap it on the ground, raise it back up! Violet, up, up!"

Was this what death felt like?

"TAP IT, VIOLET!" Tiffanni was standing over me now. I had my hips thrust as high as I could go. I was raising and tapping my right leg. I was drenched in sweat. I smelled like last week's sushi. Every single inch of me throbbed. But I was tapping. Her mouth was open like she was about to speak again. But she closed it and moved on.

Mercifully, we moved to a few exercises on our stomachs that I was able to fake my way through. Then we moved to a real cool down and stretches. My legs were trembling. It took a long time to slow down my breath. But I was still conscious, which was surprising.

"Great job," Geraldine said. She was perspiring lightly and was a pleasant pink colour. I looked like I was about to explode.

I glanced at her to see if she was kidding. "Thanks?"

Geraldine grinned. "I haven't seen her go after someone like that in a long time."

I sucked on my unicorn horn. It contained the best water I'd ever drank in my life.

Geraldine got to her feet. "Tell Irma I'm going to swing by the clinic for a visit in a bit, please."

I nodded. Even that small movement hurt. She waved as she left, and I drank some more water, ruminating about what Tiffanni might have in store for me if I didn't step lively. I now knew one thing for sure: Tiffanni was a sadist. I could totally believe she'd killed someone.

"You okay, hon?" Tiffanni said, just as I was struggling to my feet. She wore a sickly-sweet smile on her face that didn't reach her eyes. "You look a little unsteady on your feet."

I had a decision tree I used to determine what to do in situations where I didn't know what to say. But that tree was only used when I cared about how my words were perceived. "Your second position is too wide," I said instead.

"What?" she snapped.

"It's too wide. And you're turning out from your feet, not your hips. You're rolling forward on your arches."

"My turnout is perfect!"

I was almost on my feet now. I wasn't going to lie; it had taken something out of me to get there.

And I was still nauseous. I could only hope to hurl on Tiffanni.

I gathered my unicorn cup and purse and raised myself to my full height with as much dignity as I could muster. I hadn't understood before why Irma had wanted to look like she wasn't injured. I got it now. I'd eat a pointe shoe before I'd let Tiffanni see she'd almost snapped my Achilles in two.

I took a step, then another. It didn't feel fantastic, but I wasn't going to crawl out of here.

"It's perfect," she repeated. The room was mostly empty, which was nice. If I fell flat on my face and Tiffanni told people, I'd be able to lie and say it had never happened.

I walked toward the studio's exit. I could do it. I could. I was almost there. Almost at the door. All I had to do next was crawl to the sidewalk and hold my arm out. Eventually a cab would come.

"What's wrong with my second position?"

"Already told you."

"I feel fine. I have no issues at all. None!"

I was at the door. Would she notice if I leaned in the doorway? Oh, who cared. I'd survived. I was still alive. "You don't have any issues because you're twenty-whatever. In a few years you'll have arthritis in your knees if you keep it up."

She made a strangled noise.

"Oh, and another thing..." I tried to focus on Tiffanni—a challenge, since there were two of her. Nope, three. "What's this about you getting all of Lucas's stuff?"

"I can't imagine how that's any business of yours." She sniffed.

She was right, and I briefly wished Irma could have been here instead. She needed a real sidekick to help her with her investigations, instead of me and a borrowed pug who looked like he hadn't been walked since the year 2000.

"You almost hit me with your racquet the other day," I said darkly. "I'd love to know why. And why were you yelling at Imogene last night?"

"That's none of your business." She swivelled to look at the door as a happy tinkle announced the arrival of new barre flies. Two middle-aged women smiled and sat down to untie their shoes.

"I mean, everywhere I go, you're screaming your head off at people, and—"

The women's shoes were off now, but other than their eyes, they hadn't moved. They were watching us like they were at a tennis match.

"You can go right in," Tiffanni said to the women.

"Oh, just resting my ankle," the one on the left said. Then she smiled, like gossip was her gateway drug.

Tiffanni inclined her head toward the door.

I shook my head.

She stepped closer, her voice low. "I gave Lucas something I want back. That's all." She turned back to the women.

I took the hint and left after pushing myself away from the wall. I had some momentum and I wasn't going to waste it.

TWENTY-TWO—IRMA

Violet was leaning in the doorway, panting.

"Violet, dear," I exclaimed, "what on earth has happened to you?"

"Barre...class." She moved microscopically slowly to the chair beside my bed.

"Did you have fun?"

Violet threw me a dark look that almost looked scary. I felt proud of her. "I'm going to take that as a no."

"It was an advanced class," she said bitterly, then repeated, "*advanced.*"

"I see." I awaited more details.

"I have no feeling in my arms," Violet moaned.

"I'm so sorry, dear," I said. "I had no clue Tiffanni's class was so difficult. I really wish I could have gone instead of you."

"Oh, it's fine," Violet said, laboriously adjusting herself in the chair. "I just forgot how much work it is to do even a simple barre." She laid her head back on the chair. "And how old I am."

"Good heavens," I said, "you're not old at all."

She gave me another look. I tried not to laugh. She looked adorable when she was cross.

"Did you find out anything?"

"I found out you need to bring in someone else for the soft skills part of your investigations. I am just not the right girl for the job."

"Don't say that! We can work on it if you want."

"I do not want."

"Fair enough. I am sorry about your arms, dear. Hopefully the feeling will come back at some point."

"I brought donuts," she said. "But I can't get them out because my arms don't work anymore."

"Would you like me to do it?"

She made a motion that could have been a nod.

I rustled around in her knapsack and found a pink-frosted donut with sprinkles on it, and a bearclaw. "How did you know I liked bearclaws?"

The ghost of a smile flitted over her face before being replaced by misery. "I have my sources."

"I am very proud of your sneakiness! Thank you very much." I tried to put the pink pastry in her hand. When her fingers couldn't grasp the donut, I placed it gently in her mouth. Somehow, she ate the whole thing without using her hands at all. "That is quite impressive, dear."

After swallowing, she said, "The only thing Tiffanni and I talked about was how horrible I was doing, and—"

"I'm sure that's not true," I said, patting her leg. I withdrew my hand when she flinched.

"Believe it. We did not have an educational discussion."

"Oh, poo."

"Except…"

I leaned forward.

"She said she gave Lucas something. That's why she wants his stuff."

"Reallllllly."

She nodded, then sucked on a—was that a *unicorn* horn?—drink for a moment. She was a funny shade of purple, but maybe it was improving? Hard to say, really.

"Do you think she was telling the truth?"

Her shrug was so small I wasn't sure it had actually happened. I left her alone, the poor thing, while I contemplated this new intel. It wasn't much to go on. Plus, Carlton *had* just been whisked away by the police. I still wasn't sure how I felt about that. He certainly had a temper, but he was also a successful—if somewhat workshy—businessman from a family who would support him no matter what. It made no sense for him to throw all that away. Jealousy, on the other hand, was a potent drug.

Then I focused on something else that was irking me: my continued lack of admission to the poker party this Friday. I'd asked Carlton for tickets while he was being handcuffed, but he hadn't really responded. Probably had other things on his mind.

I'd promised Julian to stay here until tonight, but if Violet could distract him with a little flash-bang, maybe I could run out for a bit and—

Kendelle, the clinic's lovely receptionist, popped her head into the room. "Hiya, Irma."

"Hello, dear."

"I just got a call from Imogene at the Club. She says if you can get—" She looked down at a piece of paper, "Your nerd friend to fix the sprinklers, they'll give her two tickets to the dinner with Mr. Morceau next week."

Violet's eyes almost bugged out of her head. Mr. Morceau was a Michelin-starred chef from a restaurant in Montréal. His dinner next week had been sold out for months. I'd bought my two tickets last December and had already invited Stu.

"That's lovely, dear. Any chance we can get tickets to the Smile-a-Thon poker tournament?"

Kendelle looked from Violet to me. "They didn't say anything about that. But you can always call them."

"Excellent advice, young lady. Thank you."

"Why do you want to get into this poker game so badly?" Violet asked after Kendelle was gone. "And why can't you get into it?"

"Carlton's family's foundation holds it on his boat, which will be anchored in the lake outside the Club's bay, and there's a safety issue if it's overloaded. So they're very strict about their numbers."

"And why do you want to go so bad?"

"It brings some potentially unsavoury characters onto the island. Last year, a very dangerous gentleman popped up in town." A killer for hire, in fact, with a soft spot for Texas Hold'em. Thankfully, I'd ushered him out of town without a body count. If we had *another* murderous visitor this year, on top of the *current* murderous resident, I had to be prepared.

Violet imbibed some more unicorn drink. "You just don't want to be left out."

"That too." I grinned at her.

"Ladies." Geraldine Greenwood stood in the doorway, holding a small clutch of flowers. After her cheerful greeting, she pulled the door shut behind her. Normally, people closed doors behind themselves when they were trying to kill me. I struggled with my emotions for a brief moment.

"Hello, Violet," she said kindly. Violet looked like she was trying to raise a hand in greeting.

I finished a cycle of calming breaths. Lorraine, the town postmistress, had been at the clinic early this morning for a heavy-duty papercut and had likely told half the island where I was. So this was probably not the last visitor I was going to see today. "Geraldine. How lovely!" I took the flowers from her and sniffed. They smelled like summer.

She pulled a chair from the other side of the room over and settled herself on the opposite side of my bed from Violet. It seemed best to give her some space.

"Irma," Geraldine said quietly. "I have to tell you some difficult news."

My stomach tightened. I wasn't having the best day, frankly, and I would have really rathered she saved her bad news. Perhaps until next year sometime?

"Sorry," she said. "There's been a fire at Lucas's trailer."

I held my breath. She looked like she was searching for the right words. If another young person's life had been snuffed out, I was going to get very irate. This was my island, and I was supposed to be protecting its inhabitants. This state of affairs was intolerable.

"Someone set it on fire," she said, then swallowed hard. "It's gone."

"*Gone*?"

She nodded. "It was done early this morning. Nobody saw anything."

"Was the safe fireproof?"

She shrugged. "A Werther? Yes. But I can't get anywhere near it now. It's a crime scene, police running around all over the place. They'll keep it as evidence."

"Drat."

"Drat, indeed," she said. "I'm sorry, Irma. I wanted to help you out."

Had Tiffanni torched the trailer to destroy whatever item she wanted back from Lucas? I tamped my frustration down, squished it into a ball so small it didn't exist any more. "I know, thank you. I'll poke Mavis and see if there was anything that could be salvaged. Do the police know anything about what happened?"

She pressed her lips together. "They wouldn't say anything to me. You might have more luck. In any case, I'm sorry, Irma. It's a dead end."

"Oh, dear."

"And there's something else…"

I waited patiently.

"I was at Spa Lala getting a facial this morning, and I heard the girls talking."

"And?"

She scrunched her mouth up. "Rose isn't at work today. They haven't heard from her since last night. And they can't reach her on her cell. They think she's missing."

TWENTY-THREE — VIOLET

"Well, this is all terrible," Irma said cheerily after Geraldine left.

"What are you thinking?"

Irma glanced at the door, then said quietly, "Lucas had a very up-market safe in his Airstream."

"Can't you open it? Wait, how do you know that?"

"Suction cups and moonlight."

"*What?*"

"In any case, safes aren't in my wheelhouse, but..." She looked like she was struggling with what to say next. To say Irma was paranoid was about as understated as I could be. I gave her the moment. If she didn't want to tell me something, I didn't want to hear it. I felt like I had a better chance of staying alive that way.

"Geraldine is a master safe cracker," Irma said finally.

"Get outta here!" Geraldine always looked like she was just on the verge of baking cookies for you.

She shushed me. "It's true. They never would have got her if she hadn't whacked her terribly abusive husband on the back of the head one night."

"She—Geraldine, that nice little old lady who just left—*bonked someone on the head*?"

Irma took a deep sigh. "Yes. Then he fell down the stairs and broke…well, everything, really. That was the real issue."

"Yeah, I guess."

"So she ended up in prison for sixteen years, give or take."

I was having trouble breathing, and nobody was even asking me to do cardio. "That nice little old lady killed someone and spent sixteen years in prison?"

"Yes, I believe that sums it up quite well."

"Holy crap!"

"It's nice to see you perking up a little. You really are quite resilient."

"So is Geraldine, I guess."

"Fair point. In any case, she's retired now, but she helps people out with their safe problems every now and then."

"As one does," I said reasonably.

She nodded.

"Do you have any normal friends?"

She tilted her head and gave me a look. "Don't forget; *you* are a member of that group, my dear."

Her words landed in my chest with a warm fuzz. On the one hand, I, and pretty much everyone else, wanted to stay on Irma's good side. On the other hand, I liked her more every day, even though so far on this vacation she'd gotten me shot at, almost blown up, and had terrified me via multiple transportation methods. It was hard to explain how Irma's magic worked.

"Oh, I'm not normal," I said, trying to use a breezy tone.

She threw a look my way. "Trust me, dear. Normal is highly overrated. In any case, am I to conclude from your recent eyeball-bugging that you're willing to fix the Club's sprinkler system? You don't have to if you don't want to."

"Yeah, it's fine. I'm very excited to go to that dinner."

"It'll be wonderful. Who are you going to bring?"

"Max."

"Your business partner."

"My non-larcenous business partner, yes."

Irma frowned. "I was hoping we could speak about that."

"Shoot."

"I was wondering if you wanted any help tracking Shane down."

I suddenly felt cold and hot all in the same moment. Irma was retired British intelligence. She had a contact in Toronto who did security work and looked like she could kill you with a paper clip and a Junior Mint.

Did I want those kinds of people after Shane? What would happen if Irma broke a few of his fingers? Would he be more or less likely to give me my money if he couldn't use his left hand?

Did I care?

"Irma!" Another figure was standing in the doorway.

"This is like Grand Central Station," I said. It came out accidentally.

"It is!" Mrs. Sepp said with a smile. "I heard from your mailman that you had a fall. How are your hips, Irma?" she added cheekily.

Irma grinned. "Right as rain, Mrs. Sepp."

"This is for you." She leaned over and picked up a gorgeous bouquet of flowers; lipstick roses, raffia, hot peppers lining the sides of a cut-glass vase.

"How lovely!" Irma said.

"And I brought a friend to keep you company," Mrs. Sepp said. Mr. P was deep in her purse, and lifted his head out enough so his chin was hooked over the side. He was panting even though the room was air-conditioned.

"I don't think we can have dogs in here," Irma said. But she didn't sound like she really meant it.

"I told Dr. Harper. He said as long as Mr. P doesn't get out of your room, everything will be fine."

Irma held her hands out, and Mr. P started wiggling energetically. Before he ran out of steam and collapsed onto his jowls. Mrs. Sepp picked him up and plopped him into Irma's arms. Irma immediately pulled him in for a cuddle. He made happy whining noises, then hooked a little paw around her thumb.

"Thank you, Irma. I must go to a job now. Are you able to keep him for a few hours?"

"Well, all right," Irma said, like she was doing Mrs. Sepp a favour, even though any moron could tell she adored Mr. P. It was hard not to. He was plump and lazy and perfect.

"How long are you here?" Mrs. Sepp asked.

"Till later on today," Irma said.

"Perfect," Mrs. Sepp said, then made a face. "I must unexpectedly help Elsa Lee with the poker tournament decorations."

"Well, Carlton is currently incarcerated, Mrs. Sepp, so—"

Her eyebrows raised at that. "It doesn't matter if he is in jail or on Mars, or just around the corner. He's a *laiskvorst.* A lazy sausage."

"I see," Irma said.

"It has more impact in Estonian," Mrs. Sepp said, almost apologetically. "Elsa is so tired these days, I am becoming concerned about her."

"That must be why she snapped at me last night," Irma said. When she saw my face, she added, "She was a little perturbed that I tried to help her into her chair at the wake. It was my fault. I overstepped."

"Well, she will learn she must conserve her energy for her little one." After a glance at her watch, Mrs. Sepp exclaimed, "I must go now. Thank you, Irma!"

"Goodbye, Mrs. Sepp!" Irma said.

Mr. P sat back on his haunches, his tongue hanging out of his mouth. Then he sneezed on Irma, who took it in stride.

"I'm going to go have a nap," I said to her. "And a shower. Not sure in what exact order. I'll call the Club and tell them I'll swing by tomorrow."

"Thank you, dear," Irma said.

"No problemo. You need anything?"

She pulled Mr. P into an awkward embrace that had his arms and legs splayed out like a starfish.

"I'll be all right." Irma settled herself a bit deeper in her pillows. But then Mr. P perked up. He sniffed the air around him with his squashed little snout.

"What's wrong with him?" I said.

"To be honest, Violet, Mr. P doesn't really act like any dog I've ever met before. I'd say he's scented something, but I don't actually know if he has any canine instincts, so..."

Mr. P's legs started flailing, and he flattened himself against Irma. He looked like one of those sixties hippies performing non-violent resistance, but with more wrinkles.

He jerked to the left, then rolled off the bed.

"Mr. P!" Irma shouted.

The little guy landed on his feet, which was surprising, since I'd once seen him trip over his own tongue. Irma and I looked at each other.

Then he exploded out of his leg sockets, running to the door.

"Oh, dear."

"I'll get him," I said, an offer I regretted as soon as I started struggling to my feet. My legs felt like someone had stuck them in a drill press. But Irma was wearing a hospital jimmy and I was quite sure she wasn't going to roam around the clinic with her tiny septuagenarian behind exposed.

"Thank you!" Irma said. "Might want to pick up the pace a bit."

I mumbled something under my breath as I left. I wished Mr. P had a GPS tag on his collar. I checked in a few open patient rooms. Nothing. How bad was it to have an animal running around a medical clinic? Probably very.

I waddled along, sticking my nose into open doors, making my way to the other wing of the clinic, toward the exam rooms. The break room was also located here, and if someone asked me what I was doing, I'd tell them I was getting coffee. Which actually sounded like a good idea. Maybe caffeine would help banish the achy quivering in my legs.

"Mr. P," I called out softly. If someone was having some sort of horrible procedure performed on them, I didn't want to spook them. Or Mr. P. If he bit someone...

There was nobody in the break room, and no curly little tails poking out of anyone's door. I kept limping down the hallway.

The last time I'd been here, someone had called in a bomb threat and shot Irma. Just a little, she'd said, but it had still worried me. Even though she'd assured me that she really didn't feel pain like normal people. I didn't want to unpack that comment too much. I'd once seen her take down a two-hundred-and-fifty-pound giant with her thumb after climbing him like he was a tree. And she'd landed before he did, which was impossible if you cared about things like physics, which I did.

"Mr. P?" I crept along the hallway. The little bugger really knew how to move when he wanted to. But he was nowhere.

"Do I have to?" A man's voice broke the silence. It was coming from one of the exam rooms. Then Mr. P sneezed.

I peeked in the door and saw him, halfway wedged under the exam table. If it had been any other dog, I would have thought he was guarding something. Or someone. He was laser focused on a pair of sneakers which were currently occupied by a youngish dude with *Club Pro* stencilled on his polo shirt. Must be the Club's new tennis guy.

"There you are," I singsonged. I was hoping my cheerfulness could cover up the fact that my legs were barely working. I picked Mr. P up. He responded by licking my nose. Considering where his face had just been, I tried not to shudder.

The man was sitting on the exam table, his phone pressed to the side of his face, and he looked moderately horrified. "Can you have a dog in a hospital?"

"Uh, yes," I said, patting him on the head. "He's an emotional uh, support, uh, pug. Sorry for the bother." I turned to go. But as I did, I caught sight of the man's arms: His left was wrapped in a sloppy bandage. And it looked like it was covering up a fresh burn.

TWENTY-FOUR — IRMA

Violet hobbled back to my room with Mr. P, then shared the delicious tidbit she'd discovered while retrieving him. So, Tate the twerpy new tennis pro had a burn on his arm? How very, very interesting. And what luck, that Mr. P had been here to sniff him out.

"I'm gonna jet," Violet said. "And lie down for like the next twenty years."

"Right you are, dear. Thank you so much for all your help."

After asking me if I needed anything, she shuffled out the door. After she was gone, I looked at the ceiling again for a minute. Things were looking up. Thank goodness, or I would have died of boredom in this hospital bed. I pulled the phone close to me and dialled. I wanted to see if Rose had turned up at work yet.

"Spa Lala." Sakura Sato answered the phone perkily, her default state.

"Sakura, dear, it's Irma Abercrombie. How's your mother doing?"

"Hiya, Irma. She's great, thanks. What can I do for you?"

"I wanted to make an appointment for a massage, please. And is Rose there? I just wanted a quick word."

"Oh, uh…" I heard her hand muffle the speaker. After a moment, she came back on the line. "I'm sorry, Irma. She's not here right now."

"I see. Can you have her call me as soon as she gets back?"

There was a pause. "Uh, yes, of course, Irma, but… I think she's taking a sick day."

"You think?"

"I'm not…uh…sure. She hasn't been in today, and, well, she's not answering her cell. I'm sure it's all fine, it's just that she normally doesn't just not show up."

"I see. Well, thank you. I'll speak to her another time. Goodbye."

"Don't you want your massage?"

"Sure. I just have to sort some things out first." We rang off.

I sat back in my pillowy prison. Was Geraldine right? Was Rose really missing? I tossed that around my head for a bit, then called Rose's residence—her housekeeper hadn't seen her since last night, but said that didn't mean anything—and the voicemail on Rose's cellular telephone was picking up. I left a message.

I could not take this immobility one more minute. Plus, I had to go see what Mr. Tate Hurst had to say for himself. It took a bit longer for me to get out of bed than usual, but I was a persevere-er, as Mother had always said.

I tried to ignore the indignity of my open-backed hospital gown. It could be useful. A little old lady wrapped in flannel tended to be disarming, metaphorically speaking, although sometimes literally speaking.

After extracting my telescoping mirror from my handbag, I shuffled into the little slippers Julian had left for me. Since they had happy faces on them, I assumed they were from the children's supply. No matter. Small people got things done.

I pulled the back of the gown closed over my derriere with my left hand, secured Mr. P in my room, then shuffled over to the wing of the clinic housing the exam rooms. I saved myself from going through Reception by using a supply room with a door joining the two sides of the building.

Violet had told me Tate Hurst was in exam room five. How lovely. And so close.

I stepped into the hallway, took a deep breath to centre myself, and shuffled to exam room five. The door was slightly ajar, and the room was quiet.

I hoped the little twerp wasn't gone already.

My telescoping mirror in hand, I expanded it and peered inside the room. He was there, and he was alone.

"Hello, dear," I said, shutting the door behind me. "Let's chat, shall we?"

Tate looked like he was reading something on his phone. He glanced up briefly, then returned to his screen. "Oh, hey, Mrs. A. Wassup?"

"Not much. Have you seen a dog recently?"

His face still in his phone, he said, "Yeah, little wrinkly guy? Someone came and got him."

"Oh, how wonderful." I sat down in one of the chairs. "That's a real load off my shoulders. Whew."

"Yeah," Tate said. "For real."

"Yes, very real. Don't mind me, dear, I'm just resting for a bit. You know how old people get."

He smirked. I could feel my spleen tightening.

"Oh, my," I said, trying to inject concern into my voice. "What happened to your arm?"

He glanced at me, then pulled his sleeve over the fresh bandage someone at the clinic must have put on. I wondered when they'd be back. Best to move quickly.

"Oh, that? I don't have a BBQ in the city," he said, "I'm out of practice. I burned my arm on the fancy one they've got at the place where I'm staying."

"Really?" I tried to make my voice as flat as possible.

Tate's expression darkened. Drat.

"That's funny," I said, deciding to forge ahead. "There was actually a fire on the island early this morning."

"Oh?" he said, and it sounded like he was mimicking me. What a little wiener he was. Honestly, I was going to tie his pancreas in a knot if he kept it up.

"Yes," I said. "There's been a few recently. Lucas García's Airstream went up in flames this morning. And David Bell's car did the very same thing last night."

"I dunno, Mrs. A, I hear this is a pretty safe town."

"It is," I said meaningfully.

"Good," he said, picking up a knapsack that was resting on the floor. "I'm looking for some peace and quiet."

"So was Lucas."

"That so?"

"I hear you knew him."

"Not really." His self-satisfied expression was starting to waver around the edges.

"You were both competing at the same tournaments when you were younger, no?"

"I guess. Well, I gotta get outta Dodge, Mrs. A."

"I hear you didn't get along."

"What? What is this? I have to go."

"I mean, you can, dear, but don't you want to clear your name?"

"Are you serious right now? There's nothing wrong with my name, you nosy old lady. I'm outta here."

He slammed the door behind him. I sighed, then snuck back into my room.

I had bad tea and played with Mr. P—whatever game we were engaged in, I was almost certain he was winning—while pondering my next move. To be honest, I was disappointed in myself. My discussion with Tate had gotten me nowhere, other than being called *old*, which I didn't particularly appreciate. But why had the police wanted to speak to Carlton this morning, anyway? He hadn't actually been under arrest until he took a swing at that officer; they'd only wanted to talk to him. And where was Rose? I'd called her twice more on her cellular, and the last time her mailbox had been full. And I was very keen to see David and hear what he wanted to tell us. I'd called the mainland hospital to speak with him several times; each time I was told he was getting tests done, or was sleeping.

Julian sprung me at eight p.m., but with a number of dire warnings. I took them all in stride and skedaddled on out of there. I was crabby from doing nothing, and it was too late to go visit David in the mainland hospital. I went to bed early so I'd be fresh for tomorrow, when I would hear what David had to say about all the strange happenings on the island.

TWENTY-FIVE — VIOLET

I went back to Irma's, stretched every muscle in my body, took the hottest bath I'd ever had in my life, and slept like the future of the planet depended on it.

The next morning, I had three cups of coffee before calling Imogene to organize a time to come by and look at their sprinklers. I could already taste the Mr. Morceau dinner I was going to have with Max next week, especially since fixing the sprinkler system was probably only going to take an hour or so.

I hit the road. Irma was a terrifying driver, but it was easy to see why she Mario Andretti-ed herself around town in her little red MG convertible. It handled beautifully. It was another gorgeous summer day, and the top was down. As long as I didn't get any bugs in my teeth, it'd be a good drive.

It was strange not to see other cars on the road. In Toronto, we were all so far up in each other's business that you were never really alone.

And I liked that. But this...the country road unwinding in front of me, sun on my face...this was pretty good too.

I pulled up to the Club's locked gates. They probably recognized the car, and let me right in, which was poor security on their part. I decided not to make it into a thing.

I snagged a parking spot near the main club house, but I'd forgotten how sore my legs were from the previous day's barre from hell while I was driving. When I tried to stand, I only made it halfway up, which probably wasn't awesome. I took a deep breath and tried to focus. The door wasn't that far.

Then I started walking. Limping, really. I remembered how Irma'd been so gimpy the other day and hadn't shown a thing, but I was no Irma.

Imogene greeted me effusively at the door. For a second, I was worried she was going to hug me, but thankfully the moment passed. She ushered me to one of the back offices, which had Herman Miller desk chairs and sleek, ergonomic furnishings. The windows were huge, and most of them looked out at the docks behind the clubhouse and the lake beyond them. It was a beautiful view. I settled myself in one of the Hermans and unpacked my gear. Imogene had put a sticky note with the password I needed on the workstation's monitor.

Then I started to look at the management software the Club was using for the smart irrigation system. It took me about three minutes to determine no one had ever added a password to the master administrator account. I uploaded a small application from the encrypted USB stick on my keychain and opened a secure shell to a host machine I kept back in Toronto. I sparked up a more complex IOT search engine than the one I had on my phone and scanned to see if the irrigation system was broadcasting the details of the water system's network. It was.

I sighed. I was getting more and more concerned about the Internet of Things. All the smart appliances, the doorbell cameras, the children's toys. A lot of them weren't constructed properly because no global design standards had ever been established or agreed upon, and it was only a matter of time before a serious hack in a system like this caused real damage.

Recently, I'd helped Irma sort out a problem with some fancy new smart IV stands at the same clinic she'd recently been convalescing at, that'd been compromised by a very angry individual who'd been out for revenge. We'd been lucky we'd figured out what was really going on. A woman had died not long ago in Germany, the victim of a medjacking gone horribly wrong.

Although it was hard to imagine what damage a hacked sprinkler system could create at the Club. Bump up the water bill? Make the greens soggy? Ruin some fancy shoes? I could see it in normal situations; in a neighbourhood or a business complex, water was indispensable. Shutting off the taps could keep everyone hostage, just like medjacking—cut off a resource and ransom it back to its rightful users.

Nothing like that was going on here. But a vulnerable system was a vulnerable system. As an engineer and a sysadmin, it was my responsibility to keep those systems safe, even if they weren't my own. It was kind of like being a doctor, but for nerdy things.

I changed the administrator account's name, so it wouldn't be as easy to hack into, and added a complex password. Then I did a little research about security around systems like these. There really weren't a lot of options, but I was able to configure the network so it didn't broadcast a signal, so at least it would be harder for jerks to find. After that, I set a monitor on the master account, so the Club would be notified via email if anyone tried to log in using it.

A gust of wind rolled off the lake and rattled the windows in the office. I lifted my eyes and looked at the bay bordering the clubhouse. I'd been doing my vertigo exercises a few times a day ever since Irma had dragged me to see Julian, and *looking* at the lake no longer brought on a wave of dizziness, so I had to assume they were starting to work.

Then I turned my attention to the rows of boats neatly docked behind the Club. Most of them would contain complex computerized systems just like that tractor had. I wondered again who had commandeered the tractor, and why anyone would do such a thing. And if it was just a bunch of bored kids who'd wanted to create a kerfuffle during the ground-breaking.

It was a puzzler. But I knew Irma would figure it out. I did some more reading and tweaked a few of the settings in the irrigation system and looked through the logs to see if there'd been any breaches. Everything looked good.

I leaned back in my chair, feeling pretty satisfied with myself. Then I started packing up.

Twenty-Six — Irma

After copious amounts of tea the next morning, I called St. Jude, the mainland hospital, and was put through to the nurse's station on David's ward. I asked them to tell him I was on my way. They'd pass the message right along, I was told. Good. I needed answers from him to unravel what had happened to Lucas. Some proof or evidence would be lovely as well.

Then I waited for Stuart to come and collect me. He'd picked me up from the hospital the night before, and had been quite insistent about me not driving today. I'd capitulated because he'd been on the verge of becoming cross with me, which was not his habit.

"Morning," he greeted me cheerily, after I'd locked up and met him in the car.

"Good morning, Stuart."

He backed out of my driveway and pointed us toward the main road. We drove in silence for a bit, a comfortable one. On the ferry, we both stood at the rail to get some fresh air.

After we landed, Stu steered us toward the hospital. "I certainly hope all of this nonsense has shown you that you need to take it easier, Irmie," he finally said, after ten minutes of running his fingers through his beard like he did when he was worried about something.

"What nonsense?"

"Car fires, suction cups—"

"Who told you about that?"

"I have my own sources, Irma."

"Of course. But don't forget that if the Beaver Brooke project is going to collapse, it might just take your life savings with it."

"You're more important than money. You need to be careful, Irma. Please."

"Of course," I repeated.

"That's right." He made a humphing noise, which I decided to take as supportive. He dropped me off at the front door, and went to sit in the truck in the parking lot. He did not care for hospitals at all.

I stopped in the gift shop to get some flowers and took the elevator to the eighth floor. But when I stopped at the nurse's station, I was told to wait until they could find a supervisor. I tried to ignore the adrenaline that flooded me. Had David been kidnapped? Had—

"Mrs. Abercrombie?" A nice-looking young nurse with a short afro was standing in front of me. She was wearing pink scrubs with cats on them. Her smile was tentative but pleasant.

"Hello, dear."

She reached her hand out to shake mine. "Can we take a seat over here, please?" She motioned at a bank of chairs attached to the wall.

"Of course."

After we'd gotten ourselves situated, she said, "I'm so sorry to tell you, Mrs. Abercrombie, but—"

"Oh, dear," I said, my hand suddenly on my chest. I couldn't stop myself.

She smiled. "It's nothing like that. David is fine."

"But?"

"He's gone," she said.

"But I called an hour ago and said I was coming to visit him."

"I know. I gave him the message."

"So he got it?"

She nodded.

"Did he say anything?"

She pressed her lips together. She looked perplexed as she said, "No, not at all. He seemed fine. He just said, 'okay,' and that was that."

"Did anyone see him leave?"

"No. He must have used the back stairs."

"Are you sure?"

A nod. "All of his things are gone."

"I see. What was his condition?" After seeing the look on her face, I said, "Generally. Not looking for anything confidential."

"He was fine. A few bumps and scrapes, but he was doing remarkably well. Based on what the EMTs who brought him in told us about the accident, we were surprised, frankly. But he was about to be released, anyway, so…" She shrugged. "It's not like he ran out on his bill or anything. But I'm sorry you took the trip over for nothing, Mrs. Abercrombie."

"No worries, dear. May I take a quick look at his room?"

She pressed her lips together again. "I'm sorry. It's already been cleaned. There were no personal effects or anything like that left behind. I checked, myself."

I forced a smile to my face. Rose was missing, and now David Bell had disappeared? Could they be together?

"Thank you, dear." I convinced her to give the flowers to another patient.

She said goodbye, and I made my way back downstairs. Stuart was sitting under a tree beside his parking spot. His eyes were closed, a baseball game on the truck's radio.

I woke him up and we headed home. After catching him up on what had happened with David, I dialled Camille Beaulieu.

"Oui?" Camille answered.

"Bonjour, chérie!"

"Ah, Irma. I have been trying to get a hold of you."

"Sorry, dear. Do you have any good news for me?"

There was a heavy sigh.

"Do you have any *bad* news for me?"

She giggled. "This, I can do. Your friend Lucas was squeaky clean."

"Suspiciously so?"

"*Non*, no. He had been gradually saving for the last ten years. He'd won some professional tennis tournaments when he was younger, oui?"

"Oui."

"He banked his winnings. It appears as if he was saving for real estate. He'd put a down payment into the…Beaver Brooke apartments? It says *P* then, maybe it is an *H* on my paper here, but I cannot quite read it. I did not do this research myself, so I do not know what this means—"

"Penthouse," I breathed. Lucas was the penthouse buyer at Beaver Brooke. And he'd backed out just as the site was going to start to build. Carlton must have been furious. Furious enough to kill? Is that what David knew?

"Bon, that makes sense," she said, and I heard her scribble something. "No strange travel, he owned his Airstream trailer outright, no debt, normal banking accounts and activity. The only odd thing was his net worth. Somewhat high for a twenty-seven-year-old, but most of this was from tennis winnings from his younger days, as well as some good saving habits."

"*Merci*, Camille." *Thank you.* "What about Tate Hurst?"

A loud sigh. "Bien… Similar tennis history. He competed internationally, as Lucas did, but spent his money as quickly as he acquired it, it seems. He has six credit cards and a line of credit, all maxed out. No savings. But no criminal record at all, no complaints."

"But he's broke."

"Oui. I believe some of his recent work history is not correct, but I will need another day for this. My contact is unavailable today."

"What do you mean?"

"If I look at Mr. Hurst's résumé, he states he was employed by the Royal Toronto Tennis Club last year. I called them for a reference check. They have never heard of him."

I took in a sharp breath. "I knew he was a liar."

"I am thinking so, yes. And Carlton Carter…no criminal record of any kind, but the financial picture is very confusing at this moment. Many LLCs, some personal savings, I believe a family trust… You know how some people with generational wealth are, Irma. It can be very difficult to sort it all out."

"Is *he* broke?"

A French-sounding sigh. "Construction is not my area of expertise, but…"

"If you had to wager a guess—"

"I would say there's not much in the margins here."

"Bon," I said. So Lucas had been flush, Tate was broke, and Carlton might be having some sort of financial challenges. "Can you please see if Rose Campbell has used any of her credit cards, or purchased anything in the last few days."

"*Certainement.*"

"Merci."

"Was there anything more, Irma?"

"Yes. Please take a look at everyone in Carlton's Beaver Brooke company, just in case. Their new assistant, Elsa Lee, David Bell, whoever else you can find."

"Bien, I will," Camille said.

"Just one more thing."

"Oui?"

"Shane O'Meara." I spelled his last name for her.

"*Et c'est qui, ca?*" *And who's that?*

"You remember Violet?"

"*Bien sûr.*" *Of course.*

"Mr. O'Meara is—well, I guess he *was* her business partner. He recently emptied their business accounts and left town. I'd like to know who he owes money to, what's going on with his credit cards, that sort of thing."

"Are you planning on visiting with him?"

There was a pause. I wanted to respect Violet's wishes, but she probably didn't realise how easy it was to locate people. And convince them to do the right thing. If I played my cards right, she'd never even know I'd done anything.

"Yes," I said finally.

"Well, I shall come with you."

I said nothing. What I was going to say to that young man was only going to be heard by the two of us. But Camille would understand eventually.

"Bon, Irma. I will start on this now and call you back later."

"Merci, chérie." Thank you, dear.

"*De rien.*" *It's nothing.*

Stu lifted his eyebrows at the end of the conversation, but said nothing. He was famously tight-lipped, and I knew he'd take my secrets to the grave. The thought should have made me feel happy. Instead, worry sizzled in my stomach. If the Beaver Brooke build failed, Stu's life savings would go down the drain right with it.

Stu was happy to swing by Rose and Carlton's house to see if Rose was home. At the entrance, I could see the supplies for a gate to be installed at the foot of the driveway. Workers were also putting together a tall, wrought-iron fence around the property.

"Irma," Stu said slowly, "Why do people fence themselves in like this?"

"To keep people out."

"Maybe someone specific."

"Maybe."

The lane to the house was long and winding, with more evidence of workers sprucing up the property. Their flowerbeds put mine to shame. I needed to do my planting soon, or the whole season would be lost. Snookie would have a field day if I removed my home from the annual town garden tour.

Carlton's house was an extravagant mess; three different architectural styles smooshed together; huge white columns with a wood shake roof and bright yellow swatches painted on the side of the house. It was massive and tacky and terrible. Poor Rose.

The housekeeper informed me Rose wasn't there, but wouldn't tell me much else, which I tried to take in good humour. Then I had Stuart drop me off at Luna's Café. He did so, gave me a jaunty wave, then went to work. After picking up a few protein bran muffins, I made my way to the police station. Maybe Carlton knew where Rose was. Or why David had fled the hospital.

"Afternoon, Mrs. Abercrombie," Mavis said as she dropped off some paperwork at the front desk. Her bun seemed screwed on extra tight today.

"Hello, Chief Pickle. How are you this lovely afternoon?" Not wanting to give away the reason for my visit, I decided to stand there until she left. She'd find out eventually, of course, but I was hoping to be long gone by then.

"I'm just wonderful, Mrs. Abercrombie. I was wondering if you had a moment."

Drat. "I wish I could, dear, but I have a visit to take care of, and then I need to rest at home. Doctor's orders!"

"It's doctor's orders for you to visit someone at the jail?"

I smiled.

"We only have one prisoner at the moment."

"Yes." There was a pause. Then I asked the desk Sargent, "May I please visit your one prisoner? Thanks so much, Maurice."

Maurice pinked all the way to his ears, picked up the phone, and mumbled into it.

"Mrs. Abercrombie?" the chief said.

"Yes, dear?"

"Let's chat for a moment, shall we?"

"Oh, I'd love to, but I really need to see—"

She stepped closer. I took in her gear: a belt full of weapons, shoes that could brain a rhinoceros, and a willingness to use it all. Softly, she said, "Let's put it this way, if you want to see Mr. Campbell, you'll need to speak to me first."

There was no point in invoking my rights. I had none. I wasn't on Carlton's visitor's list; I hadn't made any arrangements to see him. "That would be lovely, Mavis."

I followed her into one of the meeting rooms and sat down, declining tea when she offered. I didn't want her to think I'd be here long.

"So, Mrs. Abercrombie."

"Yes, dear?"

"I was wondering if you could tell me where you were yesterday at about five a.m."

Well, this was a surprise. "I was at the clinic. After you had me kidnapped."

She looked affronted at that. "Dr. Harper told me you needed to be checked out. I mean, you had just dragged a man out of a burning vehicle."

"Violet helped."

"Uh-huh. So that's where you were? All night?"

"Yes." I clasped my hands together in my lap. My knee was feeling much better these days, and I was barely even affected by all that smoke. I mean, really, I'd been outside. Who got smoke inhalation from the outdoors? Julian worried too much.

"Mrs. Abercrombie, it would be so much easier if you just answered the questions I ask you when I ask them."

I looked at my lap. I had a ragged cuticle. Bother. "But I have," I said softly, still looking down. "So I really have no idea what you're talking about, dear."

"I asked you where you were at five—"

"The clinic."

She blinked a few times. "And that's your final answer?"

"Quite. And I'm sure the alarm system at the clinic will bear me out. It's on overnight. If you want to go outside for whatever reason, you have to buzz the night nurse."

"I see." She sat back in her chair and gave me an appraising look.

"You can't possibly think I had anything to do with the fire at Lucas's trailer."

Her eyes met mine. "How do you know about that?"

"I think the whole town probably knows at this point." I swallowed. My throat was unacceptably dry. Maybe I should have agreed to the Pickle's offer of terrible tea. "But why would you suspect me? I adored Lucas."

She sighed. "That's why. I thought you might have wanted to destroy something that put him in a bad light."

Again, I cursed her uncle, who'd claimed he'd been able to ferret out some information about me, which I highly doubted. My career was classified. Plus, I'd hardly ever worked with MI6. My division had been a tad more…clandestine. How irritating that her familial chitchat at a BBQ earlier in the season had filled her with such suspicious thoughts about me.

"Good heavens, dear. There are easier ways to go about something like that, if I had wanted to do any such thing."

"That so?"

I nodded. I was starting to have a real hankering for that tea. "Mavis, I did not leave the clinic, and I did not burn down Lucas's trailer. I promise."

"There's no way you tampered with the alarm system at the clinic and slipped out?"

I laughed. "Oh, you're so funny, dear. I can barely turn on a computer. Ask Violet. I promise she'll tell you all about it."

"Uh-huh."

"But I was wondering if you were aware of the fact that someone popped up at the clinic this morning with a burn on their arm."

She blinked so hard, I worried her eyelashes might fall off.

"Who?"

"I don't think I can answer that. Doctor-patient privilege, you know."

"You're not a doctor."

"Perhaps I could ask you a question?"

She settled herself back in her chair, crossed her arms.

"Why did you want to speak to Mr. Campbell? Before all the scuffling yesterday? And by the way, you have a problem with that young deputy, dear."

She threw me a *you-might-be-right-about-that* look, but said, "You know I can't comment on an ongoing investigation, Irma."

I decided to take her use of my first name as a good sign. "Just between us, dear. He's going to tell me anyway."

"If he'll agree to see you."

"Oh, he'll agree to see me." I placed my hands together in my lap again.

After a long moment where her eyebrows told me quite a story about her internal struggle to be calm, she said, "There was some physical evidence tying him to the crime."

"Really?" I sat forward in my chair. Carlton was a smarmy little twerp, but he wasn't stupid. Of course, if he'd thought Lucas was going to stay put in his shallow grave for a while, he might have popped some evidence in there with him that he planned on moving later.

"Why are you so surprised?" she said in a voice bordering on suspiciousness.

"No reason, dear. I'm just a taxpayer with a curious nature. Speaking of evidence, is there any way I can have Lucas's chain, once your investigation is done?"

"What chain?"

"The one he always wore around his neck. It had a charm, an eight. Eight was his lucky number."

She thrummed her fingers on the table. Finally, she said, "He wasn't wearing a chain when he was found. And we didn't locate anything like that at his Airstream."

"I see." I felt momentarily dejected. "Well, if there's nothing else to discuss, then—"

"Did you search Lucas's trailer?"

I pressed my lips together. "What a silly thing to say, Ms. Pickle. Why would I, an elderl—"

She held up a hand. "Just between the two of us."

"Were any of the seals on the Airstream broken?"

She shook her head. Then the silence drew itself out. Did she want me to incriminate myself? So she could hold it in her back pocket until some future date? Was she serious about it staying between the two of us? It would be our first hint of détente. My heart skipped a few beats in excitement. Not that I planned on admitting to anything, but it was a nice moment.

"Did you find anything probative at Lucas's place?" I asked.

She cracked her neck. "Lucas was getting threatening letters from someone."

"Did you find any when you searched the trailer?" I asked.

She looked at me for a moment. "There was one in a secured location."

"In his trailer?"

A nod.

So that's what was in the safe. I wondered where the other letters were. Definitely not his work office. "What did it say?"

"It was not specific. 'I'm coming for you, I'm going to get you, you better leave town,' on a printout. No fingerprints, no DNA, nothing to identify it. Did he say anything to you about any threats?"

"Lucas mentioned something to Violet the morning before his death."

She leaned forward. "What did he say?"

"We never got a chance to talk about it. Tiffanni brained him with her racquet and it all got lost in the shuffle." I rubbed my forehead. "I thought we had time."

"I see."

"Have you investigated Tiffanni Morgan's whereabouts the night of Lucas's murder?"

"I can't comment on that."

"Is she a suspect?"

"Possibly." She sighed. "Mrs. Abercrombie, has it occurred to you that we've had an unusual number of murders on the island since your retirement?"

"No."

"Before this summer, this town hadn't had a murder in eleven years. Yet so far this summer, we've had—"

"I'm not quite sure I see your point, dear," I murmured.

"That these events all took place after you came to live here permanently."

"Actually…" I met her eyes. "They also started after *you* came to live here permanently. You've been here about four months, isn't that so?"

She coughed herself purple. After recovering, she said, "Who was at the clinic with a burn?"

I tried to calculate who was winning our little game. "Are you going to let me see Carlton?"

A muscle in her jaw jumped. "If you tell me who was at the clinic."

"I see. Well, that will all work out nicely."

"And? Who was it?" she said.

"Oh, I'm going to have to insist on seeing Carlton first, dear." The Pickle had squeezed some information out of me last week under false pretences, and I wasn't going to let that happen again.

Her jaw jutted out briefly, then returned to normal. A silence that would have been perfect if there was tea ensued. Then she said, "Alright, Irma. If that's the way you want it."

"Bless your heart, dear. I do."

She grimaced, then motioned for me to follow her.

Twenty-Seven — Violet

After mailing a report to Imogene about what I'd done with the water system and sneaking into the nurse's room to do a round of vertigo exercises, I'd moseyed on down to the patio for what was sure to be a spectacular cup of coffee. While I was waiting, I pulled my phone out and continued the video game I had on pause.

"Violet?"

I looked up. Carlton's business partner, Elsa, was standing beside my table. She had a hand on her waist and was bent over a little. "I was wondering if you wanted company for lunch. Plus, I don't think I can make it to another table." She chuckled.

"Of course." I stopped my game and placed my phone on the table. The colourful pause screen cycled through a few of my best games. It was just *Tetris*, but I'd liked making all those tiny shapes fit together. I'd been cultivating my high score for years now. "How are you? And what are you doing here?"

"Working on preparations for the poker tournament," she said with a rueful shrug.

"Wow, really? When are you due?"

She eased herself into the chair opposite me. "A little less than three weeks. I'll be glad when this baby finally comes out."

"Is it a boy or a girl?"

"It's going to be a surprise," she said with a small smile.

"Well, congrats."

"Thanks."

"Irma told me you're doing this all on your own? You got a donor?"

She nodded, then drank an entire half-litre of water. When she was done, she wiped her mouth with one of the linen napkins. Most of the people from families who "summered" here patted their mouths instead. That was how I realized she hadn't grown up here.

"I'm thirty-eight. I thought it was now or never, you know? I didn't want a lot of kids, so I'm one and done. How about you, you have any?"

"I'm still making up for my own childhood," I said with a grin.

"I hear that. What are you eating?"

"Just getting a cup of coffee. I'm meeting Irma for lunch."

"Oh, that sounds heavenly…" She looked wistful.

"Well, I won't tell anyone you're drinking caffeine if you want some."

She flashed me a smile.

One of the servers came and got her order, which was fish and chips, plus a pitcher of ice water. It was hot out today. Thankfully, our umbrella was giving us excellent coverage, or I'd already be lobsterized from the sun.

"So, what are you going to do about mat leave?" I asked. "I'm always curious about how my business can make things better for new or expecting moms." If I still had a business to go back to…

"I heard about your company, the Solar Shoppe. You install solar roofs, right?"

"And panels. Along with management software and storage solutions, yeah."

"What does that mean, storage solutions?"

"The big problem with renewables is storage. Traditionally, it's been really large and bulky to use batteries, for example. And super expensive. I have a solar array set up on the roof of my condo's building, and a system in my apartment that stores it. Max—that's my business partner—he lives down the hallway from me, and we both run 100% off of solar in our apartments and feed energy back in the grid. We're using a new kind of system, a micro-flywheel, to trap the energy we generate."

"How did you get into a career like that?"

I grinned. "Max and I used to live in a rooming house in Toronto when we were kids. It froze in the winter, and boiled us alive in the summer. We got some second-hand panels from a cousin—" I didn't add that while those panels *had* come from a distant relative of Max's, they'd probably also come off the back of a truck. "And some old air conditioners, a few space heaters. We rented a/c to people at a few rooming houses on our street in the summer, heat in the winter."

"Wow, that's amazing. Beaver Brooke is a green build, you know. Or it's supposed to be." She sighed.

"What do you mean?"

"It's nothing, really." She had some more water. When she saw I wasn't going to give up, she added, "Carlton has never managed a build before. I've been doing this for years. He keeps trying to change our eco-friendly decisions with stuff that's new and shiny. And a lot more harmful to the environment."

"I guess that automated tractor was his call."

She nodded. "It's not the end of the world. It's just that he can be a little…volatile when he doesn't get his way."

"Yeah, I know." I filled her in on what had happened when he was arrested.

Her eyes widened. "Oh, dear."

"When are you guys going to actually start building?"

She made a face. "We were supposed to start the day after the ground-breaking, but we've put everything on hold for at least a week."

"I've been involved in a fair bit of construction work, on the technical side. How much buffer have you built into your time estimates?"

Another face. "Carlton did the timeline. They're very aggressive." She raised a glass in mock salute. "We're hoping to make it up later. Although, now that Carlton has been arrested, it makes things trickier, obviously."

"I'm so sorry."

"Me too." She looked down at the table for a minute, then sighed. "It's ridiculous, obviously, and I know he'll be released from jail soon, but our board of directors is agitated, and so are some of our investors." A flash of irritation crossed her face.

"He looks like he has a temper."

She played with her straw for a moment. "I think we're all just on edge right now. We've been working so hard to get ready for the ground-breaking, and Carlton's been worried about the poker tournament, and…" She shrugged.

"Any chance you have any spare tickets kicking around?"

She pressed her lips together. "No, I'm sorry."

"No problem. Have you known Carlton a long time?"

She shook her head. "Two years or so. Long enough. We're a good team."

I decided not to tell her that Shane and Max and I had been a great team once upon a time. With Carlton in the clink and a baby on the way, Elsa had other things to worry about.

"Maybe we could get your company to do some work at Beaver Brooke," she said.

My spine straightened. "Oh, I'd love that. And right now, we're beta testing an exterior paint that generates energy from moisture and solar power."

"That's fascinating, Violet. Is this being developed in Canada?"

"It's a group of Australians, actually."

"That's wonderful. How far have your tests gone?"

"We have…" I tried to think. "Ten installations in Toronto right now. They're going well. We're still data gathering. Solar paint isn't commercially available yet."

"Wonderful."

"Yeah. I've been poking at Irma to get some solar at her place. Or maybe even the Club."

"Excuse *me*." Standing in the sunlight was Snookie Smith, one of Irma's many nemeses. And the same person she'd banged into with the tractor the other day. Snookie swept the patio with a haughty gaze that made the back of my neck tighten. She looked like she was going to scream at me until I died from it. I tried not to let it bother me. I once worked for a dragon lady who'd seriously tried to cancel Christmas one year. I wasn't afraid of Snookie Smith.

"Where, pray tell, is your partner in crime, Ms. Blackheart?" Snookie said.

I looked around the empty patio. It seemed pretty obvious to me there was nowhere for Irma to hide, so I said nothing.

"Excuse me," Snookie said.

I looked up. "Are you speaking to me?"

She made an irritated noise. "Don't be ridiculous. Of course I am. Where is she?"

I thought about her question for a minute, trying to decide how to answer it. I consulted my internal decision tree. The first step was: *Will anything I'm about to say help the situation*? The answer here was no, but I still wanted to say something, if only to make Snookie stop talking to me and go away.

"I can see you get your manners from Irma," she said tersely.

"I really don't see how that's possible."

Of course, Elsa's food arrived at this exact moment, the scent of beer-swilled fish enveloping us.

"How could you eat something so unhealthy?" Snookie said. "Your baby is going to come out obese."

"Hey, knock it off," I said, my head jerking up.

Elsa's cheeks were turning a mottled pink. And her eyes were getting shiny.

"Look at the two of you," Snookie said. "She's chowing down on fatty foods and you're up to your eyeballs in these stupid video games." She gestured at my phone, the screen blinking out my *Tetris* high scores. "Why are you so childish?"

"Are you talking to me?" I asked.

"Who's the one with the ridiculous video games?"

I patted my mouth with my napkin. It was calming, in a way. Maybe that's why so many islanders did it. "Why are video games more childish than golf or sailing? Or tennis?"

She sputtered. "Those games have a function and purpose."

"Which is?"

"Good health, competitiveness—"

"Any game has competitiveness. And video games improve cognitive functioning, spatial perception, and reaction time as well as short-term and working memory. It improves problem-solving skills and reduces anxiety. Don't people just sit on their little carts most of the time when they're golfing? Why is sitting on a cart better than sitting in a normal chair?" I looked at Elsa. "I mean, they seem the same to me, what do you think?"

"Oh, I agree," she said. It looked like she was trying not to laugh.

I looked at Snookie. "Plus, I normally spend ten, twelve hours a day at the office, six days a week. On Sundays, I sleep. I'm always on call. This is my first vacation in years. And I'm going to spend my vacation doing vacation things. Things I had no time for when I was an actual child, because I had to get my first job when I was ten." I took a sip of ice water. It was spectacular. "What were you doing at ten, Ms. Smith, I wonder?"

Snookie's mouth twisted into an expression that reminded me of a startled blowfish. "I suppose I was doing childish things."

"Well," I said, as if my point was obvious. Which it was.

"Oh, you're insufferable. Take this," she said to Elsa, yanking a pile of papers out of her overstuffed purse.

"O-kaaay," she said.

Snookie took the papers and smacked them onto the table.

Elsa scanned the top sheet. "What?" She looked up, incredulous.

"That's right!" Snookie said with relish. "I'm suing your company. And Irma! Intentional infliction of emotional distress, running an unsafe work site, and just plain old running me over."

I tried not to snicker.

"You have got to be kidding me," Elsa said, looking from Snookie to me.

"I most certainly am not!" she said crisply.

"Snookie, I'm sorry you're upset. I am. But Leblanc Industries is the responsible party. They agree there was a malfunction in the machinery. I'm sure they'd be reasonable if you approached them."

"You're the ones who allowed their equipment to run amok all over me!"

I decided not to comment about my suspicions about the hack. Wrong audience. Plus, until I'd built my own remote and tried to reverse-engineer what had happened, nothing I said was provable.

"I'm very sorry," Elsa repeated. "But if you'd just moved out of the way, you would have been fine."

"Why should I have to do anything? I had every right to be there! Irma Abercrombie is not in charge of where I stand!"

Imogene Flores floated into the patio area like an apparition. "Hellooo!" she trilled. "How are we all doing?"

Snookie wiped the nasty look off her face. "Wonderful, thank you so much, Imogene."

Imogene looked at all of our faces. Elsa was bright pink. I waved hello to Imogene with my spoon.

"Snookie," she said, "remember that golf putter you wanted to look at? It just arrived, and you can try it out before anybody else."

Snookie's smile turned a little more feral. "How wonderful, Imogene. You always take such good care of me." She shot me and Elsa separate venomous glares before stalking off behind Imogene.

Elsa had her hand over her mouth. It took me a minute before I realized she was trying not to laugh.

I snickered. "I mean, good luck finding Irma and serving her with that paperwork."

"Ha!" Elsa said. "I'd like to see that." Then she sighed. "What a mess. I can't take that woman. Carlton's been arrested, buyers are backing out, and Carlton's new 'assistant' is a nightmare."

"I'm sorry," I said. "That all sucks. What's wrong with the assistant?"

"She's a moron. Carlton gave her access to our financial accounts and yesterday she 'accidently' transferred six figures into the wrong account."

"Oh, man!"

"Exactly. It's a disaster. To be frank, I might have to let her go."

"I'm sorry. It's always hard to terminate staff."

She nodded. "I think we should set up a support group for business owners."

"Probably."

"Well, I have to go. It was lovely to see you, Violet."

"Aren't you going to eat?"

"I'll get it boxed up." She motioned to a server, and someone came out and retrieved her plate. After they'd gone, she tried to stand up, and didn't quite make it. She made a face, obviously embarrassed. "Can you give me a hand?"

"You got it." I made my way over to her side of the table.

She started to giggle as I stepped beside her. She turned the chair so she was facing me and held her hands out. But she had to stop because she was laughing so hard. I caught the giggles from her and soon I was bent over laughing.

"So-orry," she managed to get out.

I got ahold of myself. "My fault. Okay, here we go." I held my hands out and pulled her up, ignoring the pain that zinged up my legs when I did.

"Thanks, Violet, I needed a good laugh."

"It's going to be okay."

She pressed her lips together, and for a minute I thought she was going to cry. Thankfully, it passed. She nodded at me, then penguin-walked out of the patio.

TWENTY-EIGHT — IRMA

There were two holding cells in the old-fashioned jail attached to the police station, and the security for both was quite good. The last chief had always asked me to break out of them whenever they did security upgrades. I'd managed to get out of cell number one every time, but cell number two had defeated me on my last attempt, and now that the Pickle was the new sheriff in town, I'd never vanquish it. I tried not to let the thought sour my mood.

Carlton was sitting on his bunk, looking at nothing.

"Carlton, dear." I'd dashed into the break room to conjure up some tea and was feeling much better as I sipped it.

"Irma? What are you doing here?"

I pulled a chair closer to his cell, which had old-fashioned bars running across its face. The station didn't have enough space to host an independent visiting room for inmates. Plus, the cells were usually empty, so there was no point to it. "I thought I'd pop in and see how you were doing, dear. Do you need anything? When are you being arraigned?"

He looked at his phone. "In a few hours."

"I'm not sure if they're going to let you out on bail."

"Oh, they are. Or someone's getting sued. And disbarred. And fired."

"That's quite a lot."

"What would you know about it?" He scowled.

"A thing or two, dear. In any case, I had a few questions for you."

"Sure, why not? I don't have anything else to do."

He sounded so petulant, I almost smiled. Instead, I said, "Isn't that nice. Why did the police want to speak to you yesterday? Before the wrestling match."

"Because Lucas had some of my DNA on him when he died."

"Huh. I'm surprised the dirt from the flowerbed didn't displace it. Did they tell you what kind?"

"What kind of what?"

"DNA. Skin under his fingernails, saliva—"

"They didn't say, but I think it was hair. They took a bunch of samples."

"I see. Had you seen Lucas the day of his death?"

"No."

Interesting. I could understand why the Pickle had wanted to speak to Carlton.

"Why do you care about any of this, anyway?"

"I've been thinking about that penthouse..." This was actually true. I'd been thinking about how Lucas had backed out of his penthouse purchase just as construction was about to start, and right before he was murdered. Had his desire to cut and run angered Carlton so much he killed him in a rage? And was fear of that rage the reason David and Rose had so recently skedaddled? "And I'm a bit concerned about buying into an organization that has any...stigma attached to it. It's not every day one is questioned for murder—"

"Manslaughter."

Manslaughter, around these parts, was a crime of passion. So they didn't think he'd planned it. "What's your motive?"

"Irma, honestly, I *have* no motive. I hardly even knew the guy. Elsa dealt with him mostly."

I thought about Lucas's schedule the night of his death: a nine o'clock lesson with Rose. It was late, for tennis, but I'd kept the courts open far later than that at times. Especially if I was winning. One time, I even—

Focus, Irma. "Why did Rose have a tennis lesson at nine on the night of Lucas's murder?"

He looked momentarily surprised. "She has a crazy schedule sometimes, and both of us like to grab exercise when we can. She didn't say anything about it to me."

"What are the police *saying* your motive is?" I said.

He made an exasperated noise. "They think I was jealous because Rose was having an affair with Lucas. That I killed him when I found out about it."

"Oh, dear." I remembered the hitch in Carlton's voice during our conversation about Lucas and Rose when we were sitting on my dock. And Snookie's gossip about Rose's extracurricular activities. "Was she?"

"Not to my knowledge." He glanced down as he said it, then met my eyes. He looked like he'd been telling the truth, but *Not to my knowledge* was the kind of slippery thing people said when they were dabbling in fabrications. The last person I'd interrogated who'd coughed up that exact phrase practically had his pants on fire.

And what if Rose and Lucas *had* been having an affair? What if *she'd* killed Lucas, and was framing Carlton for her misdeeds? There might have been evidence from their trysts in Lucas's

Airstream. Burning it to a crisp would fix that problem right up.

"Irma," he said, "I did not kill Lucas."

I gave him a look.

"I'm a businessman. I live my life behind a desk. And killing Lucas just wouldn't have gotten me anywhere."

He sounded sincere. Then his apology from the other day rolled around in my head. At least he could do that much, say he was sorry. He wasn't a terrible person. Spoiled, definitely. Lazy, absolutely. If I'd had to work with him, I would have cut his brake lines years ago, probably. But it was a giant step from being a spoiled layabout to murdering someone in cold blood and popping them into a shallow grave.

"Where were you the night of Lucas's death?" I asked.

He looked down. "I… I went for a walk over at Frenchman's Bay, on the other side of the island. My dad and I used to go there together. Sometimes I can't sleep before big events, like the ground-breaking. I wanted to blow off some steam before bed. I got home at two in the morning. Rose was already asleep."

So he had no alibi. Lucas had died around midnight. Lots of time for Carlton to bump him off, bury him, and go nighty-night back at home. Then I thought about the red streak of paint on

David's bumper. Carlton had a big bright red Hummer, and he'd left the wake before David. What if he was waiting for him? David had been on his way out of town because he was worried about something. What if he thought someone was after him? But Carlton had been locked up last night. He couldn't have set fire to Lucas's Airstream. Unless he hired someone to do his dirty work, or had a partner in crime, or someone else had been after Lucas…

"Irma, hellooooo," Carlton said.

"Senior moment, dear. I'm just trying to see how this all fits together."

"Why?"

"I like to make sure my investments are as risk-free as possible. At my age…" I trailed off to make it seem I was worried about my mortality. I could see the struggle on his face. Part of him, the smiley salesperson part, wanted to believe me. I decided to try another tack. "Carlton, where is Rose?"

"I think she went to her Aunt Adeline's. We had a fight."

"When?"

"The night of Lucas's wake."

"What about?"

He rested his head on the wall behind him for a moment, but said nothing. He looked suddenly exhausted.

"Why did you come and see me at the clinic yesterday?" I asked, when it was clear he wasn't going to answer my last question.

"I wasn't there to see you; I needed to get a prescription renewed. I just stuck my head in your room because I wanted to ask you if you'd spoken to Rose."

"I tried to reach her, but her phone's not working."

"She's been having problems with it lately. Battery issues. I keep telling her to get it fixed." He ran his hand through his hair in a frustrated motion.

"I see." And then I wondered: What if all this was a setup, and Rose had wanted to shed herself of her newly acquired bratty husband, but not his assets? Word was, the Campbell family trust could be described with all the important *s* words: *significant, substantial. Solvent.* Rose might not know Carlton could be close to broke, personally speaking. But the trust was a whole other issue. I couldn't imagine the Campbell family would want a disgruntled former Mrs. bad-mouthing Carlton. Rose was strong enough to dig a shallow grave. And shooting someone in close quarters took almost no skill at all.

But, still, I could see why the Pickle had snatched up Carlton. The story worked: he had motive, means, opportunity, no alibi, and there was physical evidence. Jealousy was a wonderful motive for murder. Juries really loved it. I wasn't loving the runaway tractor, however, although it was hard to argue with a company that claimed its equipment had malfunctioned due to a faulty design. Recalls happened all the time for vehicles. The tractor malfunction might be meaningless. I tried to smoosh it all together so it fit. It was close, I had to admit.

"Carlton, does Rose know you've been arrested?"

"No. I haven't been able to reach her either. It's driving me crazy."

A chill ran up my back. Was he telling the truth, or had he done away with Lucas...and Rose?

"How did you get along with David Bell, dear?"

He looked down at his hands, played with his wedding ring. It was nice of Mavis to let him keep it.

"I fired him a few days before the ground-breaking," he said finally.

"Why on earth was he working at the ground-breaking if you'd fired him?"

"I hired him back just to run the demonstration. I paid him a one-time fee to do it."

"Good heavens, why?"

He looked down. "I thought I could find a replacement in time, but I couldn't."

"But why did you fire him?"

"He kept on trying to push different equipment decisions down my throat." He looked up. "And it's *my* company."

"What kind of decis—"

"All of them. He was upset we were going with some slightly less eco-friendly materials. *Slightly.* And he got Elsa all worked up about it. She's an eco nut, you know. Plus, David hates any kind of automated equipment. I could barely make a decision without him telling me it was wrong."

"I'm pretty sure all that is an engineer's job, dear."

He shrugged.

I could tell there was more to his story, but he'd jammed his lips closed now. I wondered where David was and hoped he hadn't walked out of the hospital with a slow brain bleed. Missing, I could handle, from a procuring evidence perspective. Dead was much harder to work with. "Alright, dear. Do you need anything?"

"No, I'm okay. Maybe something to read." He swallowed. "If you talk to Rose, can you tell her to call me, please? I'm worried about her."

"Of course." I took a moment to pass him a protein-bran muffin through the bars to help fortify him through his incarceration. He did not look thrilled, even though I'd had to sacrifice one so Maurice could "verify it didn't have a file in it." I decided not to lecture Carlton on the health of his colon. He had enough to deal with right now.

I replaced the chair back where I'd found it, and was buzzed through all the security and found myself back in Reception before I could blink.

"Can you please make sure Carlton has something to read, dear?"

Maurice nodded and shot me a jaunty salute.

I placed a few calls from Maurice's phone and pinpointed Tiffanni Morgan's location. On to the next suspect.

I ran into Ronnie Thomas on my way out of the police station, and we took a seat under the shade of a lovely lilac tree my father had planted when he was a child.

"So, what's new?" I asked her.

Ronnie wore her regular reporter uniform: jeans, a t-shirt and blazer, with shoes that were excellent for running after people in. Today, her long braids were caught up in an impressively large bun secured to the top of her head.

She smiled. “I’ve been digging around Carlton’s life a bit. Did you know he was expelled from Upper Canada College when he was a teenager?”

UCC was a fancy-pants private school in Toronto. “So they sent him away when he was a child?”

She nodded. “His father was very controlling, from what I’ve heard.”

“Have you found anything more about Carlton’s finances?”

She shook her head. “I’ve been focusing on his earlier life. Well, and his company. It’s been up and running for two years, and this is their first actual project. They got the contract because they pitched it as a green build. But from what I hear, Carlton has been overriding all the actual eco-friendly parts of the project.”

“Oh, he’ll tell you that himself.”

“Did you speak with him?”

I nodded.

“Did he tell you anything?”

“That was it, pretty much. I’ve always gotten the impression he wants everything his own way.”

She made a noise of agreement. “Well, the company’s definitely on his side. Apparently, one of the board members tried to put Elsa in charge a while back, but the rest of the board ruled against it. Morons. She has an extensive résumé in green building, and she's done a lot of volunteer work at the communal garden near Raleigh Pier."

"I wouldn't mind hearing more about that. Which board member?"

She shook her head. "Don't know for sure. I got the lead a while back from the assistant who did the minutes for one of the meetings, but she finished her contract and left town a few months ago."

"That's a bother."

She nodded. "Yup. I'm going to try to speak to Carlton. Wish me luck."

"Good luck, dear. And please let me know if you find anything else."

"Will do."

I walked from the police station to one of the local pubs, looking at the splendour of Main Street as I went. And scanning to see if anyone was following me. The planters were overstuffed with purple and pink Peonies and some Baltic Ivy, the storefronts were polished and pretty, and the sidewalks were wide enough to park an aircraft carrier in them. A plethora of Beaver decorations celebrating the Club's regatta hung from gas lamp posts and were pressed into window fronts. My personal favourite was the bucktoothed beaver perched on a wooden boat in the front window of the music store, a telescope glued to his left eye. I stopped to admire it, then checked the reflection in the store's windows to see if anyone was lingering behind me.

Everything looked clear. I kept going.

In front of Mandy's pub, I paused. Tiffanni was sitting at a table, playing with an oversized straw that had been harpooned into a gigantic margarita glass. I personally did not approve of overly-large tequila servings before five p.m., but perhaps this would make things easier for all of us.

I made my way through the patio and pulled out the chair across from her before settling myself in it. Tiffanni's mouth hung open for so long, I considered, but then rejected, making a comment about it.

"Good afternoon, dear," I said.

"Uh, yeah," she answered. After looking at me for a moment, she stuck the straw in her mouth and sucked on it lustily.

One of the servers came by. I signalled that I wanted my usual, and they disappeared into the kitchen.

"Mrs. Abercrombie," Tiffanni said. Her eyes, behind her expensive sunglasses, looked like they might be red.

"Tiffanni," I said pleasantly.

"Is there something I can do for you?"

"Yes," I said. "But I'd also like to get some food into you. What is that you're drinking?"

"Nothin'," she mumbled around the straw in her mouth.

I leaned over and picked up her glass.

"Hey!"

I sniffed. Tequila, alright. I put it back in front of her. "Tiffanni, is this really how you want to spend your life?"

"Maybe," she said sulkily.

"How old are you, dear?" I asked, carefully placing my handbag on the empty seat beside me.

"Twenty-six."

Twenty-six. What a year I had when I was twenty-six. What a great age.

"Almost twenty-seven," she added.

"Almost thirty," I observed.

Her face blanched in horror. "Nonono, I'm still in my mid-twenties."

"Is twenty-seven mid-twenties?" I asked, my head on a tilt. Tiffanni had that bland young person's attractiveness. Everything was still where it was supposed to be, her skin was unlined, her lips plump. She didn't appear to have had any work done, although, at her age, why would she? But there was a contingent of women on the island, I'd heard, who started

Botox in their late twenties to make sure they never produced wrinkles in the first place, which was about as horrible of an idea as I'd ever heard. How could you possibly tell what juicy tidbit someone was hiding if it didn't show on their face? It was probably a good thing I'd retired. Nobody enjoyed being double-crossed by a Botox-addled foreign asset.

"I'm only twenty-six!" Tiffanni wailed.

"There, there," I said. She'd pulled her head down so she was looking in her lap. And then her hands moved.

"Good heavens," I said. "What on earth are you doing down there?"

She didn't look up. "Texting a friend to come and get me."

Ah. She was playing with her phone. "I see. I'm getting a ride home from Violet. I'd be glad to drop you off wherever you're going."

"No, that's okay." She wiped her nose on the back of her hand. It was an almost endearing gesture, like she was a little child.

She wasn't, of course.

"Tiffanni, I don't know if you knew this or not, but Lucas and I were friends."

She said nothing.

"I was at the Club the other day."

Still nothing. It was almost impressive.

"And I saw your argument."

Her head jerked up, and her eyes found mine. She pulled her sunglasses off her face. Her eyes were red.

"What was it about?"

"Nothing."

I thought about my options. We were in public, on a patio on the town's main street. Islanders and visitors were all over the place. Plus, my back was to the street, which I just hated. It was an impossible position. There was no way I could stick a knife in Tiffanni's gizzard and tell her to spill the beans. I tried to think about what I could use to threaten her. Things were so much easier in the twentieth century, when people still cared about their reputations. I stifled a sigh.

"I'm quite sure it was something," I said. "His family wants to know what happened to him, obviously."

She looked a little pale under all that makeup.

"He had a life, you know. And I'd like to know who took that life away from him."

"This literally has nothing to do with you."

"This is my town. Everything in it has something to do with me."

"Well, I can't help you. And I have to go."

I sat back in my chair. Then shrugged. One of the servers brought me a pot of tea, and I thanked him. "That's fine, Tiffanni."

"Okay." She started gathering her belongings and stood.

"Except..."

She stopped. "What?"

"Well, obviously the Club can't have members who create scenes like the one you did the other day. The Club is an oasis, a refuge from our troubles. We can't have it cluttered up with screaming almost-thirty-year-olds. But you have a lovely day, dear."

She sat back down in her chair abruptly.

I let some silence engulf us as I blew on my tea. They steeped it here just the way I liked it. Delicious.

"I mean...would they kick me out? My mom would kill me."

"I don't know," I said with a shrug. "I don't have anything to do with membership." This was actually true. Plus, everybody at the Club loved scenes; they gave them something to talk about. But Tiffanni probably didn't know that.

I took my first sip. Wonderful stuff. Then I looked across the table. Tiffanni wasn't a bad sort, at the end of the day. She was spoiled and overindulged and unless she got that sorted out, she was going to have a rotten life, from my perspective. But I'd seen a lot of spoiled people in my day. Those of us who had to police the globe with some stealth and a bit of smarts had seen it all, really. I'd take a Tiffanni over a megalomaniac dictator any day of the week. So much easier to crush her spirit.

"It was nothing," she said all of a sudden, like the words were going to explode out of her.

"I'm sure the membership committee will believe you," I said. "Have a lovely day, dear." At this point, I kind of *did* want her to leave. I really wanted her seat. Someone was going to bump me off if I stayed exposed like this.

"He cancelled my lessons," she blurted out.

"You smashed your tennis racquet into pieces in public because someone cancelled a lesson?" I repeated back to her, my inflection totally flat. It usually did the trick.

"I wanted to show my…someone. I wanted to show someone how much better I'd gotten at tennis this summer."

"And you couldn't, because *one* lesson was cancelled?"

She bit her lower left lip like she was thinking deeply about my question. I'd bet good money she'd tried that particular expression out in the mirror a few times.

"No. It was…" She looked down in her lap again.

I truly hoped she wasn't going to start wiggling her fingers around her nether regions again.

"It was my dad," she said softly. "He's coming at the end of the summer. He is. He said he is," she repeated, more to herself than me.

I frowned. "If he's not coming until the end of the summer, why would one cancelled lesson now be a problem? It's mid-June, for heaven's sake."

"Lucas didn't cancel one lesson." She took a breath. "He cancelled all of them."

I was paying attention now. "Did he say why?"

"No."

"I see." I put my teacup down carefully. I suspected that Lucas had actually cancelled their lessons because she was so volatile, and he wanted to be rid of her. "Tiffanni, why did you want Lucas's personal belongings? What did he have of yours?"

Pink flushed her cheeks. She looked down in her lap again.

"Tiffanni?" I prodded.

"There were some…" She looked around, "pictures of me."

"Pictures? Real actual photographs?"

"Polaroids."

I'd heard they were making a comeback, which made sense. No digital trail. "Did Lucas take them?"

"No. I…had a crush on him. I put some pictures in his desk." She looked away.

"When?"

"A few days before he died. I just wanted them back."

"Did he cancel your lessons before or after you put the pictures in his desk?"

"After."

I sighed. "Do you see a connection there at all, dear?"

She was looking in her lap again. "Maybe."

"Well, I understand you were upset, but there's no reason to be yelling at people in public like that, young lady."

A few tears rolled down one cheek, but I wasn't impressed. I'd known a lot of people who could make themselves cry on demand, myself included.

"I just...I get angry. And adulting is hard."

"I see. Well, some cognitive behavioural therapy will fix you right up. Nobody likes thirty-somethings who run around yelling all the time."

"I'm not thirty yet!"

"So you have lots of time to sort it all out before you *are* thirty, correct?" I gave her a dark look. She flinched. "An apology to Imogene would be a lovely start."

She mumbled an *okay*.

"Where were you the night Lucas died?"

"At home, with some friends, watching Netflix. And my mom was there."

"So they'd all tell me the same thing?"

She nodded, and when a horn sounded outside the patio, started assembling her belongings. "Well, Mrs. Abercrombie—"

"Irma, please."

"Irma." She flashed me a tentative smile. "I'm gonna go live my best life, I guess. I'll see you later."

"Looking forward to it, dear."

She vacated her seat with a little wave and a flounce. I tipped the cup into my mouth and emptied it. Excellent.

I watched her leave. I wasn't sure she was telling the truth, but then again, I always thought everyone was lying. Tiffanni seemed about as dangerous as a castrated beagle, but sometimes people put on that kind of persona so they could trick nice little old ladies like me. I noodled on that for a bit, and decided I believed her. Probably.

And then a hairy hand grabbed my shoulder.

Twenty-Nine — Violet

After Imogene cleared out Snookie and Elsa fled home for a nap, I called Max.

"Where are you?" he asked.

"You wouldn't believe me if I told you."

He laughed. "It sounds like you're having a very strange vacation."

"Yeah, pretty much. How's the office? How's everyone doing?"

"They all miss you desperately."

That felt nice. We had forty-three employees, a combination of eco-nerds and ordinary nerds, and everyone believed in our company and what we were doing. I missed it.

But I didn't miss the long days. I didn't miss not being by the water. I almost slapped a hand over my mouth. Irma must be piping hypnosis tapes into my apartment when I was sleeping.

"Well, I miss you."

"Ditto," he replied. He had a tendency of not saying big, important things, which had never bothered me. "I put your mail on your coffee table yesterday."

"Thanks," I said. "Have you thought any more about going to Shane's family at all?"

"Yeah, I think we should do it."

"Okay. Do you know where they are right now?"

There was a pause. "No."

"I want to talk to his mother." Max and I had once had dinner at Shane's parents' mansion in the Bridlepath, an über fancy-pants area of Toronto. She'd been a waifishly thin socialite who'd almost had a heart attack when I sat on her Mies van der Rohe chair without written permission.

"The mother is in St. Bart's right now. It's all over her Instagram."

I muttered a word I was pretty sure Shane's mother wouldn't like. "Do you know when she's coming back?"

"I'm not clocking her movements, Vi."

"What about the father?" He was the one who actually helmed the family business, a financial services company that boasted some very well-known names. A *conservative* financial services company.

"Yeah…that's a thought. I prefer the mom, though."

"That's because you have a baby face that always works on older women."

"It's a gift."

"I prefer the mother, too, but we can only wait so long before—"

"Yeah, I know. But how can we figure out when the mother's coming back?"

I paced a little. Then I thought about Snookie's nasty treatment of pretty much everyone she came in contact with. "Bribe the maid!" I said. There had to be people in that massive mansion who resented Shane's family, just like I was sure all Snookie's staff, if she had any, despised her. All we had to do was find them.

"That's a not-bad idea," he said.

"I know," I said modestly. A small part of me worried that Irma was rubbing off on me in ways I wouldn't be able to figure out for a long time. The rest of me was thrilled.

"Okay, I'm on it," he said, and hung up the phone. For Max, *hello* and *goodbye* were generally extraneous words.

I texted him: *And I still want you to come to the island next week.*

I'm not so sure about your island.

Then I brought out the big guns: *Mr. Marceau is making dinner and I want you to come with me.*

I'll be there.

I smiled, then finished my drink and thought about our money. After I finished my last gulp and paid the bill, I glanced over at the poster on the wall on the way out. *Smile-a-Thon Poker Tournament*, it said. *Fifty thousand-dollar purse.*

I could feel my head moving to a tilt just like Irma's, and I had to pull it back to an upright position. My phone binged with a text: *It is I, Irma! Come meet me at Mandy's pub for lunch!*

I texted her back, then pulled up the town's community forum and checked on my thread about needing tickets to the poker tournament. And then I smiled.

THIRTY — IRMA

I waited for Violet to finish up at the Club while sipping on an ice-cold beer. With Boris. The hairy, but not unpleasantly so, hand that had descended on my shoulder had been his. We'd had a nice laugh about how he was lucky to still have it. Then I'd taken Tiffanni's deserted seat and pressed my back against the wall so I could see everyone coming and going, and there would be no more grabbing of Irma today.

"You look lovely," he said for the second time. My eyes narrowed. In the world of espionage, repetition could be used for all sorts of nefarious goals. Which meant that Boris was either trying to kill me, or snog me. It was a tossup. But there was a part of me, and not a small part, that was curious about where things might go with Boris, if they ever actually got going.

"Thank you," I said. Mother had taught me to accept compliments when they came, even if they were being used to distract you from a deadly threat of some kind.

I tried to keep my eyes on Boris's face so I wasn't blinded from his Hawaiian shirt. Today's was hula girls and surfboards. If we ever did become a couple, I'd obviously burn all of them in a fire. Not close to the house, because the toxic chemicals would kill my plants, but it would be done. My mind flashed to the state of my flowerbeds, which I was supposed to be tending in my retirement, and which I'd completely ignored thus far. Drat.

"Howdy!" Violet plopped into a seat beside me.

"You remember Boris," I said.

"Of course." She smiled at him and shook his hand. "Great shirt."

"Thank you," he said modestly.

Well, there went my plan to have Violet help me with the bonfire.

Then Violet ran me through Snookie's vile behaviour at the Club. But when she came to the lawsuit part, my mood soured. "You didn't have any ragweed on you at the time, did you?"

"What?" Violet said.

"Nothing."

"This is a friend of yours?" Boris asked.

The waitress came and we all ordered: Violet, a burger and fries, Boris, the steak, and I had soup and a salad. I tried not to think about their cholesterol numbers.

"No," I said after she was gone. "She and I have been having a feud since the seventies." I sat back in my chair. "There was an issue with a tractor at the ground-breaking the other day. I tried to stop it, but…well, I ran into her."

His eyebrows sprung up to his hairline. "With a tractor?"

"Just a little."

"And not on purpose," he stated.

"That's correct. Trust me, if I ever really run Snookie over, all you'll see will be tire tracks on her caboose."

"I believe you," Violet said, at the same time Boris smiled.

Our food was deposited with a bit of fanfare, and we all dug in. I was having gazpacho, and it looked beautiful. My salad was full of local farm-fresh veggies and a homemade dressing I'd bribed the chef for a while back, it was so good. Today it all tasted like ash and cinders.

Violet finished first. It was a bit astonishing, really, how fast she could chew. I was suspicious that when she was a child she hadn't had enough to eat. The thought sat sourly in my chest. Why hadn't her parents taken better care of her? Why were people so awful?

"I have good news and bad news," Violet said.

"Oh, good. I needed some more bad news," I said in a flat voice.

Violet gave me an inquiring look and I waved it off.

"So, good news, Irma. I got a response from a posting I made about the poker game on the town website's forum."

"Oh, how wonderful!" Things were looking up.

"Yeah..." She took a sip. "Only one ticket is available, though."

Things were looking down.

"What is this?" Boris asked.

I caught him up on the Smile-a-Thon fundraiser being held tomorrow night. Naturally, he already had tickets. This information did not help my mood.

"It's just..." Violet looked down. "I know you really want to go, but I didn't realize the purse was so large. I was thinking that maybe I'd play."

"That sounds wonderful, dear," I said. I was thrilled for her, but disappointed in myself. Not only had I failed to secure tickets for both of us, I'd completely missed the fact that Violet actually wanted to participate in the tournament. And I'd bet my fanny she was agonized over it. She hated groups and strangers and especially groups of strangers. If she wanted to brave all that to compete, she must be more wound up about the money that had been stolen from her company than I'd realized. Bloody hell.

"I'm just so sorry I couldn't get two tickets, Irma..."

"Don't be sorry, dear. This is perfect. I'm happy for you. How are you going to manage the buy-in?"

Violet's smile was beautiful. "Charlotte van Oot is sponsoring me. She's a big supporter of the Smile Society. I guess they provide free dental care to needy kids, or something? Anyway, the person giving up their ticket already had Charlotte on board. When they realized they couldn't make it, they called her to make sure it was okay."

"How lovely," I said, a tug in my chest. Charlotte was a very old friend of mine, who'd been recently embroiled in an unpleasant family brouhaha, the poor thing.

"Have you spoken to her lately?" Violet asked.

"A few days ago. I'm going by her place for lunch next week."

"Oh, good," Violet said, smiling. "Please tell her I say hi. In any case, everything's perfect except for one thing."

"Which is...?" I asked.

"I can't really play poker."

We all chuckled at that. Then Boris touched his mouth with his napkin and set it on the table. "I have another appointment now, ladies, I'm sorry I have to leave you. Irma, I'll call you about that sail we talked about?"

"That sounds lovely." When he moved in to kiss my cheek, I breathed in his cologne. He put on his hat, nodded, and took his leave of us, fiddling with his cellular telephone as he went. It was possible I watched him go with a bit more attention than I usually would when a friend was departing.

"He's got the hots for you," Violet said, playing with her straw.

"Soft drinks really are terrible for your digestive system, Violet."

"I know," she said with a wicked smile. "That's why they're so delicious. So, the question is: Do you have the hots for *him*?"

"I don't know," I said, looking into my drink. I shouldn't have another. I pushed it away.

"Gonna find out?" she said cheekily.

The server deposited the cheque with a smile. Violet reached out to pick it up. "You always pay," she said, with a touch of reproach. After scanning the piece of paper, she said. "This is a receipt, not a bill."

"Oh?"

"Yes," she said. "Boris must have paid for lunch."

"How on earth? He just got up and left. He didn't pay anyone."

"He was doing something on his phone when he was walking out. I think he was paying."

"I see." Poor Violet. She would never have lasted in the field. Then I kicked myself again for not realizing she wanted to play at the tournament. But I hadn't, just like I hadn't gotten any information out of Tate or figured out who was behind Lucas's death, and all the other recent unfortunate Beaver Island happenings. Tiffanni was harmless, if annoying. Carlton was probably guilty of something, if not everything, but I had no proof of any of that either. Was Rose really missing? Was David? Were Rose and David missing *together*? It was impossible to know. Plus, I was getting sued. By Snookie, who might actually have a case.

It was not a good moment, and my lunch felt bitter in my stomach. I'd failed at my job; protecting the islanders. I wasn't even being a good host! I should have liberated Violet's money from Shane O'Meara ages ago.

Not only that, the killer would probably be at the tournament tomorrow. And Violet was going to go in without backup. It was all a complete disaster.

Thirty-One — Irma

The next morning, I slept in and eventually made myself tea on the back deck.

"Hey!" Violet called from her balcony. She held a cup of coffee aloft, and yet another computer in her other hand.

"Come down, dear!"

"Okey dokey." She shuffled back into the house and a few minutes later popped out the back door, still holding her coffee. After she sat down beside me, her eyes instantly went to the lake in front of us; blue and glittery, waves rolling to the shoreline. I loved that sound.

"Looking forward to tonight?"

"Sure am," she said with a surprising amount of enthusiasm, considering how leaving the house usually filled her with dread. "I've been studying the technical specifications of Carlton's boat. Here, take a look." She pulled up a schematic diagram of the Campbell family yacht, *The Citadel IV*, on her ever-present laptop, and pointed the screen at me. "Do you know how much horsepower this thing has? Do you see the guest cabins? Aren't they nuts? Look at this one—there's a bathtub hidden *under* the foot of the bed. Isn't that neat? I really want to take a look at the engine room. Do you think they'll show me?"

I glanced over the plans. Carlton's yacht was a bit of a behemoth, but I supposed the design was interesting. I preferred smaller boats, obviously, although I liked the misdirection of that bathtub.

"Yes, I'm sure they will." I took a sip of tea. Perfection. "They often indulge the winner of the poker tournament."

She sighed. "Yeah…I doubt I'll get past the first round."

"Nonsense. I'm sure you're a superlative poker player."

"Poker is about playing the person opposite you, Irma."

"Certainly. But I can give you some tips in that area."

"This isn't blackjack, it's poker. I don't think it's the same. You have to calculate the odds of people having particular cards, and all that jazz."

"What's 31,200 divided by seventy-eight?"

She blinked. "Four hundred."

"So you see my point, dear."

There was a pause. "I've never really thought about it like that. I mean, I've always used my nerdy powers for good."

"Fifty thousand dollars will do you and your business a lot of good."

"Yeah, you're right." Another sip of coffee. "After all this is done, you have to promise me something."

"Anything."

"I want a day where we play video games."

I held up a hand. "You can play all the video games you like, dear. I won't say a word."

"Uh-huh. I'd totally believe you, except I don't. But I want *us* to play video games, not just me."

"I see." I swallowed heavily. "Alright. But don't forget we're going sailing with Stu this week."

"No problemo."

"Sure," I said easily.

She narrowed her eyes, but graciously pretended to believe me. "What are you going to be doing while I'm playing at the tournament?"

"I'm going to be skulking around the boat."

"Uh-huh. I thought you didn't have a ticket."

"Not yet." I tried not to feel glum about it. I had a few irons in the fire. And if worst came to worst, I'd just make an amphibious approach, and become a stowaway. Wouldn't be the first time. I was very fond of those suction cups my friend had given me. One of my favourite birthday presents of all time. "Do you have to go pick up your ticket? You can use the MG."

She looked like she almost felt sorry for me. "The ticket is digital."

"Of course," I said smoothly.

"I'm sorry you can't come, Irma. It sounds like it's going to be a nice party."

"Well, I'm feeling all partied out right now, dear. I really just want to look around a little. And I'm...worried about Rose. The only place I can think she might be is on board Carlton's boat." No reason to make Violet nervous about my suspicions concerning Rose and pretty much everybody else.

"Right. Do you know what everyone will be wearing tonight? I don't think I've got anything that'll work. Everyone has seen my one black dress a million times."

"I can get Lucy to send something over." Lucy had a design boutique in town and carried wonderful clothes.

"Thanks, Irma," she said, looking relieved.

"You're very welcome, dear. Should we practice a few hands of poker? I can give you some tips."

"Sure."

So we spent the rest of the afternoon with me coaching Violet about reading the expression of the person across from her. I included tips I'd learned in my espionage training, some wisdom from Mother, and a few tidbits I'd read in *Cosmo* back in the day.

"I think you're all set," I said finally.

"I think you're a little insane," she replied. She'd wilted a bit over the afternoon, so we'd taken ourselves inside and sat in the formal dining room. It was vampiricly dark in there, so I wasn't sure why she wasn't peppier.

"Everyone is a bit mad, dear. I simply choose to embrace it."

"Most of my friends are pretty normal."

"I highly doubt that!" I said. "When you try on the outfit, let me know if we need to hem anything."

"Yeah, no problem." She bounded upstairs, and I returned to my flat to work on my own plans for the evening.

An hour later, Violet shouted down the stairs, "Could you come up here, please?"

I took them two at a time, as was my way. My knee felt a bit tweaked afterward, and I had to remind myself to slow down a bit. Violet's outfit was delightful: a pale pink halter top and matching swishy, wide-legged pants, with a lightweight pink wrap.

"Is this okay?"

"You look beautiful, dear."

"Thanks, Irma." She took a sip from a wineglass on the counter. "What are you wearing?"

I looked down. I had on a dressy black pantsuit that was impervious to stains, liquids, and incendiary devices—a knee brace on under the pants, naturally—and a pair of tennis shoes that I planned on taking off when I got on board. I'd spent a while moping around my flat and had eventually reached out to Boris. He'd agreed to my plan, rather quickly, actually. I was beginning to wonder if he was as restless in retirement as I was. I'd also reached out to Stu. Both were in.

"Oh, I managed to get a ticket for tonight," I said airily. "Isn't that nice?"

Violet nodded her agreement and poured me a glass of wine, an excellent Chablis. The night was off to a perfect start.

THIRTY-TWO — VIOLET

The outfit Irma had acquired for me was gorgeous: summery, beautifully made, perfect ballerina pink. I actually loved pink. I didn't advertise that fact a lot, but it was the truth. My all-black, monochromatic wardrobe was simply easier to navigate on a day-to-day basis. When all your clothes were the same colour, everything matched. It was science.

The pants had been too long when I tried them on, but Irma had rolled the hems up and secured them. And she only stabbed me with a pin that one time.

"Ready?" Irma said. She'd seemed like someone had stuck a pin in *her* yesterday, but now she looked like her usual chipper self. Her chipper, about-to-start-an-Ironman-competition self. I picked up the tiny purse she'd loaned me. It went perfectly with the outfit, but had no room for anything. I shoved in some lipstick and my phone.

"You look lovely, dear," she said. In these rare moments where she acted like a normal older person, I thought about how it might have been nice to grow up with Irma as an aunt. I couldn't count how many of my boyfriends she would have shot—probably all of them—but it would have been good to have someone on my side when I was young.

"So do you. How are we getting there?"

"Boris is driving you. I'm going to come along a little later."

"What? Why?"

"I have to meet with Stu before I go."

"Oh, okay. See you there?" I said. Irma nodded sweetly, but I couldn't help thinking she was up to something.

The yacht was unbelievable; a hundred feet long, beautifully designed, opulently furnished, with polished wood everywhere, a hot tub on one of the aft decks. The main salon on the upper level—the boat had three floors—had been converted into a poker saloon, with five tables. That was a lot of card sharks. I was starting to feel like I'd made a huge mistake. This was stupid. I hadn't played poker in years.

Then I realized the club soda I'd been drinking had spilled down my front, and I grabbed the little cocktail napkin that had come with the drink to mop it up. This was *also* why I always wore black. I dabbed at my cleavage and tried to look like I wasn't embarrassed. Normal people spilled things all the time, I told myself, looking around the room.

Everyone was dressed to a T—the men in expensive-looking suits, the women in dresses. Most of the women were barefoot. I was happy Irma had gotten me this outfit. It was dressy, but practical. Practical, from Irma's perspective, was: *It'll be easier for you to run away from murderous villains in pants.* Wise words. Didn't make me want to puke at all.

"I'm excited to see you play." Geraldine broke off from the crowd and sat down beside me. She swirled a mixed drink in its glass and took a dainty sip. "Irma says you're quite something."

"I'm just okay," I said. "I'm thinking I'll go out in the first round." *No, it'll be fine,* I told myself. *Just play the game, enjoy the booze after you lose, and spend some time looking at the full moon from the deck of a megayacht. The end.*

She smiled kindly. "At least all the money is going to charity."

"Yeah."

"Except the purse, obviously."

A warmth moved through my stomach when I thought about all those zeros.

The head dealer called us to our tables and Geraldine wished me luck before slipping away to meet up with friends. I looked around for Irma and Boris. Most likely she was creeping around downstairs, trying to find Rose.

I found table number one—which felt fortuitous—and settled in. There were four other players at the table, all men. They ranged in age from early twenties to early eighties.

"Evening," the elderly man across from me said, an American accent threaded through his speech. He had a full head of white hair that was styled nattily, a well-cut blue suit, and sharp brown eyes. He had a look on his face I couldn't quite place. But he reminded me of a possum. He was probably an excellent player who was used to being underestimated. I grinned back at him, showing all my teeth. It wasn't quite the wolfish smile Irma'd coached me on, but I did my best.

The twenty-something guy to my right seemed like he was closer to thirteen. "Don't worry," he said, leaning close to me while he adjusted his cuff link. "I like older chicks."

I shuddered.

The dealer announced Texas Hold'em, shuffled, burned the first card, and dealt the two hole cards.

So we started to play.

I had a pretty weak first hand. Same with the second. I bet low and tried to suss out the other players, using the tips Irma had given me, the ones that made me feel like my brain was going to explode. The possum was on to me, the Gen-Zer was leering but didn't look like he was interested in me specifically, more like he was just trying to get some practice at being a pervert. The other men were silent.

But it felt like there was energy in the room, like something important was happening. In near-silence. This was what I liked about serious poker. The thinking/silent part. The leering, I could do without.

On my next hand, after the turn, I finally had something: three kings. Spades and clubs in my hand, hearts on the table.

The dealer was a woman in her sixties and looked like she'd been through three wars with a baby wrapped under each arm. I wondered if she knew Irma. They'd either be great friends or kill each other.

The card dealt for the river was the three of clubs.

The possum smiled like a crazy person when he saw it. When I narrowed my eyes his way, he smiled back at me. He didn't care if I knew he was bluffing, and I kind of liked that about him.

Silent man number one to my left had already folded. The pervert to my right was smirking again. He reminded me of the people who got into tech to make a lot of money but could barely turn on a computer. Silent guy number two was neutral-faced, but he was tapping his foot against the table like he had a while back when he'd had a hand full of nothing.

The possum was looking at me intently. This was another thing I didn't like about poker, all the staring. It just made no sense to me: If eyes are the mirrors to your soul, why is it not impolite to stare at them? I met his gaze with one of my own, like Irma had told me to, and he smiled broadly.

There was a non-zero chance he had a better hand than me. Three of a kind was good, but it wasn't mind-blowing. Based on the cards in the river, there was a high probability someone at this table had a better hand than me. I should call.

I raised. I wanted to see what everyone else at the table was going to do.

The silent gang folded, and the little lecher raised by another hundred dollars. I was pretty sure he was bluffing, but someone that arrogant might not even know what odds he was playing.

I called.

"Showdown, please," the dealer said.

The possum showed us a beautiful pair of twos…and nothing else. The pervert had three queens, which most days was an awesome hand. I tried not to smile as I laid out my cards. The possum gave me a grudging nod, the young guy looked angry, and the dealer smiled at me in a nice, motherly way.

I let out the breath I'd been holding. That purse was starting to feel a lot more real.

THIRTY-THREE — IRMA

Stu showed up an hour after Violet and Boris left.

"You sure about all this?" he drawled.

"Quite," I said. I'd spent a fair bit of time searching my flat for weapons that would fit into the little knapsack I planned on bringing. I settled on a collapsing baton when my cellular telephone—which was attached to its charger for once, huzzah for me—beeped. It was a text from Camille, updating me about what she'd found.

She'd confirmed that Tate had been unemployed for the last year. Tiffanni had no record except for one of bad manners. Rose hadn't used any of her credit or debit cards since the day of Lucas's wake. And Carlton's business was *not* in trouble, although there appeared to be some shenanigans going on with his personal assets. Camille needed to do a bit more digging to get a clearer picture of what was going on, but that would take another day or two. She hadn't found anything odd in David's past, but he banked at a small credit union that she was having trouble squeezing information out of, and the only non-innocuous aspect of Elsa's history was that she'd been arrested in university at an eco-warrior demonstration. Hadn't even been charged.

While we were on the phone, I had Camille track down the relative Rose was supposedly staying with. Turned out Aunt Adeline had left the country for Switzerland late last week. Something squeezed in my chest when she told me. Where on earth was Rose?

After we clicked off the phone, Stu cleared his throat the way he did when he had something important to say. "What're you gonna do if you get caught? Or when you're wandering around the boat? And how are you going to get *on* the boat, anyway?"

"Suction cups," I said reasonably.

"What?"

"I'm going to go up the side of the boat and slip onto the first level with some suction cups. Violet very helpfully showed me some schematics of the boat, and there's a little alcove on the port side I can use to—"

"Up the side of the boat? Are you insane?"

I stopped my preparations. "What?"

"Isn't your knee knackered?"

"Oh, it's feeling much better. And I used the very same suction cups the other day. Worked out fine."

"I'm not gonna ask what you were doing the other day."

"Probably for the best. Shall we?"

After Stu rolled his eyes at me, we made our way to my dock. I'd pre-inflated a little ten-foot dinghy for tonight's mission. If we used my Cris Craft, it might bump the hull of Carlton's boat, making noise and possibly damaging my little speeder. This way, we could get right beside the megayacht without anyone hearing a thing.

After we hopped in the dinghy, I steered us toward the *Citadel IV*. There was a full moon tonight, but with a lot of clouds, luckily.

Stu made various grumbling noises on the way over, which wasn't like him. I finally showed him the knee brace I had on under my left pant leg, and he piped down a bit.

My dinghy had an electric motor and was as silent as the grave. We slowed down when we got near the *Citadel IV*, and glided to the spot I'd told Boris we'd be.

But there was no rope thrown over the side of the boat, as Boris and I had pre-arranged. Adrenaline flooded my limbs. Bloody hell. I did not like the idea of going up the side of an aquatic obstacle without a backup. It could be wet or have algae on it, and then I'd really be sunk.

"What's wrong?" Stu said softly.

"Bulgarians," I answered with a snap in my voice. Above us, I could hear people walking around the deck. This needed to happen fast.

I pulled the phone out and looked at it. There was a new message from Boris: *Come to stern. No problem with entry.*

"What's going on?" Stu hissed.

"Boris says to go around back."

Stu took over the tiller and motored us to the boat's stern. The aft section of the yacht was open like a drawbridge, some temporary docks lashed to the entrance. Boats like this always reminded me of going into the belly of a whale.

Boris was standing in the entrance, looking very dapper in a light summer suit. He was alone, no one there to take my ticket or clock me in. The tournament had already started; everyone must be up top.

He moved forward and held out his hand.

"Thanks, Stu," I said as I stood up. Stu threw me a *don't-get-caught* look that I pretended not to see.

"You look beautiful," Boris said after Stu had left.

"What did you do?"

"Bribed the security guard," he said simply.

"Drat," I said. I'd been looking forward to burning off some steam by rappelling up the side of the boat. Well, another time.

Boris held his arm out, and I took it as we ascended the stairs and strolled around the main deck of the boat. It really was a colossus; teak polished to a high sheen, radar, satellite, every luxurious gizmo you could possibly think of, with staff patrolling the top level for people whose drinks looked like even a few sips had been taken out of them. A little garish for my tastes, but no one was perfect.

"Lovely evening," Boris said.

I nodded.

"I hear you have a boat of your own," Boris said.

"I have a little speeder. Nothing like this. I wouldn't ever own a boat like this." I laughed.

"Oh?" he said, leaning on the rail. I joined him and looked over at the water. It was a very long way down. "What kind would you get?"

"My next one will be a sailboat," I said.

"Hard to take evasive action in a sailboat if someone is trying to kill you."

"I agree completely." I smiled. "That's why I've never gotten one up until now. But there's a gentleman on the island who helps soup up my engines. He'll get a halfway decent motor on board."

"Is that even possible with a sailboat?"

I laughed. "Probably not. But one can dream."

He joined me in laughter, and then we stood in silence for a moment. I tried to sort out how I felt with him beside me. There was something warm and wiggly in my core, but that could mean anything. Eventually, I decided I liked standing in the moonlight with Boris.

"Well, I'm off," I said, as soon as I made that revelation. "I have my cellular, but it's on silent. Just in case. I'm going to go down to the guest cabins and see what I can turn up."

"What if someone from the crew finds you?"

"I'll either go with little old British lady or drunk senior citizen. It'll depend on who it is. Can you park your caboose outside the interior?"

He chuckled softly. "Me and my caboose are at your disposal." He looked immediately horrified. "Irma, that did not…I did not…"

I waved his awkwardness off, and he looked relieved.

We walked inside, scooting past the main salon, where the game was under way. I scanned the room for miscreants, hired killers, or cat burglars. It looked clean, which should have made me feel better, but didn't. My heartbeat fluttered uncomfortably against my ribcage. Something bad always happened at this event. Always.

Violet appeared focused, and looked like she wasn't about to take any guff from anyone. Good for her. I gave her a little finger wave as we went, and she grinned at me before getting back to the game.

On the bottom floor of the ship, Boris and I stopped. We were obviously entering into the back of the house—the crew quarters and mess.

"I'll text you if anything happens," Boris said. "Good luck." Then he leaned down and kissed me on the cheek.

"Yes, er, thank you," I said, with as much dignity I could muster after getting a burst of delightfully cologned neck. I slung my handbag over my shoulder and crept down the hallway.

Most of the staff would be above decks in the wheelhouse, not down here, but it was likely that off-duty staff were hanging around.

I palmed my little telescoping mirror and crept down the hallway, sliding a pair of reading glasses onto my nose, an immediate way to look like I was old and harmless. That was part of the reason I'd gone grey, even though it pained me to do it. I'd had dark red hair all my life until it turned on me in my fifties. But management had thought it would work to our advantage. And it had.

The truth was, they hadn't wanted me to retire. But I'd had a few close calls in the last year, an op that went bad, a young person's life snuffed out. A good young person. I'd liked her immensely, even though I hadn't known her all that well. And it had been even more devastating when I'd realised she was a double agent. Oh, those Russians.

I kept going until I reached the end of the hallway. I slid the mirror around the corner. Nothing. I could hear distant radio chatter, but that was common on large boats. Boaters were required to help others in distress, and marine radios were often left on permanently on big boats. I'd always liked that there was at least one place on the planet—the water—where people had to help each other. Other than all the pirates, obviously.

I dashed around the corner. This corridor was empty as well, and I stepped forward a few paces before I heard some noise. Quickly, I opened the closest door and stuffed myself in it. If I'd stumbled upon a men's locker room, I was going to have to do some quick talking.

I held my breath as the voices came closer, then passed the door and travelled down the same way I'd come from, which meant I might bump into a few crew members on my way out. I noodled on whether drunk old person or crazy old person would be best. No matter. It would come to me, and it was best not to get married to any one course of action.

I turned around. I was in a crew bedroom, tiny and narrow with torturously small bunk beds that were made perfectly; you could bounce a quarter off them if you were so inclined.

I had a theory that Rose was on the boat. I didn't think she'd be hiding or trapped in the ensuite of this particular room, but I had to be sure. Carlton's story about her being at an aunt's was rubbish. She had to be on the boat somewhere. I made a cursory check around the little room. Nothing.

I inched the door open and thrust my mirror through it, swivelling it so I could see both ways. The corridor was empty. I made quick work of the rest of the crew cabins. There was nothing unusual in any of them.

I needed to see the master stateroom. I wondered if Carlton was holding Rose there. I also wondered if any of his financial papers were there, so I could snoop out some more info on what was going on with his financial situation. And if he was armed. I was not looking forward to patting him down during a fox trot on the aft deck. People would talk.

Then my thoughts drifted to Boris, covering the exit for me. The two of us working as a team. It was nice to have a friend who knew about the important things in life. It was nice to have a male…friend. My last husband had passed away over ten years ago from a bad ticker, and I'd been alone ever since. I'd thought at the time that that was it for me, but maybe it wasn't. Maybe retirement had more things up its sleeve for me than I'd bargained for. It certainly had so far.

I passed the engine room and took a quick look around. Unfortunately, engines had never been in my wheelhouse, so I wasn't able to do much, other than confirm it was an empty engine room, and very noisy. Violet would probably be perfectly happy in there.

I made my way back to the exit where Boris was waiting. I'd checked my phone when I was tossing the last cabin, and he'd texted an *all clear* message to me. Which was strange, because I could hear people coming down the hallway: two women and a man. They sounded young, probably crew.

I considered popping back into one of the rooms, but if they *were* crew, I might end up in one of their rooms. Bother. There were so many staircases and hallways on the boat, it would be a snap for someone to keep themselves hidden indefinitely. It was like one of Violet's video games.

I messed my hair up and tilted my reading glasses so they were askew on my face. Then I put my hand on the wall, as if I was inebriated or seasick. My heartbeat quickened while I tried to centre myself.

"Hello, there!" A young man with a broad Australian twang greeted me.

"Well, hello," I said, putting some extra oomph into my own accent.

"Lost?"

"I'm afraid so, luv. I was feeling a little under the weather, and wanted a glass of water."

"No problem," he said smoothly. "But this is the crew area. I'll take you upstairs."

I slung my arm around his. "Thank you so much. You're very kind."

We passed the two girls, who gave me friendly nods. They were both young and blonde, their hair in stylishly messy buns and their outfits crisp from an iron.

"Alright, then," the man said—his nameplate said *Ken*, and he looked like one—"There you go."

I patted him on the arm. We'd gone a different way than where I'd entered from, which meant Boris was still hanging around downstairs.

"You're welcome," Ken said politely, then turned on his heel and went back the way he came. I watched him go, then went to find Boris.

Thirty-Four — Violet

I'd moved to a new table, with four other players and a dealer who looked like he'd last dealt at the world's fair in 1967. Again, the players were all men in various stages of their life. It was my third table. I'd won the first two games with some very good cards and some less than stellar opponents, other than the possum, who I'd beat by luck only.

I was starting to get a taste for the game. If I could get my hands on that money, Max and I would have a bigger cushion. Maybe we could last a few more months. Maybe we could make it all work.

I tried to focus through the jittery feelings in my stomach. It was my turn to act. The man across from me, who had a moustache as long as my arm, raised his equally impressive eyebrows. He looked like he was sitting on a good hand. The man beside him had a small laminated card showing all the different hands in poker.

The best I could end up with was an ace high card. I folded. Moustache man's hand was garbage; his high card was a king. The laminated card man had four eights, which was a nice hand to pretend he didn't understand.

I leaned back in my chair while the dealer shuffled. I wished I was playing Blackjack.

Carlton Campbell stood at the front of the room and called for silence after the hand was done. "Thank you for coming," he said, grinning broadly. "We are so happy you have all come to help us raise money for the Smile Society." Applause. "We're going to be having a late buffet snack at ten o'clock, and please drink as much of our liquor—which has been donated by the Club—as you possibly can. We're thrilled to be a part of the Smile-a-Thon Network, and we wish you all good luck!"

"Nice to see Carlton get sprung from jail in time for the tournament," the man beside me said with a sly look.

The dealer dealt again. My hole cards were promising. Moustache man looked at his cards and shuffled them around casually. The rest of the table was either drunk or depressed. Maybe both.

I raised when it was my turn. The thought of that fifty thousand was swirling inside me with an increasing urgency.

To my left, the man made a rude noise and threw his cards down. So did the guy to his right.

It was all down to moustache man. My heart clanged in my chest. With no expression on his face whatsoever, he raised again.

Thirty-Five — Irma

It was a particularly beautiful night. The sun was gone, and the moon was affixed to the sky, a perfect, shiny circle. It might have even been a romantic moment, if I wasn't so intent on finding Rose.

I turned to look at Boris. "I got caught in the crew quarters."

He looked concerned. "Did you? Nobody came past me. I apologize for this, Irma."

"There are staircases all over the place on this boat. It's madness. I don't know how they'll take another little incursion."

"Let's find out, shall we?" he said with a broad smile.

I grinned back at him, something speeding up in my chest when I did.

This time, we made our way to the hallway for the guest cabins. Boris stationed himself outside, his phone held like he was in the middle of texting someone.

I took a quick tour of the four guest cabins. They looked like they should be stuck under glass; lush towels with spa-level bath supplies, the bed pillows karate-chopped into submission, teak gleaming in the moonlight.

The last guest cabin looked microscopically different: The bedspread not *exactly* square, the pillows not *quite* as manhandled. Maybe the steward had just been tired from all the primping by then. There was nothing there that might help me. Bother.

I exited and walked down the hallways to the master stateroom. It was massive, larger than the small apartment I'd lived in with my first husband when I was twenty-four. I shook my head when I thought about it. At twenty-four, I'd barely known how to tie my own shoelaces, and my parents were newly dead. It had just been me and my husband and a family with a history of no divorce.

I worked quickly in the stateroom. If someone was coming, Boris was going to start talking loudly to nobody on his phone.

Even though the room was enormous, it took me no time whatsoever to determine Rose wasn't here. I sighed. Then I rifled through her bedside table to see if she'd left any evidence of travel plans or something similar. Nothing.

The bathroom was perfectly clean on one side, and a mess on the other, with a double shower and an oversized bathtub. The other guest rooms only had mid-sized showers, while the crew cabins I'd seen earlier just had a faucet stuck to the wall.

Here, the men's items were on the messy side of the bathroom. I slid on a pair of latex gloves, then paused. I texted Boris to see if he could try talking, just to make sure I'd hear him if he was speaking. No reply. My breath came faster.

If Boris was off canoodling with someone else and had left me here alone, I was going to have a hard time explaining the latex, even if they bought my I'm-so-sorry-I-got-lost story. I compromised by pulling the left glove off and kept the right one on. There was nothing of interest in the bathroom, except for Carlton's Rogaine.

I focused on the bed and the storage areas. Boats were always full of sneaky little hiding places. Nothing. I unscrewed a few lightbulbs and looked in a few vents, just in case Rose or Carlton or both of them had hidden something saucy somewhere. Nothing.

Drat.

Boris still hadn't responded, and I worked as fast as I could, just in case. I sat down at the desk. It was obviously Carlton's, full of brochures and navigation charts. Under a pile of printouts about lumber and steel, I found a brochure for a Tahitian resort for singles. A date two weeks in the future had been circled. Apparently, they were having a Salsa party.

Well, that was interesting. Canadian summers weren't long, but they were beautiful. Why would Carlton be going to Tahiti in the middle of summer? Alone?

I tucked the brochure back where I found it. Just as there was a knock at the door.

THIRTY-SIX — VIOLET

It was just me and moustache man, who looked like he was about to lay an egg, he was so happy. With the turn, I had two pairs, aces and twos, not a bad hand. A nice pile of chips lay on the table in front of me.

The river gave us the ace of spades. I had a full house, aces over twos. There was a one in 4,164 chance moustache man had a four of a kind, and the odds got worse for a straight or royal flush. I tried not to let it show on my face, but I probably failed. I raised, and moustache man called.

"Players, showdown," the dealer said.

Moustache man nodded, and I laid my cards on the table. I hesitated on the last to see if I could give him a run for his money, but he simply smiled a little, one half of his moustache pulled to the side.

He had three of a kind: fives. I pressed my lips together so I wouldn't smile. My win. Warmth spread through my belly.

When I had all the chips, I moved to the final game with all the winning players. Somehow the possum had ended up here too, even though I'd beaten him at the beginning.

"I bought in twice," he said when he saw my eyes on him.

"Smart man," I said, squeezing all the emotion out of my voice. I could really smell that money now. I could keep the company going for a few more months. I could make it work. Hope fluttered inside me.

"Ms. Blackheart," the dealer said. She was the same woman from the first table. I tried a smile at her and she smiled right back. "You are the big blind."

I took a deep breath and put a few chips down. Unlike my other games, everyone at the table except for the possum was a woman, and they all looked very serious.

We started. The three women sitting at the table were all different; a Gen Z hippie who looked like she'd just rolled out of bed, a millennial with extra-pouty lips and slicked-back red hair, and a sixty-something woman who gave me a scary smile when she saw me looking. I smiled right back at her, just like Irma'd told me to.

The hole cards were dealt. The possum pretended to be asleep. Patchouli wafted over from the Gen Z hippie.

I got a handful of junk on the first deal and tried to calm the nerves jittering up and down my spine. I folded. The possum smiled faintly, then gave me an *awww* look. I smiled back at him with a bit of teeth. The game went back and forth until the millennial was out of chips.

I was happier with four players. I preferred round numbers generally, although I knew it wasn't going to last for long. The next hand was garbage too. I shot an annoyed glance at the dealer and realised the possum had caught me. I thought about staying in just to spite him before I folded to save my chips.

The possum won that game and threw a gentlemanly nod at the scary smiler, who was out. She put her hand on my shoulder as she got up, like I was a chair and not a person.

Now it was just the three of us: the possum, the hippie, the nerd.

I was dealt two kings for my hole cards.

With the cards on the table, I had four of a kind.

Players had a one in 4,060 chance of getting four of a kind. But the odds that the elderly man or the flower child could beat it were not nothing. I looked at the possum, who was studiously examining his cards. His eyes flicked up at my face. The hippie was fiddling with a button on her peasant blouse again, which was either her tell for when she had a terrible hand, or what she *wanted* to be her tell.

I had a pretty good chance of winning. I could do it. I looked at my chips; I had more than the girl, less than the crafty old man. I held my breath.

Then I raised.

But so did he. I looked at his cuff links: Tiffany. His suit was a Tom Ford, and his pocket square was crisply starched. He didn't need this money at all.

After I raised again, the dealer asked the possum if he wanted to raise, too. He nodded with a smirk, then went all in. The hippie followed suit.

I was suddenly very cold. My company was circling the drain. Forty-three employees. A shared dream. What was I going to do if it folded?

"Ms. Blackheart?" the dealer prodded. A crowd had gathered around us, and I was feeling claustrophobic. The lights were too bright, and everyone was squeezing in on me. A single drop of sweat made its way down my spine. I tried not to shiver.

"Call," I said, my voice wavering.

"Players, show your cards," the dealer directed.

"Ladies first," the possum said with a sly smile.

The hippie laid down three of a kind: aces.

I could beat it.

My heart fluttered. There was a chance I could win it all. There was. I laid my cards down one at a time, as casually as I could, even though I had a frog-sized lump stuck to the back of my throat. The possum swept his gaze over my hand, no expression on his face at all, and started to lay his cards down.

Thirty-Seven — Irma

Boris opened the door and closed it behind him as he entered the room. "Are you not getting my messages?"

"No."

"A crew member is doing some tidying up. I was worried someone would come in here. And you are not answering my texts."

"Thank you."

"Have you found anything?"

I shook my head.

"We should move," he said crisply.

"Agreed." I pulled the glove off my hand and stuffed it in my handbag. We closed the door behind us just as a gaggle of suited-up guests rounded the corner. We smiled and nodded as we passed, then found a cozy nook with some couches on the aft deck. The moon glowed brightly in the air above us. We didn't say anything, both of us lost in our thoughts.

"Dead calm," I said eventually. There was so little wind that the boat's mighty anchors were lax. Normally, even a small breeze would push a boat's nose into the wind. Dead calm could kill you, if you were a sailor in the middle of the ocean. Dead calm meant you were a sitting duck. I tried not to think about it. I had to focus. Again, I had that feeling of misdirection. There was something I was missing in all this. Maybe more than one something.

"Yes, it is," Boris said. Then he pulled my hand into his absently, rubbing his thumb against mine in a way that was making it difficult to concentrate.

We sat like this, watching the moon peek out from the clouds, then get swallowed up by them again. The wind remained still, and the dead calm of the water crept over the two of us. I liked that Boris and I didn't need to speak to be comfortable together. That was a hard thing to find, in my experience.

While we sat there, I ran through everything that had happened. David had wanted me and Violet to know something about the groundbreaking, and Carlton suspected his wife had been unfaithful. Had Carlton killed Lucas to avenge the extramarital shenanigans he thought Lucas was having with his wife? Had he run David off the road to make sure whatever he knew never came to light? Carlton had left right before David that evening. He could have lain in wait, run David off the road in his shiny red beast of a Hummer.

But could Rose be involved in all this? If she and Lucas *were* having an affair, Lucas might have wanted to make their relationship public, and she panicked. But I wasn't even sure if she *knew* David. I kicked myself for not asking her at the ground-breaking. Maybe Carlton and Rose were working together to pick off people who were inconvenient for them, somehow. But how did the tractor shenanigans fit into all this? If Violet was right about her theory, the tractor's actions had been deliberate. But maybe it didn't mean anything after all.

"Irma," Boris said, turning to me. The moon was in full effect again. The night was silent, other than the bustle of action inside at the poker game, which had picked up again. I'd have to go see how Violet was doing soon.

I closed my eyes. Something about that last cabin was bothering me. Some sort of misdirection.

But then Boris pulled me into his arms. I took in a sudden sharp breath, then let it out slowly. We fit together perfectly. I closed my eyes, leaned my head on his shoulder. He smelled heavenly, and it felt like we'd always been meant to hold each other. I let out a happy sigh, and opened my eyes.

Someone zipped past on a jet ski, pushing waves through the water. From this far up, it looked tiny, like a bathtub toy.

Bathtub.

I sprang to my feet.

"Irma!" Boris said.

I pulled him forward and kissed him on the mouth. Hard. "I have a hunch." He didn't ask any questions. Boris had seen my hunches in action before.

We made our way past the master stateroom to the guest cabins. I stopped in front of the door of the last one I'd gone through. The one that hadn't been as neat as the others.

Boris stopped beside me, raised an eyebrow.

"Violet showed me the schematics of the ship," I said, opening the door.

"And...?"

I stood at the foot of the bed. The covers were only a little bit askew, the pillows only slightly less arranged. I was probably mad.

I was definitely mad.

"There's a bathtub under the foot of the bed in this cabin," I whispered. "This whole time, I've been thinking about misdirection. Someone has re-arranged this room."

"Might just be one of the guests..."

"Yes. I hope so. But every single year, something terrible happens at this tournament.

Sometimes it attracts cat burglars and other miscreants. One time the engine room caught on fire and we had to evacuate."

Boris must have sensed my hesitation, because he stepped forward and moved the covers up the bed. There was a fold in the mattress, and he pulled it back, showing the cover of the bathtub.

He met my eyes.

"I'm probably crazy," I whispered. In my head, I was thinking: *Please don't be Rose. Please don't be David. Please don't be…*

He flashed me a quick grin. "You're definitely crazy." Then he pulled the cover off.

I gasped.

Thirty-Eight — Violet

I'd laid a good hand out, four of a kind. Jacks. But the possum had a straight flush. I felt my heart throb once and then go silent. It was hard to breathe.

"Good game," the older man said, his hand out. It was one of the only things he'd said all night. He had a broad Boston accent.

"Good game," I said as I shook it. *Don't cry don't cry.* I nodded stiffly, then left the table and headed to the bar. I needed a drink.

"Nice playing," the patchouli-wearing young woman said. She'd followed behind me.

"You too." I blinked tears back.

"I'm rusty," she said ruefully. Her eyes were a pale blue, her hair icy blonde.

"Same."

"You played a great game," she said. "I like your style."

"Thanks."

"You know what? You should come to my sister's wedding. It'll be a good time," she said, holding out a hand for me to shake. “Constance Leblanc. Bring Irma with you.”

“Uh, okay?” I tried not to be creeped out by the fact that everyone in this town knew each other while we shook.

She headed off, waving at me over her shoulder.

That’s when I heard the screaming.

Thirty-Nine — Irma

Chief Mavis Pickle's shoes made official-type noises as she walked into the interrogation room at the police station, where she'd had us all shuttled to. Boris had wanted to excuse himself from the scene before the police showed up, but one of the stewards had walked in on us and started scream-yodelling at the top of her lungs. So now he was in another room.

"Evening, Mrs. Abercrombie, Ms. Blackheart." A curt nod.

"I didn't kill Rose," I said abruptly. Might as well get it out of the way. She'd been curled up in the bathtub, wearing a blue t-shirt and jeans, and on first glance had looked like she was sleeping, the poor thing.

Mavis sat down in a chair on the opposite side of the table. "What happened?"

I took a sip from the glass of water beside me, then another. My throat felt terrible. "I was on the aft deck with a friend, and—"

"Was your friend Boris Andropov?"

I nodded.

"The same Boris Andropov you told me last week you didn't know?"

I nodded.

"I see." She wrote something in an old-timey notebook. "Go on."

I decided to leave all the hugging out of the story. "I did a quick looky-loo around the boat, and something about that room was bothering me, so I went back to check it out. And then we found Rose's body. That's really it. Were you aware she was missing?"

"No one had reported it."

"I see." Of course, the fact that Mavis had arrested the victim's husband might have put a kibosh on any desire to report anything to her.

"How did you know about the bathtub?"

"Violet showed me the boat's schematics earlier in the day."

She made some more notes. "What else?"

"That's it, really. Do you know when she died? There were a lot of staff on board. Maybe someone heard something—"

"There were very few crew on board, actually, except for the catering staff, who were all in the salon, and a few belowdecks who were off duty. The boat was at anchor, and the plan was for it to stay there. No need for crew."

"I see," I said. "Why was everybody in the salon?"

"They were watching the game. Apparently it was quite something."

I looked at Violet. "Did you win, dear?"

She wrinkled her nose. "I told you Blackjack would be better. No, I did not win."

The Pickle turned to look at her, surprise on her face. "You came second."

"Good heavens," I said to Violet, "That's incredible! Good for you." To the Pickle, I said, "Who won?"

"Jerome St. Pierre."

"Oh," I said with a little laugh. "Mr. St. Pierre is a well-known card shark."

Violet shrugged. "Yeah, he seemed pretty good. I'm just bummed about the purse."

I took a deep breath. It wasn't supposed to mean anything, but the Pickle's eyes narrowed when she saw it. Clearing her throat, she turned to Violet. "Ms. Blackheart, do you mind if we—"

"I need some coffee," Violet announced with an awkward nod. She shut the door quietly behind her.

"Was there something else you wanted to tell me, Irma?"

I took a sip of water. "Mavis, what's the DNA evidence you have from Lucas's death?"

She pressed her lips together, shook her head. She wasn't going to tell me.

"What was Rose's time of death?"

The chief took a deep breath. "I have to know this will stay between the two of us."

I nodded.

"Sometime this afternoon. That's all we know at this point."

I sat back in my chair. "If she was killed earlier in the day, the boat would have been a madhouse, everyone preparing for the tournament."

"Most likely."

"Why didn't anyone hear the gun shot? And did anyone see her come on board?"

"Not that we've been able to locate so far, but it's early stages, Mrs. Abercrombie. And I suspect a silencer was used when she was killed."

I nodded my agreement with her words before trying another tack. "Violet thinks the tractor at the ground-breaking was hacked. Apparently it's easier to compromise industrial equipment than it is to tamper with your car key fob."

Her eyebrows got a workout at that. But then she said, "Leblanc has taken full responsibility for the equipment failure. They say it was a programming issue on their end."

"Violet says that's what they always say."

A shrug. "Could be. But no one was harmed, other than Snookie Smith, who has only a minor injury. Leblanc isn't going to be charged with anything. There's not much we can do with companies who actually admit responsibility for these kinds of things, Irma."

"I do see your point, dear."

"Thank you." She crossed her arms. "Is there anything else you can tell me?"

It felt terrible to give up any of my intel, but with Rose suddenly off the board, I needed to regroup. "I've heard some gossip about Rose having an affair with Lucas Waters."

"Yes, we're aware of that rumour."

"But I have to say," I said, "I never thought of Lucas as a philanderer. Imogene Flores told me he was single. And he never spoke of any relationships with me."

"Did you talk to him about his personal life a lot?"

"We had a drink after our lessons sometimes. He never told me his deep, dark secrets, but I sometimes have gut feelings about people." I looked at her face. I'd been very wrong about a murderer recently, partly because I'd been blind to the faults of someone I'd known for a long time. And the chief knew it. "Of course, people can be excellent liars when something big is on the line."

"True."

"What if Rose wasn't having an affair with Lucas, but with David?" I asked.

"I can't comment on anything like that."

"Where's Carlton now?"

"He's being questioned. And from where I'm sitting, he looks to be the culprit here. We know he had a temper, and we've found his DNA on both the victims. He had opportunity and means. And his motive isn't so bad, either."

"I see." I nodded, folded my hands over each other. "Thank you, dear."

She stood. "You're welcome. Clearly you can see the police are on top of this investigation, alright? I don't want to hear you've been running around and—" She didn't finish the thought. She closed her notepad with a slap instead, and got up. Her smile was perfunctory.

I watched her go. She had a suspect in custody. This could all be over. I should have been happy.

But I wasn't.

FORTY — IRMA

"Morning!" Violet called out to me the next day. She brought a pot of tea for me out on the back deck, coffee for her. "Did you have a good sleep?"

"I think so," I said, smiling. Violet, bless her heart, had left the bag in the teapot. This was going to be heavenly.

"Good. Because I want to do something. Something *outdoors*!"

My heart surged. "That's wonderful, dear. I'll call Stu and we can go sailing and—"

She took a swig of her coffee. "No, we will not!"

I gave her a look.

"I want to go to Beaver Brooke," she said.

"Certainly. I'd love to sail over there."

"No, again!"

"Huh. Imagine that."

"I want to go there and test this!" She pulled a device out from a carrier bag she'd brought out with her and handed it to me. An LCD screen was carefully duct-taped to a stiff cardboard backing, its wires disappearing into a handmade cardboard box. "What on earth is this?"

"A remote for the tractor!"

"Everyone else seems to believe it was a malfunction of some kind. Mavis told me Leblanc had taken full responsibility for the whole thing."

"Well, I guess it's possible, but we can't know for sure until we try this out. I can look at the tractor's logs with it, and figure out what happened the day of the ground-breaking."

She looked thrilled, and my own heartrate had started to pick up. "I should call Elsa to make sure it's all right. But if it's outside…sure. Why not? Let's have breakfast at the Club, then go play with your machine."

"Perfect. Oh, and Stu called."

"Why didn't he call on my line?"

She gave me a look. "Because you never pick up? His grand-niece—Annie, I think?—had some sort of mission for him. He said, and I quote, 'Tell Irma to smarten up and take it easy.' Also, he's having a pig roast at his place soon to celebrate his new place at Beaver Brooke. Speaking of Beaver Brooke, can we go there now? Please?"

I smiled at her. "I'll be ready in a jiff."

After a lovely breakfast on the Club's patio—croque monsieur and a summer salad with edible flowers for me, with a dressing so tart it made my teeth tingle—I sighed happily after paying the bill. It was true, I was feeling a little more banged-up than usual, but good food and strong tea always helped fortify one's soul.

After I was done eating, I borrowed Violet's cellular and called Elsa. "Hello?" a raspy voice said.

"Hello, Elsa, darling, it's Irma. Are you all right? You sound terrible."

"Thanks," she said with a half-chuckle. She cleared her throat to regain her voice. "I'm just so sleep deprived and miserable—the air conditioning isn't working and I'm going to explode…uh, pretty much any minute now."

"Oh, my. Do you want me to send Stu over to fix it?"

"That's a great idea. I'll give him a call later after I try napping again. I've got three fans pointing at me, and I'm still convinced I can get some sleep today." She sighed. "What can I do for you, Irma?"

I hesitated, then said, "Violet has been working on a science project and she wants to try it out at the Beaver Brooke site. Is that okay with you? I don't want to disturb anyone working there."

"Well, it's Saturday, so no one's there. It should be fine, I guess." A pause. "What kind of experiment?"

"She's just...well, it's a long story. But she built a transceiver-thingie of some sort. She just wants to try it out."

"On what?"

"The tractor you have there." I took a sip. "And she wants to go through its logs to see what happened the day of the ground-breaking."

"Uh..." Her voice cracked. "You know what, Irma? I'm going to have to clear it with the firm's legal team, and I don't see how I'm going to be able to do that on the weekend. Plus, Leblanc is going to replace the tractor and do some more extensive testing on it in their lab. I think it would be better for Violet to futz around with the new one."

"Well, I won't tell if you don't, dear."

It sounded like she was trying to sit up. "It's a liability issue, and everyone's freaked out because of what happened at the ground-breaking. I'm sorry."

"No problem," I said smoothly, even though there was a catch in my throat. "We'll go sailing instead. Another time. You go back to bed and relax."

"Thanks, Irma." She sounded relieved. "I'll get on it first thing Monday morning. Promise."

"Thank you, dear." We hung up.

Violet looked dejected. "I guess she said no."

"Tell me something."

"What?"

"Do you think you'd be able to park the tractor back exactly where you found it?"

"I think so." She brightened. "We're going anyway?"

I nodded. "Why not? The site isn't visible from the road, so no one will ever know, and there's no one on site today. As long as you promise not to run amok and drive it over anyone's foot. Although if you wanted to run over Snookie again, that would be acceptable."

"Yay!" She fist-pumped the air.

I lifted my teacup to have another sip. I'd let it go cold, which was a bother. Just as my lips were parting, one of the busboys banged into our table, spilling the tea all over me.

"Oh, no!" he said. "I'm so sorry, Irma."

It was Ben, one of Stu's many nephews. "No problem at all, young man. How is your summer going?"

"Geez, I'm sorry. It's going well, Irma, thanks."

I stood up and patted him on the shoulder. "It's no trouble whatsoever. I have some spare clothes in my locker. Violet, do you mind waiting here while I get changed?"

"No problemo," she said. To Ben, she added, "Can I have another coffee, please?"

"Of course," he said, hurrying off.

"I'll be right back," I told Violet and made my way to the locker room, nodding at people I knew as I went. It was a gorgeous day, big fluffy clouds, brilliant sun. I'd rather spend it on the water than fiddling around with farm equipment, but Violet would be happy if we went, and that was the important part. Plus, I wanted to know what was in those logs.

I took a seat in front of my locker and unbuttoned the white shirt I'd been wearing. I was going to need to bleach the tea stain out. I changed into a white polo shirt I kept in my locker. I caught a glance at the tennis shoes at the bottom of the locker, then thought about Tate, flitting around in the same kind of footwear, being a twerp to his more mature clients.

It still bothered me he'd been the one to replace Lucas, and no one was suspicious of that fact. Not to mention the burn Violet had seen on his arm after Lucas's trailer went up in smoke.

Of course, I'd given Tate's name to the Pickle after visiting Carlton in the slammer earlier this week, and she might have an arrest warrant typed up in his name already, for all I knew. She might have been humouring me in our discussions, but she was most likely holding critical data back.

Local law enforcement were like that. And I could feel some facts coalescing in the recesses of my mind. I knew all of this fit together more neatly than it had when I'd been speaking to her.

I'd been standing in front of my locker, doing nothing, for too long. I roused myself and slammed it shut. The lock twirled and landed on eight. Lucas's favourite number.

I sat back down again on the bench.

Lucas's safe was a high-end piece of equipment, Geraldine had told me. It was the kind of safe you bought because you wanted to protect something important. But there had been only one letter in it. And no risqué Polaroids of Tiffanni. There had been nothing of interest in Lucas's office. There had to be something, somewhere else...

I looked around the room. All of the lockers in the Club's changerooms were for day use only. But I'd been able to wrangle a permanent one. It had cost me dearly, but it had been worth the effort. And management knew nothing about it. Had Lucas organized something similar for himself?

I rummaged through my handbag. I had my telescoping mirror and absolutely nothing else that would help me crack a lock. I opened my locker again and rifled through a little bag of tricks I kept here, just in case.

There was a small tube of Compound Nine, a nifty Silly Putty-like goo that could burn through just about anything in five seconds flat. I might have to buy a replacement lock, but that was tomorrow's problem.

I banged my locker shut.

After tucking my hair into a baseball cap and keeping my head down, I made my way into the men's locker room. I needed to be quick. I did not want to have to explain any scandalous behaviour to the board. Again.

Of course, I had no idea where Lucas's locker might be. I did a quick circuit of the room, keeping my head down. I could hear some gentlemen in the shower area, but nobody seemed to be near the lockers. Everyone must have been out on the links, and why not? It was another beautiful day.

I went to locker number eight, Lucas's favourite number. There was a little sticky note with a smiley face attached to the locker, a combination lock securing it. It looked like it could be Lucas's handwriting.

Was it his locker?

I burned through the lock quickly and with no regret, which was a wasted emotion. I took a deep breath before I opened it. Either I was going to have to cough up one hell of an apology to the rightful owner, or I had something.

The locker was neat and tidy, with a small metal box on its single shelf. I snatched it and the broken lock up and was out the door just as a gentleman rounded the corner and started setting himself up a few feet down from where I was. Time to go.

I took the box back to the ladies' changeroom and had just opened it when a group of women noisily entered. The top document was a letter addressed to Lucas. It was his locker, his things. Joy burst through me. But one of the women who'd just wandered into the room was a friend of Snookie's. I had to slam the box shut.

I took a deep breath and tried to centre myself. I'd take Violet to test out her controller. If I didn't, I was worried she was going to explode right out of her clothes. It would only take a few minutes. And then I was going to go through this box properly. There *had* to be something I could use in it.

FORTY-ONE — VIOLET

I drove Irma's MG over to the Beaver Brooke site, almost jumping up and down in my seat, I was so excited. The part I'd needed had been delivered this morning, and I'd finally finished building my remote.

"You feeling okay?" I asked as I drove at a reasonable and safe speed. Irma had been sitting quietly in her seat the whole trip, which was not like her.

"Yes, dear, I'm fine. Just thinking about a few things."

Thankfully, it didn't take long to get there. Irma'd been right; nobody would see us from the road. Frankly, I'd be happy just to get the tractor to go forward and back today, and take a look at those logs. I could do more when we had permission to be on site.

I parked in front of the construction trailer. All the other spots were empty. Across the little field, where the buffet table had been set up at the ground-breaking, the now-crushed sales office was still standing. Sort of. The wind blew off the bay and ruffled my hair. I snapped an elastic over it to keep it out of my eyes.

"So how does this all work?" Irma said, looking over my shoulder.

"I basically cloned the original RF controller, using equivalent hardware. Then I had to learn the programming language they use for construction and farm equipment."

"Very impressive, dear. And RF is radio frequency?"

"Yeah. Just like your car key fob—okay, in your case, you have a normal key, but my car has a fob. Anyway, the remote and the device it's controlling are transmitting messages at a particular frequency. So if I have a device which is also transmitting on that frequency, I'm halfway there. Then, I use some commands to assume control and send my own instructions to the equipment I'm hacking."

"Sounds very impressive."

"Thanks," I said with a grin. "You wanna see it in action?"

She nodded, and we walked over to the tractor. It was parked about twenty feet from the construction trailer, beside some new equipment that must have been dropped off recently; a backhoe and some other machinery.

Irma mounted the stairs of the tractor and did a quick inspection. "Everything looks good, dear."

I turned on the remote and tuned in to the tractor. It was transmitting a big, beautiful signal, announcing its presence. Awesome. I'd put together some complex sequences earlier, but since we didn't exactly have permission to be here, I started pulling together a few simple commands for my test.

"Are you going to be long?" Irma asked.

"No. I have to alter some sequences on the remote, but it'll only take a few minutes."

"Wonderful. I'm stiff as a board, so I'm going to stretch my legs a bit."

"Of course you are. Watch out for that knee."

She took off toward the crushed sales office, her pace faster than most people half her age, myself included. She looped around it, but didn't appear right away on the other side. She was probably hiding from me and doing pushups.

I turned back to my work and finished tweaking my sequence of commands. The engineers' union would bounce me if I didn't beta test my theory before showing it to someone. The first command I was going to send would turn the tractor on and direct it to lift the front-end loader and roll straight forward five feet. I hit *enter* and waited, my heart pounding.

Forty-Two — Irma

The sales office had two entrances, and after pulling on a pair of gloves and some booties from my handbag so I wouldn't interfere with any evidence, I entered via the entrance on the far side of the building. I didn't want Violet to see me go in and get worried, but I'd noticed that the crime scene tape had finally been removed. I'd never forgive myself if I didn't take a quick look.

The front part of the office, where the site's diorama had been displayed, was destroyed. But the back part was mostly still intact. There were two offices, and a small, squished kitchenette.

The offices were nice. The largest was Carlton's, obviously. It contained an oversized desk and a designer couch, with some fancy-looking furnishings, and at least a dozen professionally framed pictures of himself at various activities, golf, sailing, sitting on a patio being a twerp. Some of the pictures had fallen to the floor.

There was no paper on or in the desk, no evidence Carlton ever did any work whatsoever. I remembered the conversation Mrs. Sepp had had with Elsa in my backyard. Looked like Elsa had been understating Carlton's lack of work ethic.

I'd assumed the second office was for another salesperson, but I was wrong. There was a pocket door connecting the two rooms, and the nameplate on the smaller office read *Elsa Lee*. It, too, had a couch and some plush furnishings.

Huh.

It was a nice office. I wondered why she'd chosen to sit in the construction trailer the morning of the ground-breaking. Wouldn't it have been more comfortable to lie down here?

I tried to step around the broken glass, but it was everywhere. Wind blew off the lake and rattled the windows loudly as I walked around the desk, pulling open the drawers.

There was a lot of paper to do with the Beaver Brooke project, and tons of evidence that *Elsa* did a lot of work, but almost nothing of a personal nature. Perhaps, like Violet, Elsa's career left her little time for a personal life. I circled around and sat in the chair on the other side of the desk. The chair a guest would use.

I had a bad feeling, sitting there. I pulled a mini flashlight out of my purse and ran it over the room. Nothing out of the ordinary. I should go check Carlton's next.

But just before I turned the flashlight off, something caught the light, something very small and shiny under the desk. Lucas's necklace? My breath froze in my lungs.

Then, I heard the sound of car tires on gravel. A door slamming. Someone was here. A calm rippled over me.

I just bet I knew who it was.

Then I made my way carefully, quietly, to the exit on the same side as the old croquet pitch, shoved the gloves and booties into my purse, and looped around the far side of the office to make it seem like I hadn't been inside.

A little red car, a Volkswagen Beetle, was parked behind the ruins of the sales office.

"Hello, Irma," Elsa said cheerily. Her hair was caught up in a bun, and she was wearing sweats and shoes that would be excellent for running. She met my eyes briefly before injecting some air into her back tire with a little pump.

"There's a lot of glass on the ground here. Blew a tire?" I said, and she nodded. I took a step closer. I couldn't see a weapon, which cheered me immensely. I took a deep breath, then another. "What are you doing here, dear?"

"Shouldn't I be asking you the same question?"

"Oops," I said, holding out my arms. "You caught me. I'm sorry, dear. Violet's nerdishness was unstoppable."

She stopped pumping. "I hope she hasn't done anything yet, Irma. I wasn't joking about those legal issues."

"Speaking of legal issues..."

Elsa started pumping again, even though that tire looked like it was determined to stay flat. She huffed in annoyance and rummaged through her trunk for something, then slammed it shut with a recklessness that surprised me. The trunk almost clipped her belly as it whizzed past.

A few different moments crashed around in my brain, and then all the pieces came together. Elsa at the ground-breaking, running up those stairs like a teenager.

I took a step toward her.

Elsa snapping at me when I tried to help her into that chair at the wake. My elbow pressing against her soft, pregnant stomach.

I took a glance at the inside of her car. No visible weapons, but I tried not to let it make me cocky. A tire iron would make a lovely weapon, and I hadn't seen the inside of that trunk.

I took a few quick breaths, and then I was on her.

"Hey!"

I pulled up her t-shirt. Underneath was an undershirt.

"Irma!"

I lifted the undershirt. And gasped. She was wearing a prosthetic. A fake stomach.

She pulled her clothes down and jerked away from me.

"What have you done?" I whispered, horrified.

"You have no right to touch me like that, Irma." She was red in the face, but still had a pleasant undertone to her words.

"Sue me."

She smiled. "I'm assuming you have a car here."

"Just the MG. Only room for me and Violet." After a pause, I added, "You could drive that tractor right out of here, though, couldn't you?"

She said nothing, crossed her arms over the fake baby bump.

"You know what?" I said. "I really don't blame you for disliking Carlton so much. At one point this week I was thinking, myself, that I would probably just clip his brake lines if I had to work with him."

She started to giggle. I smiled to make it look like I was in on the joke.

I continued, "You did all the work. Everybody knows that. So, why not get Carlton out of the way so you could run the company? Everyone knew he had a temper, so why not concoct a story where he lost it completely? A cheating spouse is the world's oldest motive for murder; everyone knows that."

"Good heavens, Irma, you do have an imagination."

"I do, it's true." Her hands were empty. Good. "And with Carlton out of the way, you could take over the business. What did you say to me and Mrs. Sepp the other day? You don't like to be told what to do? I think you were fed up with Carlton's laziness. All he does is play golf and complain."

She snickered at that, which felt heartening.

"But why would you kill Lucas? He was a nice boy. Why, Elsa?"

She held up a hand. "Irma, I don't know what you're talking about, but I did not lay a hand on Lucas."

I gave her a pointed look. "Lucas's chain is in your office." I didn't know that for sure yet, but a little fib never hurt anyone.

Her eyes narrowed. "Lucas was in my office, or Carlton's office, all the time. It must have fell off one of those times. He had the flagship apartment. He wanted endless upgrades that drove us all crazy. And Carlton would take meetings in my room all the time, can you believe it? He'd have drinks, snacks, whatever, with clients and leave it for me to clean up."

"That's what happens when you work for a twerp, dear." I frowned. "And I know Lucas was wearing that chain the morning of his death. He had it on during my lesson that morning. The clasp was broken, and it fell off all the time."

"This is my company," she said, her voice perfectly calm and pleasant. She could be talking about the weather. "*Mine*. I'm the one who did all the work. Carlton did nothing. His rich family propped him up, so he never had to worry about failure. Have you seen his house? What is it, fifteen thousand square feet? I've worked for everything I ever had. He doesn't even understand the *contracts* we've signed for this build. It's supposed to be eco-friendly. Do you see all this gas-guzzling equipment he got? There's no future if people keep acting like this, Irma. The planet just can't take much more."

"I think—"

"And nothing personal, Irma, but your generation is at fault for all this. You people had record incomes and employment, free university educations, free everything, and all of you just took and took and took. And now it's my generation's job to fix it. And I'm going to do exactly that."

"How did you lure Lucas here?"

She pressed her lips together.

"I think you set up a phony lesson for Rose and told him to pick her up here. He was known for ferrying his clients around." I shrugged. "And I'd bet my fanny you tried to kill David the night of Lucas's wake because he discovered you had something to do with the tractor shenanigans at the ground-breaking. He wanted to tell us something the night of his accident. You were there. You could have easily run him off the road. He had a red scrape on the back of his car."

"This car?" she said, gesturing at her shiny red Beetle. "Do you see any damage to my car?"

"They have excellent forensics these days, dear. If it's been repaired, they'll find the evidence."

She laughed. "Irma, are you sure you're not having an elder moment? I'm a perfectly normal person. I don't go around murdering people."

"Normal people don't fake a pregnancy for nine months!"

"More like five, really, you don't show until then." She leaned her hip against the car. "How did you figure that out, by the way?"

"When I tried to help you into that chair at the wake, your stomach was soft. I've never been pregnant, so I didn't think anything about it at the time. But pregnant bellies are firm, not soft.

That's why you didn't want me to get close to you."

She flashed a sly smile.

I leaned against the car too. I was only three feet away from her now. "Why are you here, Elsa? Is it because I told you Violet wanted to look at the logs on the tractor? And you wanted to purge them before Leblanc picked it up and ran their checks on it?"

Horror flashed over her face. "Did you tell me that just to lure me here?"

I smiled a sly smile of my own. "I didn't want to do it, but you have to admit it was the perfect test, dear." I frowned. "But why would you bury Lucas, then dig him up? And why kill Rose? And how did you even know she'd be at the boat yesterday?"

She pursed her lips, then looked off in the distance. After a moment, it looked like she'd come to a decision of some kind. I moved my weight to the balls of my feet to get ready for it.

"She'd been there ever since she had a fight with Carlton." Elsa met my eyes. "Bribed the staff not to tell him. She called and told me all about it. Thanks to Snookie, Carlton thought Rose was having an affair with Lucas. I might have helped him believe that too, actually. Carlton was going to be the logical suspect in Lucas's death. He has no alibi for the night of the murder. *And* I tucked some of his hair in Lucas's hand. That's motive, means, and opportunity."

"Speaking of affairs, Carlton has a brochure for a Tahitian singles resort on the boat."

"I *know*," she said, smiling so much her eyes almost closed shut. "I put it there."

"But why Lucas? Everyone liked him."

A lopsided smile tugged at the corner of her mouth. "Well, that's the point, really, isn't it? Easiest way to get people worked up is take away something they like. Everyone liked Lucas. I even liked Lucas." She met my eyes and hers were suddenly soulless. "Until he backed out of his agreement. He went against his *word*, Irma. The penthouse, the flagship suite—people would hear and start to back out, and then we'd have a run. We've already had two more people try to get out of their obligations. And I can't have that. In order for me to prosper, I have to deliver a perfect build on this site. I have bigger and better plans in front of me. You understand, of course."

"Completely."

"Well, good," she said, that pleasant smile back on her face. It was almost chilling to look at.

"Why did you run David off the road that night?"

"Ugh, David," she said, her smile finally faltering. "David didn't like Carlton any more than I did. *He's* the one who came up with the idea of ruining the ground-breaking. Carlton overrode every decision he made, made his life miserable. And fired him for no reason! I told David I'd pay him ten thousand dollars to build a second remote and keep quiet about it."

"And did he?"

A nod.

"So what went wrong?"

Her mouth puckered. "After the ground-breaking, I didn't need him anymore. So why should I pay? I knew he wouldn't go to the police, because he'd helped. He was a co-conspirator, not a victim." She took a breath. "Plus, I might have told him that some of his DNA was on Lucas's body."

I exhaled. "And Rose?"

"I was doing her a favour, taking care of Carlton! But, you know, in some ways, she was just as bad as him."

"How's that?"

"She called me that afternoon, told me she was going to take him back. And alibi him for the night of Lucas's murder! Can you even believe it?"

"Someone will have seen you two together on the boat."

"No, they won't. It was a madhouse the afternoon of the tournament, everyone getting ready, people running around all over the place. I told her to wait in that guest room for me, and she did. I'll bet you nobody remembers seeing me at all."

"You had to have been planning this for a very long time, Elsa."

She smiled. "I went to one of the board members a year ago and asked him to make Carlton step down. I tried to do this the nice way, Irma, but you know what? Nice people really do finish last. Carlton does nothing. He emcees ground-breakings and sponsors charity events, but all he's really doing is buying himself a good reputation. I documented everything. The board refused to do anything other than help him ruin the company. If this build fails, I'll never work again. Because Carlton will badmouth me to everyone he can—he's not going to take responsibility for anything. Do you have any clue how competitive construction is? I mean, do you?"

"Why didn't you just kill *Carlton*? It would have been so much easier."

She snorted. "I needed a scandal so I could be the hero, coming in to save the day. Murdering someone with old money is like blowing up parliament. Brings too much attention."

"What about Rose?"

"Rose was a nobody from nowhere. Her big contribution to the world is going to be sealing

Carlton's fate. He might have gotten away with being accused of one murder, but he won't wiggle out of two of them. His wife and her affair partner. It's perfect."

I was starting to wish I'd limbered up before all this. "You should have entered that poker tournament. You're quite a gambler. You couldn't have possibly known the board wouldn't just bring in someone else to run the company instead of you. Another Campbell, maybe. They're all over the place."

She laughed. "You're kidding, right?"

"Er, no, I don't believe so, dear."

"Do you really think I would have gone through with all this without knowing it would work? The Campbell Company has a six-month hiring process for their executive positions. This build will be done before they've even finished interviewing anyone. I've been studying the company, the board, all of them, for two years now. They don't want any kind of scandal, and they need this build to be a huge success so they can look like they care about the environment to the right people on social media. It'll help take attention away from their fracking business. This is all just a shell game for people like this, Irma. You should know that. I knew if Carlton was in a scandal they'd just bump me to his position. And you know what?"

"What?"

"They already have," she said triumphantly. "Rich people aren't even interesting enough to be unpredictable. I got the call yesterday. You are looking at the first female president of a Campbell Company subsidiary."

"Well, congratulations, dear."

"That's right, Irma. So everything has gone exactly to plan. Just one final thread to snip."

"I'm assuming I'm that thread," I said calmly. "Oh, and those logs. And Violet. Threads can be like octopus legs, you know. They get away from you."

"Nobody ever suspects the pregnant woman, Irma," she said sweetly.

She wasn't wrong. "Is that why you coughed up your fake baby bump?"

"I knew I was going to have to get my hands dirty to accomplish my goals. I needed some kind of edge."

I took a sharp breath. "Did you know Ted Bundy used to do something similar? Not pregnancy, obviously, but he'd have fake casts on his arm or leg, and ask people for help. Young women, really. It gets people's guards down, makes them trust you."

"Exactly."

I didn't feel like she'd grasped the point of my comparison, that she was an addled young woman, but decided not to press the point. "How are you going to explain the lack of baby in a few weeks?"

"Oh," she said in a faux-sad voice, "Poor Elsa, what a terrible tragedy. I'll just go to the mainland—somewhere, nobody will care where—to give birth and come back full of grief. The sympathy I'll get will be perfect. It'll keep me moving right up the Campbell Company's hierarchy. Hell, I might end up running the whole thing." She smiled.

A twig snapped, and I glanced behind me. A rabbit was hopping away.

I turned back. That's when I saw the gun. A big one. And its silencer.

"Did you get that gun out of your *fake baby pouch*?" I squealed.

She nodded. Smiled.

My heart bounced around my chest for a moment. I didn't have a firearm, or body armour, or backup, because I wasn't supposed to be living a life where I needed them anymore. So I was on my own. With Violet only steps away from us. I took a deep breath while I tried to assess my odds of getting Swiss-cheesed by Elsa's enormous gun. She was not a well woman, and I was standing in her way.

"Where are your car keys, Irma?" She stepped toward me calmly. If she came closer, I might just be able to get that gun away from her. My heartbeat thudded in my ears. I tried not to let it show on my face.

"I mean, can you drive a stick shift, dear?" I asked.

She put both hands on the gun, steadying it. I'd been hoping the recoil from the first shot would knock it out of her grasp, so this development obviously did not thrill me.

"I'll figure it out. I'm pretty smart. And I told you not to come here. This is all your fault. Not mine. I really don't think you understand the meaning of the word *no*."

She had me there.

"The keys, Irma. *Now*."

"It's not nice to shoot unarmed senior citizens, dear."

"I know," she said. "I really am sorry about all this, Irma."

Then she raised the gun.

FORTY-THREE — IRMA

The problem with civilians who know nothing about firearms is that they think it's all so easy.

Which was why Elsa never even pulled the trigger. I closed the gap between us, and cracked my elbow in her larynx. She fell over and grasped at her throat, a bunch of strangled noises erupting from her. I felt no remorse. She was a monster in sensible shoes. And now I had her.

I relieved her of the gun, emptied the chamber, and ejected the magazine. I stowed it all in my handbag and slung the strap over my head, before pressing down on a spot on her neck that would disrupt the flow of blood to her brain. She'd be out for a while.

I took the keys out of Elsa's ignition, glad she hadn't realized that was exactly where mine were, and kicked her right in the bottom.

Then I took two quick breaths. I had to get Violet to safety. The gun cheered me up, but it was too big and bulky for me. I made sure Elsa was still out, then ran back to the field where Violet was working, waving my arms.

"What's up?" she said. "Did you see the tractor? I got it working! Isn't that awesome?"

"That's wonderful, dear, you have to leave immediately."

"Why?"

"Elsa's the killer, she's got some emotional issues, and she isn't actually pregnant. Let's go."

"*What*? Where?"

I took a second to catch my breath. "You're going to drive to town and get help. I'm going to stay here and make sure Elsa doesn't go anywhere." Of course, we'd call 911 first, but I wanted Violet as far from here as possible.

"Oh, okay."

"Thank you, dear. You're always such a good girl."

"Uh, thanks." She came down from the tractor. I hadn't realized there was a new backhoe beside her. Leblanc must have dropped off some more equipment.

But then the backhoe roared to life. Bloody hell, Elsa wasn't out at all. Violet ran toward the road, and I joined her, the backhoe hot on our heels.

"Get back to the tractor and use it as a shield!" I yelled.

Violet pivoted and ran to the tractor. I peeled off and ran the other way, the backhoe following me. I had to get the bloody killer-robot-machine away from Violet. There was no way I was going to let a lunatic assassinate one of my house guests.

The machine turned toward Violet.

Bollocks.

I ran after the backhoe, trying to figure out how to climb up to the cab where the driver's seat was located. The cab was covered and complicated-looking and I'd never actually driven a backhoe. And it did not feel like the kind of thing one should do at speed.

The backhoe crashed into the tractor and stopped, its arm winding up to smash the exposed seat where Violet was crouching. It looked like she was trying to put the tractor in reverse.

I grabbed a handle on the backhoe's cab and stepped up the stairs. I tried to open the door of the cab, but it was locked. About fifteen naughty words crowded into my brain. I took the compound I'd used to snap open Lucas's lock from my handbag and slapped it on the window. It cracked open enough that I could stick my hand in and open the door.

The backhoe jerked into reverse, then started to spin in a circle. I tried to keep my eyes on a single spot so I wouldn't get dizzy, but it was impossible. The arm of the backhoe wound up again to take a shot at the tractor. And Violet.

Violet finally got the tractor into reverse and steered it away from the backhoe. I tried to find the same kind of kill switch that had been located beside the tractor's steering wheel. But there was nothing. My heart pounded in my ears. I looked for anything red, anything that looked like the controls on the other machine.

Nothing. Time for plan B.

I started to rip wires out from under the steering console, while the backhoe rolled forward at a horrific pace, toward a stand of trees. Elsa was going to smash me right into them.

My heart galloped in my chest. This couldn't be it. I couldn't die like this, in peacetime, on my island, surrounded by killer robot construction equipment. I looked around to make sure Violet was safe, but I couldn't see her. Bloody hell!

The backhoe—and I—roared toward the trees, massive old Maples that weren't going to budge, no matter how hard I hit them. I looked at the door. Which would be worse? Me doing a drop and roll from the cab of a backhoe at fifty miles an hour, or the backhoe hitting the trees? My hips twinged in anticipation, and a strangled noise emerged from my throat. It was an impossible situation.

And the trees came closer. I held my breath.

But then the backhoe was...slowing down? It was. Ten feet from the stand of trees, it came to a gentle stop that didn't even jar my neck.

I was out and on the ground before you could say *fake baby bump.* Quickly, I checked my hips. Still there. Bloody marvellous. "Violet, are you all right?"

"I'm over here," she called, hoisting her controller in the air. "I stopped it for you!"

"Oh, you brilliant girl," I said, with an enormous exhale.

She smiled modestly.

"Is it going to start again?"

"No, I changed all the passwords."

Relief surged through me. "Thank you so much, dear, you're just lovely in a crisis."

"Years of dealing with internet outages and screaming customers."

"Wonderful," I said. "But I need you to get yourself somewhere safe. Our killer seems to be more resilient than I gave her credit for." Plus, I was obviously out of practice with my neck-vein-squishing technique, which really was irksome.

"Okay, should I sit in your car?"

"No." I looked around. "It's a convertible, dear. If Elsa has another gun in that bump, it's not going to help us much. Stay behind me, please."

“Gotcha.” She hunched over so much it felt like a commentary on my height. “Did you say she had a gun in her *bump*?”

“Let’s chit chat a little later please, dear.”

I marched Violet to the construction trailer, popping the lock and doing a quick sweep: empty. “Okay, Violet, you go in and lock the door. Oh, and can you please pass me the two-by-four at your feet? That’s a good girl.”

She dutifully handed it over and slammed the door.

FORTY-FOUR — VIOLET

Irma picked up the two-by-four I'd given her at the same time Elsa came out from behind the sales office, running like a crazy woman. She threw a box at Irma's head as she ran—probably her sneaky second remote, which was now useless thanks to me changing all those passwords. Elsa had pretty good aim for a maniac, and it hit Irma right in the forehead. Irma stumbled back and slipped in a patch of mud fed by something leaking from the construction trailer.

Then Elsa kicked Irma in the leg and took off toward Irma's little MG. The keys were in the ignition, and she had it started in seconds.

I looked at Irma. She had her knee in her hands and was trying to sit up, but the mud kept sucking her back in. There was no way she'd be able to stop Elsa. There wasn't enough time.

My breath froze in my chest.

I had to do it.

I moved to the other side of the office and peered out the window. Elsa was driving over the corn field, straight to the main road.

Right over those big, beautiful, industrial sprinklers.

From my phone, I opened a connection to Carlton's irrigation system and turned on the sprinklers, every single sprinkler head, full blast, and pointed them at the little red MG.

Like Irma'd said before, her car *was* a convertible, and the water gushed over it, around it, and into it. Elsa put her hand over her eyes to shield them as she steered.

Right into a tree.

FORTY-FIVE — IRMA

The Pickle and her staff came and arrested Elsa after Violet finally turned off those sprinklers. And after an enormous amount of questioning, let me and Violet leave. Violet was so excited about her remote working, it was hard to calm her down afterward. I considered testing my technique for shutting off blood to the brain to get her to go to sleep, since I'd obviously failed miserably when I'd done it to Elsa. But Violet sorted herself out eventually, and I'd headed back into town to watch Elsa's interrogation.

Later, I got the phone call I'd been waiting on, and drove to the house where Tate Hurst was living for the summer. Poor Lucas. He'd had so many people after him that it had been a sticky undertaking to unravel who had done what to the poor boy. And why. But Elsa hadn't sent any threatening letters to Lucas or burned down his Airstream.

I picked a spot under a lovely maple tree to wait. It didn't take long. And when Tate saw me, he burst out laughing.

"Oh, hey, Mrs. A. Watcha doing sitting in the dark?"

"Waiting for you, dear."

"Oh, yeah?" He raised an eyebrow.

"Yes. Why don't you take a seat?"

He made a rude noise. "I'm pretty busy, actually."

"Sit," I said with a touch of quiet menace. After he'd settled himself in the chair beside me, I said, "So Imogene has told you I'm involved in the Club's management, hasn't she?"

"I guess."

"Part of what I do is help out with security sometimes."

Another laugh burst out of him. And who could blame him? He was used to thinking of old people as feeble. Just like we were all used to thinking of pregnant women as delicate and in need of our protection, even if that was all balderdash. It was a beautiful little ruse Elsa had put together for herself, and I, for one, should have seen right through it. I was going to be annoyed with myself over it for a while.

Once Tate had finished laughing, I stood. "I'd planned a longer speech, but I spent the afternoon with a murderer, and I'm out of patience. You're fired."

"What?"

"You heard me. Fired. Imogene will send you your things, if you have any at the Club. Just give her your forwarding address."

He snorted. "I'm staying right where I am."

"On the contrary, you're leaving town first thing tomorrow."

"You can't make me do anything."

"Mr. Hurst, you sent threatening letters to Lucas, and you burned down his trailer."

"You can't prove that."

"You wrote him a bunch of letters telling him to *Get out of Dodge*." I'd spent part of the afternoon going through the box from Lucas's locker. That particular saying had been popular.

"Lots of people use that expression."

"That's true. But lots of people don't lie on their résumés."

"What?"

"You lied on your résumé about the Royal Toronto Tennis Club. You've never worked there."

He blanched.

It wasn't quite the magic bullet I was looking for, but Capone had been put away for tax evasion, after all. And lying on his résumé had been enough to get Tate fired from the Club, even though I didn't have enough to get him arrested for arson and his little letters. It was not a perfect solution, but sometimes it was important not to let perfect be the enemy of good enough. Plus, Camille was going to be keeping an eye on him.

"And I think you'll find that your hosts no longer want a lying arsonist in their pool house."

"You can't do this."

"It's already done. And if you're still here tomorrow morning, I am going to make you wish you were never born. This is my island, sonny, and don't you forget it."

His mouth hung open so far, I was sure he'd eventually swallow a moth. Good. I hoped he'd choke on it.

It can be a challenge to stomp off when you're as petite as I am, but I managed to make it work anyway.

"You're doing excellently, dear," I said to Violet the next day.

She muttered something.

"I'm very proud of you," I added.

Violet was sitting behind the oversized steering wheel of Stu's lovely Grampian 30 sailboat, and we were almost two hundred feet from land, a new record for her. Stu, Julian, and Boris took up the rest of the cockpit.

"So, what did the chief say to you about all this?" Julian asked.

"She thanked us for our help," I said primly.

"Speaking of the chief," Stu said, stretching like a cat, "Did she really let you listen in on Elsa's interrogation?"

I nodded. It had been very nice of her, although I'd had to promise not to bash through the two-way mirror and strangle Elsa to death. On the bright side, she'd assigned Officer Matty Jones to supervise me, and we'd had a nice catch-up session. His wife was expecting a baby. A real one. I made a mental note to get a nice little onesie for them.

"Maybe you and the Pickle will become friends," Violet said.

"Maybe." Although probably not.

"So, let me understand this," Stu said. "Elsa planned this all out months ago?"

"Indeed," I said, sipping on some water. It was another perfect Beaver Island summer day: sun, waves, water, good friends.

"Why go after Lucas, though?"

I pressed my lips together. Poor Lucas. "The rumour about him and Rose had been zipping around the Club for some time, apparently, courtesy of Snookie. Elsa knew she was setting

Carlton up for a fall, but didn't have a specific victim picked out until Lucas backed out of his agreement to buy the penthouse at Beaver Brooke."

Violet looked like she was going to stand again. I was no fan of sitting, but with the water as rough as it was right now—

She sat down abruptly.

Well, it was nice she was trying something new, and we were outside. I made a supportive noise.

"So, she ran David off the road the night of the wake?" Stu prodded.

"That's right," I said, putting my feet up on one of the seats. On the bright side, Elsa had kicked my good leg, so I wasn't too terribly banged up. I'd always had excellent luck like that. "She saw him talking to Violet at Lucas's wake and realized he was about to spill the beans about making that second remote for her, especially since he'd been acting distant with her after Lucas's body was unearthed at the ground-breaking. So, she left before he did and laid in wait."

"And the fake pregnancy? That's intense," Violet said, her teeth clenched. The wind had picked up a bit, but she was still at her post. I was starting to think she was a sailing natural. I raised my face to the sun, felt the wind. I tried to let it wear away the sad feelings left over from finding Lucas's killer. Lucas was gone. I didn't want that to be the truth, but it was. Nothing could change that.

"Wow," Stu said. "She's really awful."

"Oh my, yes. Terrible. Poor Lucas. And Rose." After a pause, I added, "And Carlton. He never even saw her coming."

"What made you suspect her?" Stu asked.

I sighed. "There had been a few moments I thought she was acting oddly, like when she ran up the stairs of the construction trailer at the ground-breaking. I thought at the time she just really wanted to get out of the sun, but she must have forgotten herself. And at Lucas's wake, I tried to help her into her chair, and she became quite upset. She wanted to keep everyone from touching her so no one could get close enough to realize her baby bump was a little faker."

"Wow," Violet said.

"Plus, her voice was funny after I told her Violet was going to look at the logs on the tractor. I don't think she realized such a thing was even a possibility. David was the nerdy one in that particular conspiracy."

"So, she came to wipe the logs?" Stu said.

"Exactly. She thought I had listened to her, and wouldn't be there until Monday. She thought she had lots of time. Ironically, she didn't see *me* as a threat either." I smiled.

"But why did you tell her about the logs in the first place?" Violet said.

I pressed my lips together. "I wanted to make sure it wasn't her. Carlton is not the most pleasant fellow, but I didn't want him to go to jail for something he didn't do. Luckily, Camille has located David, and will convince him to testify against Elsa."

"Where was he?" Violet asked.

"A Motel 6 in Saskatchewan, surrounded by video games and Cheetos."

Violet snickered.

"What did the logs on that tractor say, anyway?" Julian asked.

"That the remote that Elsa was found with was responsible for the tractor's actions at the ground-breaking," Violet said.

She was right. After I'd verified that the shiny object under Elsa's desk was, indeed, Lucas's necklace, Violet had coaxed out the tractor's secrets while I guarded Elsa and waited for the Pickle.

"And Elsa sent those threatening letters to Lucas, and burned down his trailer?" Julian asked.

"No. That was Tate Hurst," I said with triumph in my voice. I'd also found Tiffanni's risqué pictures in Lucas's box, which had now been returned to her.

"That's why he left town on the ferry first thing this morning?" Stu said cheekily.

I gave him a *Who, me*? look.

Violet moved her head so she was facing Julian, but immediately turned away to look forward. I couldn't blame her. We had wind coming off the bow, with waves hitting the side of the boat, and rolling under us. It was a recipe for nausea. Frankly, I thought she was doing a bang-up job so far.

"I'm impressed you're the one who brought Elsa down, Vi," Stu drawled. "Although I don't know if Irma's been a good influence on you."

Violet's mouth was scrunched up in a funny way. Then she glanced over her shoulder at me. "I think she's been an awesome influence," she said, before whipping her head back around.

What a lovely girl she was. And how happy she would be when she learned I had a fresh lead on Shane, her embezzling former CEO. I'd scare the pants off him before telling her, naturally.

"Oh, and I forgot to let you know that we're invited to Constance Leblanc's sister's wedding, Irma," Violet said.

My stomach tightened. The Leblanc family owned Leblanc Industries, the company that made all those killer robot tractors. Plus, Cynthia had kicked me in the shin that one time. I could already tell there would be some sort of shenanigans at that particular wedding.

"Sounds lovely, dear," I said.

"Plus, everyone, Irma and I are playing video games tomorrow!"

"This, I gotta see," Julian said with a grin.

"And don't forget," Stu said, pulling his hat over his eyes so he could take a catnap, "pig roast at my place the day after tomorrow!"

Julian said, "Can't wait."

"We'll be there," Violet said.

I looked out at the water again. And then I thought: *Lucas isn't gone.* Not really. He'd live on in his friends, the people who remembered him. He would live on in me forever. And then gratitude swept over me. I'd been lucky to have him in my life.

"We certainly will," I replied to Violet. Boris smiled at me. Ahead of us, the sky was blue, with streaks of red starting to glow on the horizon. Our whole world was the sound of the waves and the rolling movement of the boat under us, a rhythm as old as time itself. I looked around at my friends and sighed happily.

And then we sailed off into the sunset.

Also By This Author

Vitamin Sea: Book 1 of the Beaver Island Mysteries

Dead Calm: Book 2 of the Beaver Island Mysteries

High and Dry: Book 3 of the Beaver Island Mysteries

Water Town: Book 4 of the Beaver Island Mysteries (summer 2022)

Irmageddon: A Beaver Island Novelette (for newsletter subscribers only)

Peace on Earth: An Irma Saves Christmas Novella (Ebook only)

About the Author

Maia Ross is the author of the *Beaver Island* mystery series, featuring retired spy Irma Abercrombie and couch-locked nerd Violet Blackheart, along with the spin-off series, *Irma Saves Christmas,* and the *Beaver Island* prequel novelette, *Irmagedddon.*

Maia spent almost twenty years in the tech sector, and is an avid sailor. She makes her home in Toronto with her better half, John.

To be notified about new releases, contests, and giveaways, and to get a free copy of *Irmageddon,* please sign up for Maia's monthly newsletter. You can find her online at www.maiarossbooks.com.

Acknowledgements

A big shout out to all my editors for their terrific work: Dustin Porta, Anna Albo, Flora from Brockway Gatehouse Literary Services, Lee from Ocean's Edge Editing, Marta from The Cursed Books, and Elizabeth at Binocular Edits.

Finally, thanks so much to my smismar, John. *Ma armastan sind*, babe.

Maia
April 2021

Made in the USA
Las Vegas, NV
17 July 2024

92389275R00249